LOVE
CHARMS

and
other

CATASTROPHES

KIMBERLY KARALIUS

Swoon Reads   New York

MAR   2017

A SWOON READS BOOK

An Imprint of Feiwel and Friends

Our books may be purchased in bulk for promotional, educational, or business use. Please contact your local bookseller or the Macmillan Corporate and Premium Sales Department at (800) 221-7945 ext. 5442 or by e-mail at MacmillanSpecialMarkets@macmillan.com.

Library of Congress Cataloging-in-Publication Data

Names: Karalius, Kimberly, author.
Title: Love charms and other catastrophes / Kimberly Karalius.
Description: First Edition. | New York : Swoon Reads, 2016. |
Sequel to: Love fortunes and other disasters. | Summary: "Aspiring love charm maker Hijiri Kitamura, her friends, and her new boyfriend (given to her by Love itself), must find and stop a rogue charm maker from taking over Grimbaud"—Provided by publisher.
Identifiers: LCCN 2015036230 | ISBN 9781250084040 (paperback) | ISBN 9781250084019 (ebook)
Subjects: | CYAC: Love—Fiction. | Fate and fatalism—Fiction. | Magic—Fiction. | Friendship—Fiction. | Contests—Fiction. | High schools—Fiction. | Schools—Fiction. | Japanese Americans—Fiction. | BISAC: JUVENILE FICTION / Love & Romance. | JUVENILE FICTION / Fantasy & Magic.
Classification: LCC PZ7.1.K36 Lp 2016 | DDC [Fic]—dc23
LC record available at http://lccn.loc.gov/2015036230

Book design by Eileen Savage

First Edition—2016

1 3 5 7 9 10 8 6 4 2

swoonreads.com

To those with small hearts:
They're much bigger than you think.

THE BARGAIN

L ove played with the key around his neck as he strolled through Grimbaud. Ran his thumb along the rough ridges. Felt the teeth against his skin. He was *home*. The streets were filled with high school students exploring with their parents, gathering school supplies and charms for the new school year. Love tried to be gentle with them as he passed—a touch on the shoulder, a breath on the back of the neck—and they never saw him.

"Turn around again," he whispered in a senior girl's ear. "That boy with the glasses. You should say hello."

The senior girl rubbed her ear, frowning, and noticed the boy.

Love laughed like a toddler, bright and happy. He didn't need to look back to know the teens were talking; tendrils of attraction curled around them like vines. But for every new romance blooming, another withered. Love sighed when he saw a couple bickering over a bruised plum at the fruit stand. The poor stand owner tried to show them other plums, but the argument went far beyond that. Love knew a breakup was coming. For once, he didn't have the stomach to stick around and hear it.

His town was lovely but lost, off-kilter without Zita's love fortunes to anchor it. Sure, the townspeople would listen to him, even if they didn't know it, but he hadn't the time to repair Grimbaud cobblestone by cobblestone. Not when the rest of the world grabbed at his ankles, always tugging him this way and that. He couldn't stay long. But he also couldn't abandon the town, not after Zita.

At first, Grimbaud had seemed to benefit from the bargain he'd struck with her; he shared his power with her and Zita used it to craft love fortunes that revealed each person's romantic future with 100 percent accuracy. But as time passed, Zita had abused that power and twisted the fortunes for her own gain, ruining lives and loves in the process. It was only thanks to a few brave teenagers that Love finally took back the town and set it to rights.

Not to rights, exactly, Love thought, *not yet*, as he saw the town council gathered around the flyer they'd just taped to a lamppost. He slipped behind a café, shifting his form until he looked like Mrs. Visser, the missing council member. Love patted her perfect blond perm and walked over.

"There you are," said one of the council members. "The new flyers are up. Verbeke Square is an odd choice for the competition venue, what with Zita's shop gone."

"That's precisely why I pushed for it," Love said. Thankfully, Mrs. Visser had suffered from chronic stomach cramps all summer, allowing Love to take her place and encourage critical decisions. "Grimbaud needs a new beginning. Sometimes, in order to do that you must build upon the past."

Sensing the real Mrs. Visser on her way to the council, Love excused herself and took his previous form again.

Grimbaud was recovering, on the way to becoming Love's town once more, but attracting love charm-makers back after Zita's monopoly had been harder than he thought. The love charm-makers who *had* set up shop over the summer worried him and made Love think more and more about Hijiri Kitamura.

Hijiri's talent in love charm-making was exceptional for a girl her age. Yet when Love had offered her Zita's position, Hijiri refused. Maybe he had been too hasty with his offer, but he had felt her potential as fireworks under his skin. She still needed to grow. Her heart was cold, despite her love charms, and Love was determined to show her what she was truly capable of.

"Almost time," Love said, checking his watch. He changed direction, crossing clogged streets as he made his way to the Student Housing Complex, a boardinghouse for nonlocal high schoolers to live in while attending Grimbaud High.

He had taken the form of a man with a hard jaw and

a clear gaze, someone trustworthy. He needed Hijiri to trust him.

He'd made a new bargain on behalf of Hijiri. This time, he had the upper hand. No mistakes. No bending and twisting his rules.

Love's stomach rumbled. One quick detour first. He needed a chocolate-drizzled waffle.

Chapter 1
PARTY

H ijiri Kitamura suspected that her heart had a limited capacity for love. A *small amount*. Her friends took up enough room already. There just wasn't room for a boyfriend. She spent the summer trying to measure it, to put math to her frustration, but no ruler or calculator in the world helped.

"Put the ruler in your suitcase," her mother said, "before you end up poking someone with it."

"Never mind the ruler," Mr. Kitamura said, grimacing at his watch. "Hurry to the platform. You can't be late."

You can't be late either, she thought, reluctantly shoving the ruler in the suitcase's front pocket. The train whistle blew. Lejeune's train station had been built outside the city limits, where the tracks ran uninterrupted by the city's numerous lakes and skyscrapers.

The Kitamuras worked for the same insurance company, though in different departments. On the drive over, her parents had complained about the meetings they were missing. Hijiri tried to ignore how often they checked the time and muttered about their bosses. They were *here* right now and she wanted to enjoy that. She carefully grabbed her overstuffed suitcase; she didn't trust the porters to be gentle with her precious supplies.

Mrs. Kitamura kissed Hijiri on both cheeks, leaving faint pink marks from her lipstick. "Do well this year," she said.

Mr. Kitamura squeezed Hijiri's shoulder affectionately before pushing her forward. "Try to get some fresh air."

When the train arrived, she ran through the open doors. The first passenger in her train car, Hijiri chose a window seat and settled in. *Grimbaud's only a few hours' ride away*, she reminded herself, curling up tighter when a heavyset man took the seat next to her.

If only the train could fly. She couldn't wait to be back.

The town of Grimbaud no longer smelled like roses, but Hijiri enjoyed the other scents that took their place: musky canals and bitter chocolates sprinkled with salt. Teetering on the end of summer, the town was hot and bright. Hijiri pulled her hair into a bun, leaving long pieces in front to frame her face—a curtain for when she felt anxious. Her bangs were uneven from having trimmed them herself over the summer; Sebastian needed to fix them. Fortunately, Fallon and Sebastian were probably in the Student Housing Complex already. They always came early before the new semester.

Hijiri dragged her suitcase into a cab; the distance wasn't too great, but her arms already hurt from tugging on the suitcase handle. Even with upkeep, the Student Housing Complex had a lived-in, well-loved energy to it, with chipped paint on the doors and a creaky wooden gate separating the three-story stone building from the street. Mrs. Smedt, the caretaker, waved at Hijiri before disappearing around the corner. Hijiri had helped Mrs. Smedt take care of the complex last year as a part-time job—a job she hoped to have again, since she enjoyed the solitude that came with it.

Her apartment was the same as last year's. First floor. Hijiri slid her key into the lock and pushed, surprised when the door got stuck. A thick piece of folded paper wedged under the door was the culprit. She bent down to pick it up and was pleased to find the De Keysers' weather-charm shop logo: swirling font surrounded by a halo of storm clouds, lightning, and a beacon-like sun at the top. Femke's careful handwriting covered the page:

Dear Hijiri,
Your summer could not have been as fun
without us. Mirthe and I (mostly Mirthe)

*firmly believe this. Time to
right that wrong with a party at our
house!*

*Drop your suitcase off and come now.
Yes, right now. Our little rebellion must
reunite before the new school year starts.
We have gossip to discuss and plenty of
good food to eat. Besides, today's supposed
to be hot. If you come to the party, Mirthe
and I promise cool breezes. You might even
need a sweater.*

*Your troublemaking seniors,
Femke and Mirthe De Keyser*

Hijiri re-folded the letter with a grin. The invitation
warmed her. Her usual anxiety flared up at the thought of
crossing town to see the group again, but she quickly pushed
it down. Fallon, Sebastian, Nico, Martin, and the twins
were her friends. She *wanted* to see them. *I'm just rusty
after a summer at home,* she thought. Her voice had been
severely underused with her parents at work every day and
having the entire house to herself. Alone. Just the way she
had liked it.

Her suitcase fell over when she let go of it, but she
didn't care. Hijiri unzipped the front pocket, withdrew
a crumpled cardigan, and dashed out the door.

The eggplant-colored cardigan came in handy when she reached the De Keysers' house. The weather had been sticky hot on her way through town but fall had taken up residence at the blue colonial house. Promised breezes cooled her face and blew her bangs back. The pinwheels in the shrubbery bled colors as they spun.

Years of abuse from weather charms showed. Cracked windows. Leaking gutters. A sliver of roof partially exposed. The twins said they couldn't keep up with the repairs. Femke and Mirthe had spent their summer paying their parents back for using potent (and expensive) weather charms against Zita. They had even traveled with their mother to replenish their collection of earthquake tremors—dangerous business. Hijiri didn't envy them, except that she loved the feel of the De Keysers' property. The air was electric—charged and thick with a history of used weather charms. After passing the broken sundial, she heard the sound of laughter coming from behind the house.

Grass turned to sand. The sun intensified the blue of the ocean, dazzling Hijiri as much as the cool, salty air.

"You made it," Femke said, jogging across the sand to meet her. Mirthe was bent over a table, making sure the waves wouldn't carry it away.

Femke and Mirthe were twins, but they didn't look

alike. Dark, coiling hair and nut-brown skin were their only matching features, so their continuing attempts at looking identical occasionally bordered on comical. Today, they both wore tan shorts, long-sleeved turtlenecks, and silver octopus necklaces. But their hair, Hijiri noticed, didn't match at all.

Femke's hair was pulled back in a tight bun, while Mirthe's tumbled wildly down her back. Hijiri was so surprised that she missed Femke's question.

"Did you bring something?" Femke asked again, eyeing the bag in Hijiri's hands.

"I stopped for some cookies," Hijiri said, handing Femke the bag. Luckily cafés were plentiful in Grimbaud. The cookies were still hot, the chocolate chips gooey.

Mirthe was at their sides in seconds, her brown eyes hungry. "Are you trying to torture me? They smell heavenly."

"Dessert," Femke warned her.

Mirthe rolled her eyes and took the cookies to the table.

Femke watched her sister go. Her green eyes slid back to Hijiri. "Happy to be back?"

Hijiri took a deep breath. Let it out. "Surprisingly, yes. This party is quite a welcome."

"What are friends for?"

Hijiri bit back a smile. *Friends.* No matter how many times they used the word, it still gave her the tingles.

Someone called her name. When Hijiri turned around, she saw Fallon Dupree emerge from the house with a steaming dish in her mitted hands.

"Do you need help?" Hijiri asked, because she wanted an excuse to talk to Fallon, who, in all probability, was the closest person she'd ever had to a best friend.

"Sebastian's watching the stew on the stove," Fallon said, grunting as she shifted the dish in her arms, "but sure. Help would be nice. Without me, none of us would be eating."

Mirthe laughed. "Well, without decorations, we wouldn't be having much of a party either."

After Fallon put the dish of honey-roasted endives and parsnips on the table, Hijiri followed her into the house. Despite not having seen her all summer, Hijiri thought Fallon looked the same as always. Her hair was cut in a straight bob ending at her chin, its plainness balanced by Fallon's hawklike gaze and neat appearance. That gaze turned on Hijiri as they reached the steps. "Your bangs look like they need a touch-up," Fallon said.

Hijiri blew at her bangs, but they fell right back into her eyes. "Think Sebastian can take care of it?"

"He's been carrying his shears everywhere since getting a job at the groomer's."

"What about for humans?"

"Don't worry. He's fully prepared for any hair emergency."

The De Keysers' house smelled like burning wood and clean laundry. There were little disasters here and there— a broken vase, a pile of pillows knocked off a couch—no doubt caused by the family's habit of using weather charms indoors. The kitchen was in the darkest part of the house. Three big hanging lamps threw spotlights on the counters and island. And on the boy stirring a pot of savory fish stew.

When Sebastian looked up, Hijiri didn't miss the quick smile that spread on Fallon's face. Previously known as Grimbaud High's resident heartbreaker, Sebastian Barringer still had his charmingly disheveled look. The slant of his dark eyebrows made him look irritated or bored (as did his attitude at times), but underneath, he was a kind person. Hijiri didn't have to try to sense their love for each other. It was quiet but strong.

"Hijiri needs a trim," Fallon said.

"You know, most high schoolers get their hair cut *before* the new school year," he teased.

"Ah. But you're a Hijiri Kitamura hair specialist. I couldn't possibly trust the stylists back home," Hijiri said.

Sebastian laughed. "It's a good thing I can cut both dogs and humans."

Fallon peeked at the stew. She looked pleased. "Almost ready. Good job."

Sebastian asked Hijiri to stand under one of the lamps so that he could see her bangs better. He wore a leather hip holster for his scissors and comb. Strangely enough, it didn't look weird. While he snipped, he told her about the job. Three nights a week, he would work at a groomer close to the Student Housing Complex. The work would consist of him sweeping up after the other groomers, and maybe even shampooing a dog once in a while, but he was happy to start. He measured her bangs between his fingers and carefully snipped while Fallon took the pot off the burner.

"Just one more," he whispered, finding a stray hair that had been tickling her eye. "There. You're ready for school."

"Thanks." She shook her head, relieved when her bangs stayed out of her eyelashes.

"Bring out the stew," Mirthe shouted from the back door. "Nico and Martin are here! We can start the party!"

Sebastian volunteered to carry the pot outside, but Fallon hovered beside him, her fingers twitching as if she expected him to drop it before reaching the table. The stew pot *was* heavy. Sebastian gritted his teeth and tried to take bigger steps.

Hijiri carried the bowls out. She ran ahead, eager to see the last members of their rebellion again.

Nico was in the middle of dumping a massive amount of twice-baked fries on one of the serving platters. Martin took the lid off the sauce container and drizzled mayonnaise over the fries; they must have bought half the vendor's supply in sauce and fries before coming here. The smell made Hijiri's mouth water.

When Nico spotted her, he opened his arms for a hug. Hijiri obliged, albeit stiffly, her chin bumping against his shoulder. He was tan and smelled damp like canal water, the brown hair on his head burned almost blond by the sun. She had never expected to become good friends with Nico, but helping him when Martin fell under the spell of Camille's love charm had solidified a bond between them. Like Fallon, Nico had stayed in touch with her over the summer with occasional phone calls.

"No more bank statements this year," Hijiri said, remembering their last phone call. Nico had moved up in student government from treasurer to vice president, a role he was happy to take on since it meant spending more time with Martin.

"I know," he said. "Do you think I can handle being vice president?"

Hijiri shrugged, smiling. "Ask your boyfriend."

Nico brightened. "He believes in me."

Martin Pauwels hung back, fiddling with the mayonnaise container. He looked healthier than the last time she saw him; his pale skin had some color to it, and his glasses were smudge-free. He took his job as student government president seriously; he even showed up to the party in his casual uniform: khakis and a polo shirt embroidered with the school logo.

"If he does more than the last vice president, he'll be perfect," Martin said, putting the cap back on the empty container. "Nicolas promised that I would be spending less time on paperwork this year."

"He still isn't using your nickname," Hijiri whispered.

"I don't mind," Nico whispered back. "Whenever he says my name, it *feels* like a nickname."

Martin sat in one of the chairs and pulled a bundle of papers out of his back pocket. He smoothed the creases and muttered something about a fifth draft.

Nico leaned on the back of Martin's chair. "Put that speech away. We're at a party," he said softly.

"I'm not happy with it," Martin said.

"The freshmen are going to be bored and overexcited at orientation anyway. You don't have to put in so much effort."

"But it's my last speech." Martin put the papers away and sighed. "Being a senior feels . . . so final. It's all going to be over soon."

Worry flashed in Nico's eyes, but he squeezed the back of Martin's chair and said nothing.

Hijiri fidgeted. She was about to speak when the twins asked everyone to come to the table. She grabbed the nearest chair, facing the ocean, while Fallon and Nico sat on either side of her. The twins sat on opposite ends of the table, raising their goblets of raspberry lemonade like queens.

"A toast to the rebellion," Femke said.

Everyone lifted their goblets.

"A rebellion without a cause," Sebastian added, "now that Zita is gone."

"But we still have our friendships," Fallon said.

"And bravery," Nico said, smiling at Martin.

"And a new mission," Mirthe said. All eyes locked on her. "Later. Let's enjoy the food."

Hijiri filled her bowl to the top with fish stew. She ate quietly, listening to everyone talk about their plans for the semester. The stew was thick with carp, carrots, onions, and potatoes, seasoned with bay leaves and sage. The richness warmed her inside and out. Sand swirled at her ankles, stirred by the breeze. The party was delightfully caught between hot and cold. Maybe it was that dreamlike juxtaposition that made Hijiri anxious for the punch line—what new adventure could the twins reveal?

"Do we have something to worry about?" Hijiri said into her bowl.

Femke dipped a fry into the mayonnaise and chewed thoughtfully. "What, indeed?"

Hijiri's head snapped up. She hadn't realized she had spoken aloud.

Mirthe's eyes twinkled. "The town needs us again. So we're going to enter the love charm competition."

Hijiri's stomach twisted. "What competition?"

"News has been spreading locally since last month,"

Nico said, his brow furrowing. "Grimbaud hasn't done well since losing Zita. A love charm revival just isn't happening yet, and the town council is concerned that the lack of, well, *love* in Grimbaud will turn tourists off."

"So the council came up with a love charm-making competition to inspire town spirit," Mirthe said. "The three love charm-makers that moved here over the summer will be participating . . . but they're *outsiders*, guys. None of them should win. Someone homegrown, with true affection for this town, needs to win."

Hijiri regretted not keeping up with Grimbaud news over the summer. She stirred her soup but didn't feel like eating anymore. All eyes fell on her. She started to sweat. "Why are you looking at me? This isn't my hometown."

"You're the best we've got," Mirthe said firmly. "And you love Grimbaud, right? Your charm-making skills are already indisputable. Winning will be easy. The other love charm-makers don't stand a chance."

"You won't be alone," Fallon said softly.

"We're entering as a team, just like the shops did," Femke said.

"We'll use our standing as a club to enter the competition. Principal Bemelmans will have to approve it first, but I'm sure we can convince him," Mirthe said.

"So long as Fallon waits in the hallway," Sebastian said wryly. "He's probably still sensitive about her refusing to eat his famous casserole last year."

Fallon crossed her arms but agreed.

Martin wiped his mouth on a napkin and said that he could get them a meeting with the principal on Monday.

Hijiri felt the world spinning out from under her feet. Her friends spoke faster than normal, more buzzing than words, and her stomach imitated the roll of the ocean. The idea of being in a competition—onstage, in front of hundreds of people—made her want to hop on the first train back to Lejeune. But underneath that, the challenge of crafting the best love charms she could was enticing.

This could be the year I make my mark as a great love charm-maker, said a little voice in her head. *Are you watching, Love?*

Hijiri put down her spoon and twisted the tablecloth in her hands. When she looked up, she tried to sound braver than she felt. "Okay. Let's do it."

By the time the party ended, the sun hung low in the sky. The pink of a blooming sunset crept on the edges of the horizon. Sebastian and Fallon walked ahead of her, holding hands, while Hijiri wrestled with her thoughts. During the group hug that ensued after Hijiri had agreed to join the competition, her hairband had snapped. Without the weather charm's breeze, her long, ink-black hair stuck to her spine.

"We'll check out the competition tomorrow, okay?" Fallon said as they reached the wooden gate of the complex. "You'll feel better when we see them. I'm curious about these new love charm-makers too."

Hijiri nodded and wished her and Sebastian good night. She couldn't imagine sleeping.

She fished her key out of her pocket—and nearly bumped into a giant present sitting outside her apartment door. The present was a cardboard box wrapped in iridescent white paper with a red ribbon around it.

What was it doing there? Who did it belong to? It couldn't possibly be for her. Her parents didn't surprise her with gifts. She hadn't ordered any new charm-making supplies either. Despite that, the box was perfectly lined up with Hijiri's door. And when she checked again, leaning in close, she saw her name printed on a tag hanging from the ribbon.

"Are you Hijiri Kitamura?" said a muffled voice from inside the box.

A squeak escaped Hijiri's mouth as she jumped away from the box. Her heart beat wildly.

"*Are* you?"

"Y-yes?"

"That sounded like a question," the voice said, amused. "Can I come out now?"

She wasn't sure if she wanted a talking thing in a box to *ever* come out. She couldn't say anything, but her sharp intake of breath must have been enough.

The box trembled as the *something* in the inside pushed. The ribbon fell away. The top flaps opened with a loud tear of tape and wrapping paper.

A boy stepped out of the box.

Chapter 2

MADE WITH LOVE

ijiri's heart roared in her ears, making it hard to think. *A boy just stepped out of that box. A living, breathing boy*, she thought. *Or is he?* Nothing was making sense.

The boy had ink-black hair like a duckling, soft and wild on the top of his head, while flat against his cheeks in front of his ears. He had narrow shoulders and a sharp chin, softened by full lips. *He's certainly thin enough to have fit inside the box*, she thought with some worry. The dusky rose coat and white shirt he wore hung off of him.

"How do you know who I am?" Hijiri asked. "Who are you?"

The boy's dark eyes roamed her face. "I'm a gift."

"I see that," Hijiri said, taking in the torn wrapping paper and the ribbon draped around his neck like a scarf. There was confetti too. From inside the box. Pieces of it stuck to his clothes and skin.

Hot wind blew across the complex, momentarily blinding Hijiri. She shielded her eyes with her hand. With the wind came a man finishing the last bites of a chocolate-drizzled waffle. Grayed at the temples with pressed khakis, a sweater vest, and owlishly round glasses, the man looked like an academic.

"Hello, Hijiri," the man said, licking a drop of chocolate off his thumb. The key around his neck told her exactly who he was.

"Hello, Love," she said with a smile.

Love put his arm around the boy like a proud parent. "Allow me to introduce you to Kentaro Oshiro. He's starting school here. A transfer student. Your age. Please be kind to him," he said, "because I created him just for you."

"Ken," the boy corrected, holding his hand out to her.

Hijiri blinked. Without thinking, she shook hands with him. His grip was firm, his hand swallowing hers.

"Go on, admire my handiwork," Love said, gesturing at Ken. "I'm sure you'll find him to your taste. I can already sense your heart beating a little harder."

"You made him," Hijiri whispered.

Love nodded.

"For me?" If her stomach had twisted at news of the competition, this pain was much worse: her insides hollowed out, anxiety ricocheting against the lining.

Throughout the exchange, Ken's eyes never left hers. The pleasant smile he wore morphed into a concerned frown. "Are you okay?" he asked, reaching for her again.

Hijiri flinched and stepped back. "He's a charm," she

said, staring at the boy's feet. "He's just a charm, and you want me to accept him as my boyfriend?"

Love crossed his arms. "You know, I don't do this for just anyone. Most people spend their entire lives searching for their true loves. I'm simply giving you yours now. It's a present. Clever, right?" He picked up a scrap of wrapping paper and waved it at her. "I've been keeping my eye on you since Zita's fall. You seem to be having a difficult time with love."

"My charms are coming out just fine," she snapped.

"Not charms. I mean your love life."

Heat crawled up her cheeks. She was about to say it was none of his business, but that wasn't true. He was Love, the very essence of it in a physical form, and getting on his bad side was a terrible idea.

"Your heart is so small," Love said quietly. "There's no room for love. Or so you *believe*. Let me prove you wrong. Give Ken a chance."

But he's fake. No more a boy than an illusion, Hijiri thought. Tears burned the back of her throat, but she refused to show them how upset she was.

Love exhaled loudly and wiped his face. He let the scrap of wrapping paper fall from his hand. "The time has come for me to take inventory again. I must measure the state of love in the world, and that means I won't be here to watch how Grimbaud fares in the next few months without me. There will be challenges, Hijiri. Pay special attention to the new love charm-makers."

"You know about the love charms competition, then?" Hijiri said, grateful for the slight change in topic. She tried not to look at Ken.

Love's smug smile was all the answer she needed. He had to be involved somehow. "The town is in good hands with you here."

The praise made her squirm. "But you gave me this charmed boy. Like I actually need the help. Which I don't."

"Then *solve* him," Love said, losing patience, "if he's such a puzzle to you."

Ken shrugged with a shy smile.

"Find me if you need me. The cupids have ears," Love said, raising his hand in a mock salute. He stepped back on his heel and the wind returned, tossing her hair in her face. When the air settled, Love was gone. So was the box.

The red ribbon still hung around Ken's neck, but the wind must have stolen his pink coat. He wasn't wearing it anymore. Instead, he slung a large duffel bag over his shoulder and smiled at her. "You miss the coat," he said.

"Not really," Hijiri said. "What was the point of it?"

"Love's idea. He thinks pink is my color," Ken said.

Hijiri stared at him. He looked almost normal now, with the duffel bag and the plain white shirt and the fact that his chest expanded and shrank with each breath. Like a person. *But he's not a person. He's a charm.* She rubbed her eyes, squinted at him, and then rubbed them again.

Unease made her fidgety. She turned on her heel without another word and climbed the staircase. When she heard footsteps on the stairs below her, she looked over her shoulder. "Are you following me?"

Ken grabbed the handrail. "My room is on the second floor."

Hijiri sucked in a breath.

"You don't have to show me where it is."

"You're living here?"

"I have a scholarship," he said. "Love is paying for everything."

Hijiri nodded, as if his answer made perfect sense. Then she reached Fallon's door and knocked as hard as she could.

Fallon opened the door within seconds, her hands red and slightly soapy from the kitchen sink. "What's the matter?" she asked, wiping her hands on her skirt. "Who's that behind you?"

"Kentaro Oshiro," the charm-boy said, brushing past Hijiri to shake Fallon's hand. "Love sent me here as a gift to Hijiri. I hope she'll fall in love with me."

Fallon chewed on her lip, amused. "Is that so?"

Hijiri's hands started shaking. She curled them into fists. First the love charm-making competition. Now this. She needed Fallon on her side, to understand. "He's serious. I found him wrapped up in a box outside my door. Like, with a ribbon and everything."

Ken slid the red ribbon off his shoulders and handed it to Fallon for inspection.

Fallon rubbed the ribbon between her fingers. She raised it to her nose and sniffed. "Grosgrain ribbon, nice," Fallon murmured. "And a little . . . The ribbon's humming with charm magic. Even I can feel it."

"Do I hear the evaluation of clothing material?" called Sebastian, from inside Fallon's apartment.

"Almost," Fallon called back with a laugh.

"Seriously, focus," Hijiri said, digging her nails into her skin. "This is a big problem."

Fallon turned her sharp gaze on Ken. "So it's true, then?"

Ken opened his mouth, only to gasp on the first word. His face turned red when he tried again.

Hijiri's heart lurched. Was he okay? He looked like he was choking . . . on what? Air?

He touched his throat, frowning, and said, "Love sent me here."

"And you're supposed to get Hijiri to love you. That sounds like manipulation," Fallon said.

"*I* may be a charm," he said, "but I don't know what kind."

"So you don't know how you were made?" Hijiri relaxed a little. Curiosity made her fingers itch. "You must know *something*."

Ken coughed and shook his head. "I guess that's where you come in. Love said you could solve me."

"Doesn't mean I'll love you."

"Then figure me out," Ken said with a soft smile. "I'll enjoy the attention."

Hijiri sighed.

Sebastian came to the door, wrapping an arm around Fallon's waist. He wore his usual smirk, the curl of his lip rising when he spotted Ken. "Hi there, charm-boy. Did I hear right? Love gave Hijiri this guy, and then what?"

Hijiri rehashed the last few minutes to them both, from Ken popping out of the present to Love's windy exit. She told them about Love's hand in the love charm-making competition, and how he would be away from Grimbaud while taking inventory for the next few months. "He also said to keep watch over the new love charm-makers. If Love's concerned about them . . ."

"Then we have to be too," Fallon said. "The twins were onto something when they said that a local should be competing."

"All the more reason to meet these charm-makers tomorrow," Sebastian said. "While you two go love charm shopping, I can show Ken around town. He looks lost already."

Ken's smile widened. "Thank you."

"Don't be so nice to him," Hijiri said, fidgeting. "He could . . . disappear into a puff of smoke or collapse into a pile of glitter when you're not looking."

"Do you think Love made me so flimsy?" Ken said, his eyebrows lifting.

"You *are* flimsy." He was too thin. Probably lacking muscles of any kind. She'd never understand Love. If only she could identify the charms that held him together. What had Love done to make him?

He caught her intense stare. "You're trying to dissect me. I think that means it's time for me to go."

"Do the puff of smoke thing," Sebastian said.

"Sorry, I just have my two feet." Ken took his key out of the front zipper of his duffel bag. His eyes landed on Hijiri once more. "Tomorrow."

"Good night," Hijiri muttered. She pressed her fist against her heart, trying to muffle its beating.

After a fitful sleep, Hijiri tumbled out of bed early the next morning and started unpacking her suitcase. The few clothes she brought fit easily in her closet. The rest— her charm-making materials—were more complicated to reorganize and find a place for in her bedroom.

Hijiri gathered a few potion bottles and notes in her arms and looked for a place to put them. Last year, she had used a corner of her bedroom for charm-making: the perfect spot to hide from prying eyes and conduct her crafting in secret. As an extra precaution, she always covered her worktable with a shoji screen. *I couldn't let anyone find out I made love charms. Not with Zita monopolizing the craft,*

Hijiri thought, remembering how careful she had been. She could have been kicked out of town like Grimbaud's past love charm-makers . . . or worse.

She had tried to tell her parents numerous times last year that she couldn't get a good education in Grimbaud with the situation the way it was, but they hadn't believed her.

Her parents had always supported her dreams but never looked too closely at them.

"Nothing to fear now," Hijiri said to herself, adjusting the supplies in her arms. "Zita's gone. It's okay be a love charm-maker here again."

It was okay to be public about it.

Hijiri shuddered. It might be okay, but it still scared her.

Her current problem was finding out what to do with her newfound freedom. Where should she put her charm supplies now? The bedroom and bathroom were off of the kitchen. The kitchen overlooked the living room and the front door—a long, unused stretch of space. And very, very out in the open.

Hijiri swallowed thickly and mumbled, "I'll figure it out later. Fallon will help me. For now, I'll put everything where it used to be."

She set up her table with the supplies she had left in her closet over the summer. Then arranged everything so that it made sense to her. By the time she finished, she decided to put off unpacking the rest of her suitcase and shoved it under her bed. Hijiri stopped to breathe. Her body ached and her head felt cottony from nerves. After a dull summer, so much had happened. Surely Ken was a figment of her imagination. There wasn't enough room in her reality for him.

None at all.

Hijiri had two problems already this school year: solving Ken and preparing for the impending love charm-making competition. Making a dent in one of them would turn her day around—and she was ready to set aside her thoughts of the charm-boy for a while.

"What do you think the love charm-makers are going to be like?" Fallon asked.

Hijiri pursed her lips. From what she had seen back home in Lejeune, love charm-makers were an eccentric lot but usually warm and welcoming. It came with the territory. But what kind of love charm-makers were these people? Moving to Grimbaud so soon after Zita's loss was a risk. Did they want to make this town a better place? Or, as the twins feared, were they here for more selfish reasons?

She knew the twins could be overly dramatic; they liked getting a rise out of people. But if Love was concerned too . . . should *she* be?

"Well, I'm familiar with the first shop we're going to," Hijiri said.

"Really? Have you been to "—Fallon checked her directions—"Metamorphosis before?"

"Absolutely not," Hijiri said, frowning. "But there's a branch in Lejeune."

As they approached Metamorphosis, Hijiri sensed the air thicken. Her eyes flicked to the shop's name above the door, written in reflective cursive. Two round windows on either side of the entrance had been shaped like mirrors with little golden bulbs framing them, drawing towns-people to peek in the windows. The lights stung, too dramatically lit compared with the neighboring shops.

"What are they selling?" Fallon asked, squinting. "We need a closer look."

"Exactly what they want," Hijiri muttered. They came to see the shops though, so she put her misgivings aside and tried to tolerate it. Shading her eyes to block out the golden lights, she saw that the left window revealed a makeup station with a chair already occupied by an excited customer. A Metamorphosis employee fussed over the customer's face, smoothing on blush and lip gloss that warmed up the skin.

Hijiri sighed. "So Grimbaud really has one of these now."

"You've heard of us," said a small, dark woman with a jagged pixie cut. It wasn't a question. The woman's eyelids were dusted shimmery bronze, the hollows of her cheeks defined with more metal-hued powder. Her black smock had crystal butterflies pinned below the straps. "Don't be shy," she said. "My name's Clea Deyrem, co-owner of Metamorphosis. Mandy's inside."

"You're beautiful," Fallon blurted at Clea.

Hijiri pinched her arm.

Fallon flinched and rubbed her arm. She thanked Hijiri under her breath.

Clea modeled her face, letting the charmed makeup shimmer in the light and shadow. "Our newest color palette for the fall. You're feeling its effects already. The eye shadow and bronzer are charmed to encourage compliments."

Compliments pulled like taffy from people's mouths the moment they set eyes on her, Hijiri thought with a shiver. Clea was trying to make her customers infatuated with her. The warmth Hijiri started to feel went away when she tore her eyes away from Clea's face. That kind of charm reminded her too much of how Zita's assistant Camille had controlled Martin with her charmed perfume—and made her doubly repelled by Clea's products.

Fallon must have been thinking the same thing, because she narrowed her eyes and said, "I'd rather form my own opinion of you."

"That's not the point," Clea said dismissively. "We design our love charms to fit our motto: 'If you love you, love will love you too.'"

"So if I look beautiful on the outside, I'll feel beautiful inside, and love will surely follow," Hijiri said.

Clea clapped her hands. "Exactly! It's magnetism. Love is pulled toward positive feelings, don't you think? That's what *we* think."

Hijiri wasn't sure if that was true, though it was a nice sentiment. The Love she knew appreciated mischief. After all, it was mischief in the form of a rebellion that allowed Love to take back Grimbaud from Zita's clutches. Then there was the present Love had left her yesterday.

"New customers are often overwhelmed by our love charms. Let's take a look at you," Clea said, unconcerned with the fact that they were still standing outside the shop. She leaned down to examine Hijiri's face. "You've got such long hair. So well taken care of. Nothing to change there. Clear skin. Good. You need to take better care of your lips. We have a line of glosses that will plump them up and draw boys in like bees to honey."

Hijiri's ears burned from blushing. "I—I don't want that. No kissing."

"You say that now," Clea said, laughing. "Well, what about your eyes, your cheeks? No makeup at all. That's a shame. You could be attracting more attention if you paid more attention to yourself."

Hijiri broke into a sweat, her pulse pounding. She didn't want any more attention, especially from boys. Clea's remarks dredged up memories of last spring when she had tried to go on a few dates. After Hijiri had helped defeat Zita, a few of the braver boys had asked her out, and she had said yes out of curiosity and a sense that a love charm-maker should have experience in these matters. Yet she never made it past the first fifteen minutes. Instead of focusing on her dates, she would start itching to return to her charm-making. *Must be my small heart*, she had decided, *the reason I can't feel even a flutter of attraction.* "I've heard enough. Thanks," she snapped at Clea, grabbing Fallon's hand and turning on her heel.

Clea called after her, but Hijiri didn't waver.

"Do you think she treats all her customers like that?" Fallon asked. "So pushy."

Hijiri pressed her hand over her heart, willing it to slow down. She couldn't believe how quickly and effortlessly Clea had dissected her. *How did she know in one glance that I've failed at love? What can she do to me because of that knowledge?*

Fallon touched her elbow. "Maybe we should take a break."

"No," Hijiri said, shaking her head. "We have two more shops. It can't wait. . . ."

"It *can*," Fallon said firmly. "We both need lunch. I know of a place that makes omelets with organic ingredients. You'll feel better with some nice, clean food in your stomach."

"Will that really make a difference?"

"Fresh food, fresh mind," Fallon said. "One of my parents' mottos."

Hijiri cracked a smile.

⇥

No matter how high quality her omelet was, Hijiri's stomach twisted into knots as they entered a rougher part of Grimbaud. "Rougher" wasn't quite the right word, considering how the town was built, each brick carefully laid and cracked only with age, but some townspeople took better care of their homes and shops than others.

Fallon reread her directions a few times, crinkling her nose. "Is there really a love charms shop here?"

Hijiri looked around. Most of the shops catered to locals since tourists usually didn't wander off the main streets. They passed a lawyer's office and a gym. After counting the numbers on the sidewalks, they found the second shop. Maybe.

Heartwrench was a dingy extension of the car repair shop next door, with oil stains on the pavement and a crumbling shingled roof. Blacked-out windows gave no hint of what was inside, except for the flickering neon-pink sign that read HEARTWRENCH, with a wrench for the *T* and a heart framing the shop's name. Fallon avoided stepping on the oil stains. When Hijiri and Fallon stepped inside, a bell made of nuts and bolts clattered against the door.

Despite having been open for months, the shelves were dusty and empty. Boxes still sealed with masking tape were piled by the cashier's desk. The shop was dark except for the hanging lightbulbs overhead, spotlighting the display tables below.

Fallon ran her finger over one of the display tables, making a trail in the dust. She crinkled her nose.

If Hijiri hadn't known that this was a love charm shop, she would have thought the items on display were junk parts. She studied a charm sitting on a table to her left; the metal had been sculpted to look like an anatomically correct heart, and messy wiring tangled around it like bramble. When Hijiri poked the heart, the charm sprang to life, rattling on the table and shooting sparks.

"It's not done yet," yelled a man in his late sixties, emerging from the back room. His blue overalls strained against his belly, and oil spotted the mauve button-down shirt underneath. The man's jowls jiggled as he walked, his thinning hair buried underneath a baseball cap.

Hijiri leapt away from the table when the heart started rolling. "What does it do?"

The man ran over to the table and caught the heart before it fell. He struggled to turn it in his hands while it still rattled, but after pulling a red wire, it stopped moving. "It's a breakable heart," the man said. "If you're afraid of a broken heart, just wear this one strapped to your chest instead. It absorbs all the feelings you get while dating someone and keeps it away from your real heart. So when the relationship ends . . ." The old man chuckled. "This heart breaks instead and your real one is safe."

"To date someone with no risk to yourself . . ." Hijiri felt sick. "That doesn't seem fair. It's like you're telling people it's *okay* to close themselves off from experiencing love fully."

"Only cowards would buy it," Fallon said, glaring at the mechanical heart.

The man's smile dropped.

"Uncle Gage, I need some help here," said a college-aged boy, popping his head out from the back room.

"We have customers, Ryker!" Gage said.

Ryker sighed and pushed his glasses up the bridge of his nose. He had a handsome face with dark blue eyes and a straight nose, his hair smoothed back against his head with gel. Like his uncle, he wore overalls and a button-down shirt. "What are they going to buy? You haven't unpacked the boxes yet."

Gage grunted. "We're ready enough. The sign's lit up outside."

The emptiness of the shop made Hijiri uneasy, and the one charm they saw didn't tell her much about her competition. "I was wondering what kind of charms you make," she asked.

Ryker's gaze flickered from Hijiri to Fallon and back again. His blue eyes were magnified by his thick prescription glasses. "Uncle and I decided to go into the love charm business with one goal in mind: to make charms that whet the appetite of customers who prefer technology to the magic of charms."

"So you mask your charms in wires and gears," Hijiri said. While Grimbaud had always been accepting of charms, other places were not. In Lejeune, charms were used frequently, but most people preferred using modern technology rather than charms to heat their homes or monitor their heart rates. Hijiri always saw it as a matter of practicality—but that was why love charms were so interesting. *Love is magic,* she thought, *and nothing can change that. Technology is no equal to love.*

"We marry the two," Ryker said before his uncle could speak. "Watching a charm interact with the metal body we've built it into is *exhilarating.*"

Hijiri shivered. The wired, metal heart on the table still hadn't moved since Gage turned it off, but she half-expected it to start rattling again. Unnerved, she said good-bye, thankful that Fallon took her cue to leave.

"Tell your friends about us," Gage called after them.

We will, Hijiri thought with a grimace.

Chapter 3

SWEATER WEATHER

Hijiri's feet dragged. Her heart had gotten stuck underneath her shoe; she heard it *squish*, *squish*, *squish* in her head as they came close to the third and final love charms shop. After two rather disconcerting shops, she doubted the last one would restore her hope.

"Love For All is just around the corner," Fallon said, folding her directions to go back into her skirt pocket.

Hijiri grabbed Fallon's wrist. "Did you say Love For All?"

"Yes, why?"

Forget her hope. This one was going to be a disaster. "It's a discount store."

As common as supermarkets and nail salons, Love For All sold discounted love charms. The charms were cheap because Love For All notoriously bought them from apprentices or hobbyists and sold the charms at a slightly higher price to unaware customers. The company stayed in business because people preferred buying more charms for less money.

The love charms that came from that store were unreliable. Hijiri had heard numerous stories of those love charms fizzling out after the first use or not working the way they were advertised. *Still, Love For All never gets in trouble. They hang disclaimers all over their stores to protect themselves,* she thought with disgust. *Why would Grimbaud have approved of Love For All opening here?*

"I thought this town had standards," Hijiri whispered.

"Now you sound like me," Fallon said wryly.

"You're not going to like this shop either," Hijiri warned her friend.

"I haven't liked any of them yet. Metamorphosis was pushy and manipulative. Heartwrench was . . . kind of strange. Creepy, even," Fallon said, shrugging. "I can't blame Love for being concerned."

Hijiri had to agree.

Love For All had set up shop in a time-worn brick building. Stone cupids joyously danced on the ledges. Giant yellow posters advertising back-to-school deals disfigured the old building, but it drew in crowds of middle school and high school students with small allowances.

Seeing the crowds of eager customers made her eyes misty. Grimbaudians wanted their love charms. They were moving on. There was something beautiful about that. After Zita's defeat, Hijiri felt the town darken with loss. They hadn't known how horrible and twisted Zita's love fortunes had been. They had no idea.

Most of the townspeople had considered Zita the heart of the town. Losing a heart completely . . . is a death. *But the town's living again, little by little*, she thought, softening.

But watching them dig through bargain bins of badly made love charms wasn't okay either. Hijiri stood taller and lifted her chin. She felt more resolved than ever to win this competition.

The generous floor space inside had aisles and more bins. Big signs hung over each section with labels like UNREQUITED LOVE, BREAKUPS, and REKINDLING OLD LOVE. Customers searched through racks for charmed clothing with various love-related properties. Even with the signs, the sections themselves offered the same plethora of love charms mixed together in boxes, bins, and drawers. Most of them didn't have labels either; how could people tell just what some of these love charms did?

Fallon kept her hands at her sides. "I don't want to think of the material," she said when she saw a woman carrying a pile of charmed shirts in her arms.

"Ignore the clothes," Hijiri said, tapping Fallon's shoulder. "Look at the back corner. I wonder what's there. That line's so long."

The main attraction that had caused the line was a candy station. Flashing bulbs along the top of the station beckoned customers closer for a taste of the treats inside the dispensers. Children grabbed plastic bags and scoops that were tied to each dispenser. Hijiri watched with fascination as customers scooped gummy mice, blackberry chews, miniature sugar waffles, and unsurprisingly numerous chocolate and chocolate-flavored confections.

Hijiri slowly nudged her way to the dispensers to see the sweets. She spotted what looked like chocolate-covered black licorice, each one in a tubelike shape. Bending down to read the description, she was startled to find it carried a love charm:

Sweet on the outside, bitter on the inside.
Feed this to your angry loved one and find out
why he or she's mad—helps resolve lover's
quarrels with honesty.

Forced honesty, Hijiri thought, flinching slightly, but that was how most love charms worked. "I thought they were just candy," she said, meeting Fallon's eyes.

Fallon threw her a panicked look and checked another one. The gummy mice. She read it once, then motioned for Hijiri to join her. It read:

Temporary heightened sense of hearing
when eaten. Use your spy ears wisely.

"For the stalker boyfriends and girlfriends in all of us," Hijiri said dryly, her nose crinkling. "Why would people eat these? They're sure to cause trouble."

"Why are *kids* eating them?" Fallon stressed. Her eyes flung daggers. "This is *not* okay, Hijiri. Worse than loose threads and dirty ice."

For once, her quality-obsessed friend wasn't overreacting.

Back in Lejeune, there was an age restriction on buying certain kinds of charms. For safety's sake, love charms had been included on that list of monitored charms. While not intentionally harmful, love charms impacted a person's emotions and thoughts. Manipulating the mind and heart *too much* had consequences. A few years back, a love charm-maker in Lejeune had been arrested for selling love potions that turned the drinkers into little more than slaves—never eating, sleeping, or having a thought stray from the person they had been forced to love. Worse than the perfume Camille crafted, those love potions had been irreversible.

As far as she knew, those poor people were still suffering from the potions' effects while the crooked love charm-maker rotted in jail.

Recalling that story gave her the shivers. Hijiri knew there was a fine line between a good love charm and a bad one. That was why rules existed. Middle schoolers needed permission from their parents to buy love charms, but once reaching high school, they gained the freedom to buy and use them as they liked.

Grimbaud had not needed such rules during Zita's reign. She had closely monitored who had access to her charms. But now that the town was free, Grimbaud's police force should have been catching up with the rest of the world.

"Where's the manager?" Fallon said, raising her voice. She stomped away from the line, cupping her hands around her mouth. "I need a manager *right now*."

A weedy man with a sour face approached. His blond hair was cut short, his forehead riddled with acne. "Sanders Lemmens," he said, crossing his arms. "Not a manager. *Owner*."

"You're selling charmed candy to underage children," Fallon said loudly.

Sanders curled his lip. "Of course I am. Don't they teach the basics of supply and demand here? My *customers* want the candy, and if I don't sell it to them, they will just steal it. Shoplifting seems to be particularly prevalent in this 'sweet' little town."

Fallon made a strangled sound. Her cheeks flushed. "You can't get away with this."

Sanders crossed his arms tighter but otherwise appeared unfazed. He blinked slowly. "Are you done?"

"What kind of love charm-maker are you? If you're one at all," Hijiri said.

"My charm-making skills will speak for me once the competition begins. Feel free to join the audience. I hear Verbeke Square will be packed."

Hijiri wanted to say she'd be there too—onstage, ready

to show off her own skills—but her participation wasn't secured yet. Her jaw hurt when she clenched it. "We'll see you there," she said as pleasantly as she could manage.

Fallon didn't bother being nice. Instead, she complained about the stickiness of the tile floor before shooting Sanders one last withering glare.

Sanders merely waved good-bye.

☘→

When Hijiri got back to the complex, she paused at the gate. Then she crouched and looked through the cracks in the wooden gate. *Not now, please,* she mentally groaned when she confirmed Ken was waiting for her outside her door. *I can't handle him right now. Not after everything.*

"Are you hiding?" Fallon whispered.

"I don't want to talk to Ken," Hijiri said, rubbing her face. Her head hurt and her fingers itched for therapy in the form of love charm-making. "I can't deal with him right now."

Fallon sighed. "I'll tell him to come back later."

Hijiri grabbed Fallon's ankle. "Not later. Tomorrow."

"Are you sure?"

"Please."

Fallon tucked her hair behind her ears. "Okay, then."

Hijiri stayed in her hiding spot as Fallon closed the gate behind her and said hello to Ken. She hoped that this plan would work—she couldn't sneak into her apartment through the windows since they were locked, unless she wanted to risk Mrs. Smedt's wrath by breaking one. Which seemed ridiculous just to avoid a charm-boy.

She couldn't hear what they were saying, but she saw Ken's smile flatten and his shoulders slump when Fallon must have told him that she wasn't home . . . or something like that. *Whatever excuse Fallon's giving him is probably a sound one, knowing her.*

After Ken left to go back upstairs, Fallon gave Hijiri a thumbs-up. All clear. "I told him you were at the library reading up on love charms," Fallon said. "You could be there all night, so he shouldn't wait up."

"Thank you. That sounds like me," Hijiri said, re-lieved.

"Good. Get some sleep, then. School's starting tomorrow. Don't forget."

Hijiri nodded and nearly leapt into her apartment. The day's events left her restless. Nothing but silence and charm-making could mend her frazzled thoughts now. Her fingers darted across her worktable, pinching sugar, smoothing rose petals, and drawing diagrams of the few love charms she hadn't gotten to making over the summer. Her hair fell over her shoulder, landing in the bottle of ink she had open on the table. She hadn't realized she'd been so preoccupied until her hair left black streaks on her shirt when she leaned back.

"Maybe Fallon's right," she muttered, rubbing her thumb over the stains. Charm-making usually calmed her, but she felt like she was racing. *I want to outrun today,* she thought with a snort. *But the only way I can do that is to leave it behind. Time for bed.*

〜▷

Monday morning, Hijiri took a shower and donned her Grimbaud High uniform. If her mirror was being truthful, she somewhat resembled a human being. Good. When she heard a knock on her door, she finger-combed her bangs into place before jogging over to answer it.

Kentaro stood on the other side, holding a paper bag that smelled deliciously of lemon and blueberry.

Her stomach gurgled; she slapped a hand over it, as if it would smother the sound.

"Good morning to you too," he said, his lips twitching with suppressed laughter.

Hijiri felt at least three levels of embarrassment at once. Her stomach betrayed her by growling. "You're outside my door. Again."

"This time, not in a box," he said cheerfully. "I bought muffins from the café a few blocks from here. The smell was incredible."

Her stomach let out a whine of agreement.

"The muffins are bribery, if you must know," Ken said,

lowering his voice. He looked nervous. "I came here to ask . . . if it's okay to walk to school together."

She felt for him. School wasn't that great, after all; as a charm-boy, he probably had no idea what he was in for. "Of course we're walking together," she said. "Come inside. I haven't restocked the kitchen yet, but if you're okay with tap water . . ."

He nodded. "Thanks."

Ken must be a morning person, she thought with some envy. His eyes weren't crusty from sleep, and not even a whisper of a yawn touched his lips as he took in her plain apartment. He wore the standard Grimbaud High uniform: brown slacks and a white polo shirt worn underneath a brown-and-gold sweater. It took Hijiri a minute to realize he was wearing the winter uniform. In August.

"Why are you wearing that?" she asked.

"Sweater's part of the uniform."

"Yeah, when it's actually cold out."

"I get cold easily."

Hijiri chewed her lip. "Could be a flaw in your design," she said, staring at him. "Love shouldn't have missed such an important detail. I wish I had a thermometer on me."

"My body temperature is normal," Ken insisted, brushing past her to place the bag of muffins on the kitchen table. "I just like sweaters and being warm. I heard that high schools have frosty air-conditioning systems, despite the weather outdoors."

"You heard?"

"Love told me."

"So you've never been . . . to school?"

Ken looked almost relieved when he said, "Never."

Hijiri wanted to slap herself. *Of course he's never been to school. He's a charm. He hasn't experienced anything besides being squished in a box.*

Ken began searching the cabinets for glasses.

"I can do that," she said, scrambling after him.

"You were in a different world just now," he said.

"I was thinking."

Ken raised his eyebrows. He handed her two glasses from the cabinet. They were dusty, so Hijiri took them to the sink to wash them.

He pulled a few more items from the cabinets. Then she heard the paper bag rustle behind her. The scent of muffins filled the room. Running water masked her stomach this time. Hijiri hustled to fill the glasses with water, knowing that as the seconds wore on, her hunger grew. Turning from the sink, she gasped.

Although she hadn't been at the sink long, he had managed to dress the table with whatever she had left lying around the living room. Her plastic utensils framed the plates like little soldiers. The vase of begonias she was saving for charm-making made a pretty centerpiece. He had even managed to fold the paper napkins into knots.

Ken hummed as he placed each muffin on its plate; the muffins were big enough to have to cut with a knife and fork. "Come sit down," he said.

Hijiri slowly sat in her chair. Then she poked the folded napkin. Had Love programmed him to set tables? This was *only* breakfast. What could he do with a candlelit dinner?

"What's the matter?" Ken asked, grabbing his fork. She poked the napkin again and stared at the table. She stared hard enough to make her head hurt. "I know what this is," she said, blinking. "You're *flirting* with me." Ken dropped his fork, startled by her bluntness.

Hijiri frowned, even as she cut into her muffin; it was still warm, the heat drifting like smoke. The first bite melted on her tongue.

"About this," he said, tapping the table with his fingers, "it just comes naturally. I wasn't trying to flirt . . ."

She huffed.

"Intentionally."

Hijiri put her elbows on the table. "Tell me how you work."

Ken laughed. "The same way you do. An anatomy textbook would explain everything."

"I don't believe you. Maybe on the outside you look normal, but you're not. You're a charm."

"What do you hope to gain by figuring me out?" Ken asked softly.

Hijiri's gaze dropped to her hands. "I want to be the

best love charm-maker ever. I know I'm already on the way to achieving that dream, especially since I have contact with Love, but you're a charm I haven't made myself. Even Zita hadn't crafted anything like you, and she was the greatest love charm-maker we've had. If I could figure out how you were made, then maybe I could make a charm-boy or charm-girl too."

"What would you do with them?"

Hijiri shrugged. "I can't think of any uses off the top of my head."

Ken didn't try to hide the hurt in his eyes or the tightness around his mouth. "I'm useless?"

Hijiri shifted uncomfortably in her chair. "I meant that you're dangerous to fall in love with. Since you're . . . you know . . . not real." *Love wants me to fall in love with him, but there's no way I can. This will only end badly,* she thought. But he was upset, and she didn't like that. She changed her answer a little. Made it not about her. "I'd never want to put customers in such a position where they fall in love with something so transitory, but I do want to have the skills to craft something as complicated as you. That knowledge might lead me to bigger and better love charms."

Ken shredded his napkin, then reached for another. She watched his fingers tear at the paper. How realistic each movement was. After a few minutes, he sighed and pasted a peacemaking smile on his face. "Okay, I can live with that for now."

"I'll solve you, puzzle-boy," Hijiri warned, taking a bite of her muffin.

"And I'll make you change your mind," Ken said, matching her tone. "I'm irresistible. Just like these muffins."

Hijiri snorted. "Now you're desperate."

Ken laughed.

They ate the rest of their breakfast in silence. The silence wasn't uncomfortable, but it was strange all the same. Ken seemed unfazed. He was perfectly calm, lost in relishing the taste of his muffin and looking around the room. Their eyes met often. She fidgeted and kicked her feet under the table.

When they were done, Ken took the plates and cups to the sink. "Would you like me to wash up?"

"No, that's okay. You bought the food." She paused. "Thanks."

"You're welcome." Ken crossed the room and dug his own keys out of his pocket. "Will you be leaving for school soon?"

"In a few minutes." She had to brush her teeth and toss some pens and notebooks in her bag.

Kentaro waited for her at the complex's gate. Most Grimbaud High boys used briefcase-style or messenger bags to lug their textbooks, but again, Ken had chosen a strange alternative: a backpack that had a strap across his chest. A bad choice, she thought, since it made him look dorky.

Hijiri nodded her thanks when he opened the gate for her. "Okay. Explain the backpack."

"These straps help distribute weight properly," he explained. "I figure that carrying textbooks around all day would be bad for my back. Anything helps."

"Maybe Love should have made you stronger." Hijiri had noticed his slight, somewhat scrawny frame from the first.

Ken shrugged. "I don't know what can and can't hurt me. Might as well be prepared."

"You look . . . sturdy enough."

The corners of his eyes crinkled when he smiled. A big smile. "Thanks."

As they walked, Ken barely watched where he was going. His eyes swept the streets and rooftops, sucking in the details that made up Grimbaud. Hijiri was glad that she didn't have to make small talk, but she found herself sneaking glances at him, just to see what he was looking at. Cafés with open doors, coaxing in hungry passersby with strong coffee and flaky pastries. Children in their elementary school uniforms, holding hands with their parents or sitting in the backseats of cars, fogging the windows with their noses.

"Are we almost there?" he asked.

"One more street," Hijiri said, her steps slowing. She

wasn't looking forward to the crush of students in the hall-ways or the pop quizzes.

A girl riding a bicycle flew past. Ken moved closer to Hijiri to avoid getting clipped. And stayed there. The back of his hand brushed hers. "Do you have any advice," he said quietly, "on how to make friends?"

Grimbaud High loomed before them. They both stopped, marveling at the stonework of the wings flank-ing the original building: a gatehouse with a tunnel running through it, marking the western edge of town. The cam-pus had a big lawn; the old, trampled grass had been re-placed over the summer, and chattering students already occupied the benches.

"Hijiri?" Ken asked.

Right. His question.

"I'm not the person to ask." Hijiri had never been able to make friends before Grimbaud. And the friends she did have . . . they just happened. Like fate.

Strangely, her answer made him smile. His hand brushed hers deliberately. He found the spaces between her fingers and slipped his through, his skin warm and surprisingly comforting. But Ken was still nervous; she could tell by the way his other hand squeezed his shoul-der strap.

"You don't have to be afraid," she said impulsively. "My friends will be your friends."

Without waiting to see his response, she tugged him

forward. The usual meeting spot in the tunnel was already crowded with students eager to escape the hot sun. Hijiri squeezed through a group of confused freshmen, finally spotting her friends. Her hold on Ken's hand stayed firm. Fallon and Sebastian waved, but Femke and Mirthe barreled toward Hijiri.

"Hello, Love-thing," Mirthe said. Without warning, she grabbed Ken's head and stared into his eyes, as if expecting to find an answer there. Then she told him to smile so she could inspect his teeth.

Femke felt Ken's pulse. "Feels real to me."

"What are you doing?" Hijiri's voice broke. "Don't touch him!"

Her cheeks felt like they were on fire. Which was silly, since Hijiri wasn't going to get involved with Ken. He wasn't real and she didn't want to invest even a sliver of her heart in a very clever charm. Except perhaps to study it. Watching the twins poke and prod at Ken made her itch to do the same.

The twins dropped their hands. Mirthe pulled off the biggest pout she'd ever seen.

Ken scratched the back of his head. He wiped his mouth where Mirthe's fingers had been before and sucked in his breath. "I have a heartbeat," he said, "and I need air to live. By the way, my name's Ken."

"Oh, he's good," Mirthe whispered.

"We're sorry," Fallon said, looking as mortified as

Hijiri felt. "Sebastian and I told the twins about Ken before you two got here, but we didn't think he'd be attacked."

"You handled it well, actually," Sebastian said to Ken. "I think you'll fit in."

"Are you really what Fallon said?" Mirthe asked. "Love made you?"

When he tried speaking, his voice caught in his throat and he coughed into his fist. Ken looked down at his hands, staring at his palms as if he could see through them. He tried again. This time, his voice was soft but firm. "Love created me for Hijiri. I already love her. If my feelings are returned, then I suppose I've done my job. Regardless, I belong to her. It's as simple as that."

Hijiri hadn't thought it was possible for her cheeks to burn even worse. *He just said he loved me.* The burning spread down her neck and back. If her skin hadn't turned the color of a candy apple within seconds, she'd count it as a miracle. The entire confession made her dizzy, confused, and achy. Hijiri quickly shoved his words to the back of her head, where the darkness and cobwebs were.

Her friends were equally stunned. Sebastian coughed, his own cheeks pink. Fallon had her sharp gaze on Ken, her mouth turned up in a smile. When they finally found their voices, Mirthe was predictably the one with more questions.

"So tell me," she said, her eyes aglitter, "did Love give you superpowers?"

Hijiri sputtered.

"Why would you think that?" Ken said, interested.

Femke cut in. "Because that's how it's *done*. Love must have given you some powers to aid Hijiri in her love charm-making."

"I don't think she needs my help with her craft," Ken said. He broke into a boyish grin. "But there *is* something cool I can do."

Chapter 4

IMPRESSING THE PRINCIPAL

Ken walked to the back of the tunnel. Hijiri's curiosity flared as she followed him. The greenbelt separating Grimbaud from the roads leading to the next town over had been overlooked during the pre-school-year cleanup. Plastic wrappers and empty bottles were scattered in the overgrowth. Ken unsnapped his chest strap and rooted around in his backpack until he found a slingshot. "Pick any target," he said, gesturing to the litter, "and I'll hit it."

"From here?" Sebastian asked.

Ken stood in the shade of the tunnel; the overgrowth had to be at least a hundred feet away. Bending down to pick up a pebble, he said, "Anything."

From their distance, the bottles and wrappers were spots of color, half-obscured by the weeds and scraggly plants. Hijiri squinted. A teal-colored soda can caught her eye. "How about that one?" she asked, pointing.

Ken nodded. He notched the pebble. The muscles in

his forearms quivered as he took aim. When he let go, the pebble whistled through the air and knocked into the can's already-bent middle, sending it flying.

The twins let out whoops and clapped Ken on the back.

Confident before, Ken seemed to deflate after showing off. "How'd I do?" he asked Hijiri.

"Impressive," she nearly whispered.

He flashed a shy smile.

"Where did you learn to do that?" Sebastian asked. "I played with a slingshot as a kid, but I had terrible aim."

Ken hesitated. He toyed with the rubber strips. "I'm decent with a bow and arrow too, but not as comfortable with them as a slingshot."

"Makes perfect sense," Hijiri said. He hadn't answered Sebastian's question, but how could he? He hadn't lived long enough to have practiced at a skill. Love obviously gave him some remarkable talents. "Think of the cupids. As one of Love's creations, Ken must have the same abilities."

"I can't fly," he admitted.

Mirthe sighed. "Now, that's a shame."

Ken was going to give another demonstration with his slingshot when Martin came running, Nico on his heels.

"Weapons and horseplay are strictly forbidden on campus," Martin said, every inch the student government president.

"Good morning to you too," Sebastian said.

Martin held out his hand. "I'm going to have to confiscate your slingshot. You can have it back at the end of the day."

"Can the president do that?" Mirthe whispered.

"Better him than an assistant principal," Femke whispered back.

Being separated from his slingshot was not an appealing option to Ken. His eyes darted from the slingshot and back to Martin. With a sigh, he handed it over.

Hijiri placed her hand on Martin's wrist. "Ken doesn't know the rules."

"Kentaro Oshiro, transfer student?" Martin asked. His expression relaxed. "I'm sorry, but I really can't give you back the slingshot until school's over. I'm aware of your situation. If you have any questions, don't be embarrassed to ask us."

"Did we miss Ken's interrogation?" Nico asked cheerfully.

"We'll fill you in later," Fallon said.

"You told Nico and Martin too?" Hijiri asked.

Fallon flashed an apologetic smile. "I thought it would be best if everyone in our club knew."

Hijiri nodded.

The seconds scattered. Ken's eyes met hers. He was nervous all over again. She could tell because he grabbed both straps in a white-knuckled grip. He wasn't even paying attention to the twins' theories on why Love hadn't given him wings.

She wanted to tell him that he would be okay. That his slingshot would be returned. That tomorrow wouldn't be as bad as the first day. But she wasn't used to offering comfort beyond giving people love charms. "Don't worry so much," she finally said. "You'll find a way to blend in."

Ken's grip on his backpack straps loosened, just a little.

The bell rang. Students dispersed in different directions. Hijiri looked at her class schedule; first period would be algebra with Mr. De Pelsmaeker. Before leaving, she asked Ken if he needed help finding his class.

"I'm going to the orientation," he said.

Fallon froze. "Don't eat the casserole."

"Actually, you probably should," Sebastian said. "Don't want to upset Principal Bemelmans."

"Just be careful. Food poisoning is not fun." Fallon cracked a smile. Punctual to a fault, she hooked her arm through Sebastian's and said good-bye to the group.

At the mention of orientation, Martin paled and searched his file folder for the latest rewrite of his speech. When he couldn't find it, he started shaking.

Ken shifted his weight. "Maybe we should get going."

"Wait," Hijiri said.

Nico gently took the folder from Martin and searched through each of the pockets. He found the speech toward the back, stuck against an old syllabus. "Even without this, you'll do just fine," Nico said.

"My last speech," Martin said wistfully.

"Yes, and it will be your best. I've got just the charm

for you." Nico wiggled his fingers and cupped Martin's face. He pressed a short but soft kiss to his boyfriend's lips.

Martin kept his eyes closed a little longer, as if hoping Nico's charm needed more time to work. He was blushing, but not as flustered as he had been when he and Nico started dating last spring.

Hijiri felt proud of the two boys. "We can go now," she told Ken.

Ken fell into step beside her as they joined the rush of students crossing the lawn. "That wasn't a charm, was it?" Ken asked.

She shook her head. "Nico would never use a charm on Martin."

"That's good," Ken said.

Hijiri frowned. "Shouldn't you know a love charm when you see it?"

"Maybe Love forgot that with the wings," he said.

Now that Hijiri was a sophomore, she had earned the privilege of wasting time during homeroom watching orientation from the third-floor windows. Mr. De Pelsmaeker even opened the classroom windows for them so that they could smell the casserole and excitement wafting while they peered down at the freshmen.

Freshmen orientation had been a blur for her. Tables

enticed the new students to become part of the community early. Local charm-makers talked about their disciplines and interviewed for potential apprentices, should a freshman already know what type of charm-making he or she wanted to pursue. Other tables gave out information on clubs and school programs.

Hijiri tried to see if Ken had taken a piece of the principal's casserole, but he was hard to spot from that height. She thought she might have seen him at the office-experience program booth, but she couldn't be sure with students rushing from table to table. She gave up after a few minutes and found her seat. When homeroom ended, Hijiri didn't have to move since Mr. De Pelsmaeker was her first-period teacher too for algebra. Mr. De Pelsmaeker stapled the class's worksheets while reminiscing about his own freshmen orientation many years ago. His white hair was almost translucent and his vest had seen better days, but Hijiri was glad that when it came down to teaching, the man could explain exponents perfectly.

She drifted through the school day in much the same fashion as she had last year. She found seats in the back of classrooms, where she could either stare out a window or stare at inspirational posters on the dull, cream-colored walls. She took notes as each teacher discussed major projects and exam dates, but her margins were dedicated to doodles and ideas about love charms. Ken wasn't in any of her classes.

Martin made good on his promise of getting them an appointment with Principal Bemelmans that day. The principal's office was located at the very top of the main office—the rooms above the old gate. Hijiri had never been beyond the front office, where sleepy secretaries and office-experience program students fielded calls and took care of minor emergencies. As she climbed the steps to his office, she felt dizzy. Everything was riding on earning the principal's approval. If they failed here, they wouldn't be able to compete.

Principal Bemelmans's square-shaped office had windows on three walls that provided an excellent view of the campus below. Because of the constant sunlight, his certificates and degrees had faded in their frames. The principal himself was tall, tanned, and handsome, with a graying mustache and sideburns. Hijiri tried to pick out the details Fallon would have noticed in order to share them with her later. The exercise distracted her from her thumping heart. She wiped her sweaty palms on her skirt.

"Entering the competition is a heavy commitment," Principal Bemelmans said, steepling his fingers.

"One that we can handle," Femke said.

"Or would you rather let three outsiders compete for the title of Grimbaud's Best Love Charm-Maker?" Mirthe asked.

Femke jabbed her twin with her elbow, but it was too late.

Principal Bemelmans frowned. "It doesn't matter where they've come from. These are the love charm-makers we have now, and they deserve our respect."

"Then it doesn't matter what age we are," Mirthe said, "or how far along with our charm-making skills. Our club has a love charm-maker. Let her participate."

"Which one of you?"

Hijiri stepped forward.

The principal appraised her. He untangled his fingers and rubbed his chin. "Miss Kitamura, why do you and your club want to participate? Tell me in your own words."

Hijiri pulled an acorn out of her pocket. She held the acorn between her thumb and index finger. This was a simple charm, but one that took a great bit of effort and earned her numerous paper cuts over the summer. She twisted the top off the acorn, and a garden of miniature paper roses floated out and spun in the air. The words *I love you* burned like a firework and the paper roses crumbled to dust. Easy cleanup for a surprise romantic gesture.

Principal Bemelmans had watched the little charm with unmasked awe. His gaze flickered from the empty acorn to her eyes.

"Words aren't as powerful," she said, tucking the acorn back in her pocket, "but if you want an answer, it's simply this: because I must."

The twins were smiling so hard their cheeks looked ready to split. She didn't look behind her to see Sebastian's, Martin's, and Nico's reactions, but she felt their support. The cramped office buzzed with energy.

Principal Bemelmans reached across his desk to shake her hand.

Hijiri swore that the bobblehead cupid on the desk winked at her.

After school, Hijiri came over to Fallon's apartment. Fallon kept her apartment tidy and covered her walls with vintage restaurant posters. Her furnishings looked like new because of the high-quality antiques she bought. The space could be a little uncomfortable with its cleanliness, but Hijiri noticed with some amusement that Sebastian's touches showed up here and there: a magnetized list of fast-food numbers on the fridge and cassette tapes stacked haphazardly on her desk.

They brewed mint tea. Hijiri sat cross-legged on the floor, taking small sips from her clay cup, while Fallon tried finding the most efficient way to pack her school supplies in the new leather bag her brother had bought her. While the feminine briefcase with golden locks looked very smart, it was impractical. The pockets were stiff. Fallon's folder just barely fit when she wedged it inside between her pencil case and planner.

"At least it's pretty," Hijiri said. "And obviously quality."

"That's exactly what I told Robbie. But I really wish I could use it. There's just not enough room," Fallon said.

Hijiri had left her own school supplies where they were in her bag, a messy heap of loose pens and pencils, her notebook cover already creased when crushed between two textbooks. She bit her lip and blurted, "What do you think about Ken?"

Fallon unzipped her pencil case. "He seems nice."

"What I mean is the idea of him. It's not fair. Love just shoved this guy at me. Said I'm bound to fall in love with him. I hate it. I don't want to be forced to like him, just because Love said so. Plus, he's made of charms. I love charm-making, but I'd never *marry* my own charms."

Fallon separated her pens and pencils on the floor. She rubbed her upper lip, considering each one. "If it were me, I'd be happy to have met The Boy so easily."

Hijiri groaned. "That's because you *expected* to meet him."

"And you didn't?" Fallon looked up. "I remember our first rebellion meeting. How you cried because you wanted someone to love you as you were."

She did remember that. At the time, what she wanted had been so clear. Loneliness gnawed at her, from her empty home to watching the people around her come together as couples, two by two. When she came to Grimbaud, she wanted a romance of her own. But what she got had been more valuable: friends, *real* friends, and a chance to become a great love charm-maker. The few dates she had gone on were disappointing and made her question her own heart. It was more a secret to her than ever.

"I don't understand my heart," Hijiri confessed.

Fallon grabbed Hijiri's hands and squeezed. "Hearts are complicated. It's okay."

"No, it's not."

Fallon frowned. "You can't know everything. Try this: while you're studying Ken, pay attention to what your own heart is doing."

Hijiri huffed, smoothing down her bangs. Her friend was right, somewhat. She needed to look at this like an experiment. Experiments were simple: engage and observe. Record results. She could handle that.

"Trust Love," Fallon said.

"What does that mean?"

Fallon laughed. "It means relax. Besides, you have a competition to start thinking about."

Hijiri cracked a smile. They spent another hour talking and trying to arrange Fallon's supplies in the bag before saying good night.

When the stars came out, Hijiri stepped outside her apartment and breathed in the humidity. The complex wasn't quiet. Lights were on in many of the apartments. Students shared first-day stories with their friends out on the patio.

She put on her sheer cardigan before climbing the stairs. The higher she rose, the more she could see. When she reached the top, she sat on the highest step and rested her elbows on her knees. Moonlight covered the town in shadows and silver strokes of light.

Then she felt a presence beside her.

Ken mimicked her pose. He wore the free T-shirt that the student government officers gave out during orientation; it looked the same as last year's, with the school's crest on the front.

"What are you doing here?" she asked.

"I recognized your silhouette on the stairs," Ken said, brushing his knee against hers. He smelled clean, like evergreen with a touch of sweetness.

Hijiri forgot Fallon's challenge and mentally shoved her heart into a box before it could react. "Did you hear about the love charm-making competition?"

"You've entered," he said, nodding. He'd heard the news from Sebastian when he bumped into him at the complex. "I'm proud to be a member of such a prestigious club."

"You're joining?"

"Of course."

Hijiri picked at her cardigan's sleeve. "Our club has a lot of history, you know. We've changed this town."

Ken nodded solemnly. "Tell me about it?"

Hijiri drew in a sharp breath. Should she? It wasn't information she could share with just anyone. Even Fallon's friends, Anais and Bear, didn't know about the rebellion.

Ken nudged her knee with his. "If I'm a fake-boy, then telling me shouldn't be dangerous. I could disappear at any moment and your secrets would die with me."

Hijiri squirmed at the mention of death, but he had a point. While she couldn't trust him with her heart, she *could* share this story with him. He was one of them, figment or not, because of his undeniable connection to Love. She felt sure that Love would want him to know.

"You're thinking," Ken said with a smile.

"Love didn't say anything to you?"

"I think Love wants me to find the answers on my own," Ken said. "I want to hear it from you."

Hijiri blushed and looked away. "You know how the club's entered the charm-making competition?"

Ken flashed her an encouraging smile. "Yes. Go on."

"Well, it's not about me, really."

"But you want to be the best love charm-maker, right? This is the perfect way to show Grimbaud how talented you are," Ken said, eyebrows furrowed.

His easy belief in her threatened to knock the lid off her mental box. Hijiri crushed it back down with her skepticism. *How would he know how good I am at crafting love charms? Where is his confidence coming from?* She shook her head. "I want that, yes, but there's so much more at stake. Fallon and I saw the new love charm-makers yesterday."

"Your competition," Ken said.

"Each of them is a threat to this town," Hijiri whispered. "We hoped that having new love charm-makers in Grimbaud after years of no one but Zita would be a positive start for the town. But I'm scared, Ken. These charm-makers have the potential to wreak havoc on Grimbaud just as Zita did."

Ken hesitated. "I've heard of Zita."

"From Love?"

"Of course," Ken said, looking down at his knees. "I know that she took over this town because her fortunes were so perfect. Love said she sold one-hundred-percent-accurate love fortunes. They were never wrong. So what happened to her? Why is she gone?"

"Zita only made it look like her fortunes were perfect," Hijiri whispered. He had to lean in to hear her. "She had made a bargain with Love and had too much of their power at her disposal. Over the years, she let her own heartbreak fester until her thirst for revenge took over. But destroying the lives of the man who left her at the altar and his family wasn't enough. I think she enjoyed the thrill of playing with people's hearts and lives. She decided who would fall in love, who would break up, who would marry and divorce. Whether true or not, some people got fortunes saying that they would never fall in love. Zita controlled them too. She made sure she broke their spirits with the town's help. They became spinsters and bachelors because she said so."

"No one fought back?"

"How can you fight fate?" Hijiri asked. "If people tried fighting her in the past, she either drove them out of town or silenced them."

Ken raised his eyebrows. "Where does the charm theory club come in?"

"The club was just a cover for us. Femke and Mirthe started our rebellion. I don't think Grimbaud's ever been home to two people as stubborn or mischievous as the twins." Hijiri laughed softly. "We worked together to fight Zita. The twins used their fiercest weather charms. Fallon was the bravest I've ever seen her. Sebastian almost lost his life that night. But thanks to Love, one of my charms helped save him."

Ken soaked up her words, barely breathing. "And Zita's really gone now?"

"Forever."

"But these love charm-makers can hurt the town in a similar way if they gain the town's trust through this competition. I understand." Ken slid his hand on top of hers. "Thank you for telling me. I know it wasn't easy."

Hijiri tried not to look at their hands, but she couldn't ignore the simple comfort that came from the contact.

"Well, you need to know what you're getting into by joining our club."

The apartment lights started going out around them.

Ken was the first to notice the time. "Better get some sleep," he said, helping her up. "Are we walking to school together again tomorrow?"

"I suppose so," she said coolly. Hijiri didn't want him to think she was looking forward to it in the same way a new girlfriend couldn't wait to see the boy she was dating. *Just because I shared these things with him doesn't mean we're anywhere close to dating. Walking with him in the mornings is a good excuse to study him more. Figure out how he works. It's nothing more than that.*

"Good night, then, Hijiri," Ken said, smiling so his eyes crinkled. "Pleasant dreams."

Hijiri ran down the stairs to her apartment. Leaning against the door, she took Fallon's advice and paid attention to her heart. It was warm and trembling. Remembering how intently he had listened to her, even when her voice went hoarse, made her heart melt into a sticky puddle in her chest. She didn't understand what it meant, but it made her nervous.

Chapter 5

THE QUESTIONABLE DATING GAME

Hijiri's anxiety about the upcoming competition took on a life of its own as the first week of school passed. When she wasn't charm-making, the hours she spent at school dragged. Nothing a teacher taught or a friend said distracted her for long. When Saturday arrived, she breathed a sigh of relief before her stomach immediately twisted into new and tighter knots.

"Finally," she almost sobbed, ducking her head under the sheets. "It's finally today."

August had quietly given up its crown to September, which meant that cooler weather was on the way. Hijiri searched her limited closet with that in mind. Unlike Fallon, who had strong opinions about things like polyester and thread count, Hijiri never gave much thought to her clothing. She shopped for clothes only when her old ones had gotten stained from her crafting; searching through racks of sweaters and jeans was more of a chore than a fun activity.

Her mother had picked out some tasteful outfits for her, though. The ones she only wore for special occasions. Hijiri decided on one of those: a soft plum blazer over a black elastic-waist dress. She dusted off her black leather sandals just as Fallon arrived early to braid her hair.

"You should leave it long," Fallon said, standing behind Hijiri at the kitchen table. "Let's just put a tiny braid on the left side, and keep it in place with a gold clip."

Hijiri stayed as still as she could while eating her breakfast. The oatmeal was too thick and too sweet.

After brushing her teeth and wiping her sweaty hands on her dress, Hijiri was ready to walk over to Verbeke Square for the opening ceremony. Without pockets, she kept a few charms in a messenger bag.

"Sebastian and Ken are supposed to be waiting for us at the gate," Fallon said as they left the apartment. "So try not to look so nervous. You'll worry them."

Hijiri nodded stiffly.

Sebastian leaned on the wooden gate, yawning.

"Sorry I'm late," Ken yelled from the staircase. He didn't seem to notice Hijiri and Fallon as he flew down the stairs and ran for the gate.

The two boys shook hands, linking fingers and making a whooshing sound when they pulled back.

"A secret handshake?" Fallon said loudly. She raised her eyebrows and nudged Hijiri. "Should we feel left out?"

"We came up with the handshake yesterday in gym class," Ken explained as they started walking. "After too many fouls on the basketball court, our teacher made us sit out."

"Ken kept traveling instead of bouncing the ball," Sebastian said. "I tried covering for him, but I ended up making a few mistakes of my own. Mrs. Flits misses *nothing*."

Hijiri knew Sebastian's old reputation as a heartbreaker and that it hadn't made him popular with other boys. Having a close guy friend would be good for Sebastian. The secret handshake had been quite charming. . . .

No, no, no, what are you thinking? Hijiri thought, shaking her head. *This is so bad for Sebastian! He'll get hurt if Ken vanishes.*

But no matter how temporary Ken might be for all of them, she didn't have the heart to wrench Ken away from her friends. So she tried to see this development in a different light. One that made her less likely to ruin her blazer with anxious sweat. *He's not trying to win the love of anyone else in town*, she reminded herself. *So seeing how he acts with other people might give me clues to solving him. Charmboy, I'm onto you.*

Her thoughts turned and turned in circles, distracting her right up until they entered Verbeke Square. The square had been decorated and scrubbed up for the occasion. Lace shops opened their windows so that their workmanship was on display, flickering in the wind. Vendors were hard at work cooking; inspired by the competition, they sold foamy pink drinks and frosted heart-shaped desserts. The square was usually crowded because tourists and locals alike loved the old buildings crammed together with their gingerbread roofs, and the shops and cafés were always welcoming. People used to come far and wide to receive their love fortunes from Zita here, but her shop had collapsed into a pile of rubble after Love ended her reign.

A stage had been built where Zita's shop used to be. Hijiri thought it was an ominous spot to hold a love charms competition.

She knew just from looking at the stage that this opening ceremony would have surprises. The stage was divided in half by a partition: a single chair on the left side of the partition and three chairs on the right side. A table in front of the stage held four empty jars, each one made of a different colored glass, and a bowl full of red marbles.

Since Hijiri was the only love charm-maker in the club, she had to go onstage alone. However, her friends were right in front, ready to cheer her on. Ken waved at her as she took her place next to the other love charm-makers. She gave him a weak, unsteady smile.

Her heart pounded when the crowd started clapping. Bram De Groote climbed onto the stage, wearing his infamous tan trench coat and fedora. Ever since he revealed his identity as Hard-Boiled Hal, the host of Grimbaud's anti-love radio show, he'd been more or less pressured into emceeing the town's events.

"How backward is it that I'm here, about to introduce you to a bunch of *love* charm-makers?" he asked, his voice booming across the square thanks to his microphone. "Love gives me heartburn. I'd rather be anywhere else."

The crowd burst into laughter. More clapping. Some men raised their glasses and drank deeply.

Hijiri grimaced only because it was a close cousin to a proper smile. She knew Bram wasn't trying to be funny. He was still jaded when it came to love.

"As much as I hate to admit it, there's no denying that this town has a history of remarkable love charm-makers and their creations. This kind of history shouldn't change. Grimbaud must keep creating. Now that we're moving into a new era, friendly competition is a healthy start." He was careful not to mention Zita. "Let's see what these charm-makers are made of."

Hijiri felt the muscles in her shoulder tighten. Bram reminded her yet again why she was risking public humiliation and extreme discomfort onstage. Despite the nerves, she wanted to be here and make her own mark on Grimbaud. A good one.

"Our competitors have three months to work on their greatest love charms. Not a bad amount of time, but not generous either. That's just the way of competitions," Bram said unsympathetically. "The love charms will be presented for voting on November thirtieth. And guess what? The judges are *you*, Grimbaudians! You will decide by voting for the charm you love the most!"

So that's the way this is going to go, Hijiri thought. *Grimbaud had no interest in picking so-called "experts" to judge the contest. This is more about the town itself picking its next Zita: the love charm-maker they love, respect, and welcome here.*

"Cheating is strictly prohibited, children," Bram said, wagging his finger at the charm-makers. "I wish I didn't have to say it, but the temptation could be too strong for some of you. Using charms to distract, disorient, or hamper your opponents is grounds for an instant disqualification. Maybe even legal action, depending upon the charm. Same goes for sabotage. Please concentrate on crafting your own charms, not destroying someone else's. Here with us today is Grimbaud's new charm-crime specialist, Detective Desiree Archambault. She's going to make sure you play fair."

Detective Archambault looked less than pleased to be singled out in the crowd, but she raised her hand anyway. The detective didn't need to wear a trench coat like Bram to look as if she stepped off the pages of a noir novel; her high cheekbones and grim, tight mouth spoke volumes. Hijiri wouldn't dream of crossing her. She looked over at her friends to see Fallon watching the detective with admiration.

"The winner will receive a shiny certificate and a sizable trophy," Bram said, smirking, "but most important, bragging rights."

And business, Hijiri thought, looking at the charm-makers beside her. Winning a competition like this would earn them respect and even a little faith. One baby step away from Zita's legacy.

"Here's how it's going to go. I will be introducing you to our fine love experts. Keep your attention on this stage. You won't want to miss what we have in store for you today. Let's talk to the ladies behind Metamorphosis first!"

Clea grabbed the microphone from Bram. "I thought we'd never get to talk," she said, batting her unnaturally long eyelashes at him. Her pixie cut was extra spiky and her dark skin glowed with shimmering charms.

Bram's jaw worked. He didn't look away from her face. He didn't blink, and it looked like it hurt.

Hijiri dug her nails into her palms and took deep breaths. She kept her gaze from Clea's face and instead tentatively glanced at the co-owner, Mandy. Mandy's skin was equally stunning, her freckled cheeks the color of ripe peaches. Hijiri waited for the force of the Metamorphosis charms to hit her, but Mandy's products were more subdued. She was short and round and had a motherly vibe about her.

"You people look like you can use some of our bronzers," Clea said, strolling to the edge of the stage. "Just because it's the end of summer doesn't mean you need to sacrifice your tans and the compliments that come with them. Just stop by the store and—"

"Anyway. We believe that beauty makes you a stronger you," Mandy said, cutting Clea off, "and that kind of confidence welcomes love."

"Like us," Clea said, raising Mandy's left hand. Then she wiggled her fingers on her own hand. Both women wore matching engagement rings: the diamonds reflected the sunlight as beautifully as their charmed makeup did.

Clea and Mandy shared a quick kiss onstage while the crowd cheered. Bram rolled his eyes, and a few people chuckled. Hijiri took Bram's recovery as a good sign, but nothing, not even a seemingly sweet fiancée, would stop Clea from hawking her shop's products and bringing the townspeople's desires for beauty and love to the surface. Hijiri kept her eyes averted as Clea passed by. Her skin broke out in goose bumps.

"We've got plenty of time to swap romantic stories later," Bram said. "For now, let's say hello to Heartwrench!"

Ryker and his uncle Gage kept their mechanic uniforms but dressed up by wearing clean overalls and shiny, pressed shirts underneath. Neither man wore a hat this time. They both looked hopeful after seeing the turnout.

"Heartwrench is a truly innovative love charms shop," Gage said with enthusiasm. "We combine technology and charm magic. We push the boundaries of the two mediums in all our efforts." When the crowd didn't return his fierce grins and used-car-salesman pitch, he sweated so heavily that his armpits and the back of his shirt darkened. "Our shop hasn't gotten too many visitors," he admitted. "You do know we're open, right?"

Hijiri cringed when she heard the laughter in the crowd. *There's no way I'll be as awkward as Gage*, she thought. It wasn't reassuring. The knots in her stomach didn't budge.

Ryker stole the microphone from his uncle. "Our shop has a lot to offer," he said smoothly. "Just you watch."

Bram moved on to the last new love charm-maker, the owner of Love For All. Sanders Lemmens took the microphone, nonchalance oozing from his slouched posture and cool gaze. His brown-and-orange plaid suit hung on his frame.

"Love For All doesn't need an introduction," Sanders said.

"What tricks do you have up your sleeve?" Bram said, trying to pry a response from the man. "Many of us are familiar with your shop's products. Do you think you'll do better than what you sell?"

Sanders turned purple. "My products are the finest love charms."

No one cheered, but a few people had the decency to

clap. One boy in the back said he wanted his money back for the charm he bought yesterday.

"No refunds," Sanders snapped. "Read the signs."

Bram snorted.

Sanders drew himself up to his full height. "The confections my shop offers rival Grimbaud's best sweet shops. Even better, my chocolate is charmed."

Hijiri was surprised by the sudden eruption of cheers from the children in the audience. Fallon's and Martin's expressions darkened with fury. The local pastry chefs in the audience weren't happy either, but the children were louder. Hijiri felt her own anger rise. She had to defeat this man.

"Let's not forget about the home team," Bram said. When he reached Hijiri's side, he spared her a smile. Just for her. Then he turned back to the crowd and said, "She wasn't born in Grimbaud, but she might as well have been. Let's give a big hand for someone who loves this town as much as we do: Hijiri Kitamura, sophomore at Grimbaud High!"

Unsure of what to do, Hijiri bowed. Her heart tried to crawl up her throat. Everyone was looking at her now. Everyone.

"You're an aspiring love charm-maker, but you're not alone in this competition. Am I right?" Bram asked.

Hijiri dragged her eyes up to the microphone and stared at it. She swallowed thickly.

Bram inched the microphone closer to her.

She jumped back as if it were a coiled snake.

"You're not alone," Bram said again, softer this time. "Am I right?"

Hijiri took a shaky breath. She may have been standing onstage by herself, but her friends were as close as they could get to the stage. They were there. *She wasn't alone.* She pulled herself together long enough to finally speak. "I couldn't have gotten here on my own. I have the entire charm theory club behind me."

"Round of applause for the charm theory club," Bram said.

The twins ate up the applause. While the others waved, Ken paid no attention. His focus was on her.

Hijiri lifted an eyebrow and motioned for him to join in. Charm-boy or not, she didn't want him to be an outsider at a time like this.

He pointed at himself, bemused, and turned around to smile at the crowd.

"Now then," Bram said, rubbing his palms together. "We can't go easy on our love charm-makers, can we? Just to keep things interesting, we'll have monthly check-ins and challenges so we can see them in action. How about we throw a challenge at them now?"

Hijiri gasped. Her knees buckled. Her nerves shot ice-cold panic through her veins as the crowd cheered and stomped.

Bram pulled a young woman up from the audience. "This is Sofie, an art teacher from Grimbaud Elementary. Sofie here wants to fall in love," he said, rolling his eyes as Sofie made her way to the lone chair on the left of the partition. "In a town like this, she shouldn't have a problem. We have many eligible men."

With a sweep of his hand, three young men stepped onto the stage and took their seats in the chairs to the right of the partition. Sofie couldn't see the men because of the partition; she fidgeted with her patchwork dress as each man was given a number from left to right.

"These three men know nothing about Sofie, but they trust us when we say that she could be the perfect girl— for one of them. Which man? Our love charm-makers must help Sofie do the choosing," Bram said. "But not with their charms."

Hijiri thought she heard him wrong. Wasn't this a love charm-making competition? Why wouldn't they be tested by *making charms?*

Bram held up an index finger. "Each love charm-maker gets one question. Sofie will ask her eligible suitors these questions to find out which of them she'd like to go on a date with. So they better be good questions. Think hard." Bram paused and caught Hijiri's eye. "And use your teammates."

Hijiri felt a pinch of relief. She was still part of a team, even if she was the only love charm-maker in the club.

Working with her friends was completely within the rules. They had entered as a club, after all.

After Bram handed each of the charm-makers a card to write their questions on, Hijiri left the stage to join the Grimbaud High's charm theory club already in a huddle. Ken and Nico broke apart to let her in.

Bram looked at his watch. "You have five minutes."

Hijiri felt the seconds start to crawl across her skin. Away.

"This shouldn't be hard," Mirthe insisted. "Just have her ask what their favorite colors are. Or favorite animals!"

"Not important enough," Sebastian said. "We're not playing a trivia game."

"It's harder than it seems," Femke said.

Fallon agreed. "Sofie only has their answers to work with. What matters most to her? What does she need to know about them?"

Luckily for Sofie, she had four questions to ask. Hijiri wanted to have the strongest one. She looked at the men sitting in their chairs. Guy #1 was stout, with a shaved head and gold-rimmed glasses. The chair bent under his weight. Guy #2 rested his fist on his chin, one leg crossed and bobbing at the ankle. Unlike the other two, Guy #3's ginger beard hid his mouth, but that didn't stop him from talking to the crowd. Detective Archambault climbed onto the stage, her hand on Guy #3's shoulder. He quieted immediately.

"Can you tell anything about them?" Ken asked.

Hijiri shook her head. "Not enough. We don't even know their names."

"Then Sofie is the important one," he said.

Hijiri's eyes widened. They knew her profession and how involved she was with art by the way she dressed and held herself. Even now, Sofie waited by running her finger over her dress in patterns.

"Will you look at that? Heartwrench turned in its question first," Bram said, holding up a teal card.

Ryker high-fived his uncle.

Detective Archambault plucked the card from Bram and inspected it. Smelled it. Closed one eye and turned it upside down in her hands.

"Why did she smell the card?" Fallon asked, more to herself than anyone.

"Does it matter right now? I have the question," Hijiri said, shoving the card at her. "Can you write it down? You have better handwriting."

Fallon blinked and took the card, uncapping the pen Sebastian handed her.

"You weren't entirely wrong when you suggested a favorites question," Hijiri said, looking at Mirthe. "But we can do better. Something more pointed, situational."

"Don't keep us in suspense," Nico said. "We have to approve it before time runs out."

"Our solemn duty as your fellow club members," Martin said.

Clea and Mandy ran to Bram next with their pink card. Sanders elbowed his way through the crowd. Instead of giving his orange card to Bram, he handed it straight to Detective Archambault. Both cards got the same inspection from the detective.

Hijiri lowered her voice to a whisper. When everyone leaned their heads into the circle, close enough to brush one another's foreheads, she told them the question.

Mirthe said it sounded too long. Femke argued that it wasn't long enough. Nico thought it was fine since it fit Sofie's passion. Martin wondered what would happen if one of the men couldn't come up with an answer.

"That's simple," Ken said. "It would mean he isn't the one for Sofie."

Fallon held the pencil over the card, her eyebrows furrowed as she waited for the outcome. "Ready?"

Hijiri said the question again, this time a little sharper, a little different, and the club approved. After Fallon finished the dot on the question mark, Hijiri ran as fast as she could as Bram counted down the last seconds. Detective Archambault plucked the purple card out of Hijiri's fingers just in time.

The charm theory club exploded into cheers. Hijiri looked back at them and smiled, pushing her hair away from her face.

"Everyone's in," Bram said, waving the cards. "Get ready, Grimbaud. After all the questions are asked, you must cast your vote for the question you believe was the best. See the bowl of red marbles? Take one marble only and drop it into the jar with the color that matches the index cards." Bram held up the purple one. "If you liked the purple question, put your marble in the purple jar. Simple as that."

Hijiri's stomach twisted. No wonder Bram hadn't talked about the voting right away. She couldn't look at the people around her—the crowd, the voters—so she kept her eyes glued to Sofie. The young woman was nervous too; she shuffled the colored cards until they fell out of order.

"First question from the pink card," Sofie said, her voice loud against Bram's microphone.

"Pink," Bram echoed. Then he pointed at Clea and Mandy to remind the audience which shop the color belonged to, for anyone who had daydreamed when the colored cards had been passed out. Metamorphosis's card.

"What is your favorite part of your morning beauty routine?" Sofie asked.

Sebastian snorted. A few surprised bursts of laughter followed after, but Clea and Mandy remained untroubled. In fact, Clea's smug expression showed she was confident that their question was excellent. *Maybe she always asks her clients that*, Hijiri thought.

A trickle of sweat ran down Guy #1's face.

Bram was thoroughly amused. "Well, what do you have to say, men? Be honest."

"I don't have a routine," Guy #1 admitted. "Waking up is hard enough."

Sofie nodded vigorously, even though neither could see the other.

Guy #2 said he loved seeing his clothes laid out on his bedside chair from the night before. Being prepared like that, especially when he hit the snooze button a few times, made him feel confident about facing a new day.

"Hair gel," Guy #3 said, stroking his beard. "But never on the beard. My friends have been trying to get me to buy a beard grooming kit, but I refuse. The natural look is the best. It's my pride and joy."

Sofie scrunched her nose. She played with the corner of her card.

Bram shook his head and walked the length of the stage, saying, "I'm with Number One on this question. But you know, there *might* be something romantic about brushing your teeth in the morning."

Fallon frowned and whispered, "Of course there is. Personal hygiene."

Sebastian wrapped his arm around her waist and hugged her close.

"Second question is from the orange card," Sofie said, holding up the card.

That one belongs to Love For All. Hijiri leaned forward, eager to hear what sort of question Sanders had come up with.

"Bitter or sweet?" Sofie said.

"That's it?" Bram said, looking over Sofie's shoulder to read the card. "So it is. Well, then. Interpret as you like."

Sanders's expression hadn't wavered from smugness. He crossed his arms.

Guy #1 was quick with his answer. "Anything that's sweet. Especially with marshmallows. When I was a kid, I used to get in trouble for building snowmen out of them."

Guy #2 must have taken that story as a challenge, because he said, "I'm the same way with spinach."

"You made snowmen out of spinach?" Bram asked.

Guy #2 sighed heavily. "My brothers were horrible at the dinner table, so I used to make them laugh by taping spinach to my lip. A spinach mustache. But I secretly loved the bitter taste. My mother never served it with salad dressing."

When Guy #3 got the mic, he said, "Sour."

Hijiri shifted her weight. Listening to the other questions going first was difficult. When Heartwrench's card was raised, her stomach twisted again. Last. They were going last.

"Hey," Ken said, his face suddenly in front of hers. "Deep breaths."

"I'm not nervous," she mumbled.

"Deep breaths," he repeated.

Hijiri followed his directions. Inhale. Exhale. One after the other. The anxious twisting in her stomach shrank. "I'm not . . . This isn't about my charms."

The more she thought about it, the sicker she felt. The absurd challenge wasn't a true showcase of her skills. *Just let me have five more minutes,* she thought, *and a few words and fern leaves and—*

Ken brushed his knuckle against her chin. It was a ghostlike touch, but enough to send a shiver through her body. "This is a test of instinct," he told her. "It's something you already possess. You don't need a charm to show how good you are."

Hijiri's thoughts frayed. Instincts? Was that true?

Sofie looked at the teal index card. Her brow furrowed when she read the question, but she eventually said it out loud. "How did you get over your last heartbreak?"

Ryker and Gage shared a proud look with each other, but the mood in the square changed. This was a more serious, private question. None of the men answered for some time; Hijiri couldn't blame them for hesitating.

Guy #3 asked for the mic. "I've never had my heart broken," he insisted, though his voice caught. "My ex-girlfriend left me because I refused to shave off my beard. Not that it bothered me to lose her, mind you. My love for my beard runs deeper. She just couldn't accept me for who I am."

"Time," Guy #2 said. "If it's long enough since the breakup, your heart will heal. Mine did."

"Does it ever heal?" Guy #1 asked. "Really? I don't believe that. We can move on, but the scars will always be there."

"That's a depressing attitude," Guy #2 said.

"It's a lot less depressing with ice cream," he replied with a smile.

Bram cut them off before the discussion could turn into a debate. "Why don't we see what the last question asks," he said. "Sofie, the honors?"

"This is it," Mirthe hissed.

Ken grabbed Hijiri's left hand, while Fallon grabbed her right hand.

Sofie gratefully lifted the purple card. Her eyebrows rose when her eyes scanned the question. A small smile touched her lips. Then she asked, "If you were in a museum, which exhibit would you go see first and why?"

Hijiri exhaled loudly. This was it. Her question.

Guy #2 brightened. He uncrossed his legs. "Anything contemporary, so that I have the chance to meet the artists."

Guy #3 said he found museums to be boring.

When Bram asked Guy #1 for his answer, the man took off his glasses, wiped them, and put them back on crooked. "Some people like the traveling exhibits because they're new and temporary. But me, I like the permanent displays. I can't choose which type of art I like best, except that seeing the same paintings and sculptures each time is like saying hello to old friends."

Hijiri drew a sharp breath.

Sofie blushed, smiling, and the patchwork on her skirt was safe from her picking for the first time that morning.

We could win this, Hijiri thought.

Chapter 6

INSTINCT

Bram asked the townspeople to vote for their favorite question while Sofie pondered her big decision. The crowd was the sea, ebbing and flowing its way around the table with the marbles. Detective Archambault stalked the stage, her eyes moving so quickly over the crowd that it was dizzying to watch.

After a few minutes, the voting trickled to an end. Sofie left her chair and hugged the mic to her chest. With a small, bashful voice, she said, "I'd like to go on a date . . . with Guy Number One."

Guy #1 blushed straight to his ears, a look of utter shock on his round face. His glasses slipped down his nose as he struggled out of his chair.

Before he could see her, Bram stepped in the way. "Lucky Number One, why don't you tell us your name?"

"Lars," he said, breathless.

"Lars," Bram repeated, smiling. He stepped back and pushed the wall out of the way. "Meet Sofie."

A glint of light caught Hijiri's eye. She looked up, spotting a stone cupid perched on the upper floor of a lace shop, its arrow aimed at Sofie's back. Then another glint—from a different stone cupid whose arrow lined up with Lars. Both arrows were painted gold. *Have I seen them before?* Hijiri wondered, while the crowd sighed. Grimbaud had too many stone cupids to keep track of, especially since they'd been put back after Zita's defeat.

"Look at the cupids," Hijiri said, grabbing Ken's forearm.

Ken looked from where her hand squeezed his arm to the cupids. "You know," he said, "it's possible that Love is still watching us, inventory or not."

"I thought of that."

"It's comforting, right?"

Not with the game Love was playing with her.

Sofie held out her charcoal-stained hands. Lars took them. They stared into each other's eyes before breaking apart, blushing and grinning as the townspeople clapped.

The other two men shrugged off their losses. They shook hands with Sofie and Lars and left the stage.

"Love," Bram said dryly.

Hijiri and her friends inched closer to the stage when Bram started counting the marbles. Detective Archambault conducted the second count, just to make sure the accountant-by-day-and-radio-host-by-night didn't mess up.

"In fourth place," Bram said, "is Metamorphosis."

Clea gasped. Mandy chewed her nails.

Detective Archambault took the mic and said that third place belonged to Heartwrench. Her voice was deep and husky.

Ryker shrugged and pretended to dust off his shoulders. Gage followed his nephew's lead but wasn't as convincing with red-rimmed eyes.

"Two more," Mirthe said, bouncing on her toes.

Bram plucked the mic back. He looked upset for a moment. Then his expression smoothed. "Second place goes to Grimbaud High's charm theory club."

Hijiri's ears itched. Had she heard right?

"You know what that means," Bram said.

Detective Archambault drew close to the mic. "After fairly being counted, the winner of the most votes is Love For All."

"Come on up, Sanders," Bram said. As the cheering commenced, he added, "Who knew that talk of spinach mustaches would win the day?"

Sebastian groaned. "That's not right. It should have been about the *best* question, not the funniest."

"It's a popularity contest," Martin said.

Nico grimaced. "Seems like it."

Hijiri blotted out the noise of the crowd as Sanders shook hands with Bram and Detective Archambault. He looked as bewildered as Hijiri felt, but he managed to give an awkward wave at the townspeople.

"Hijiri," Ken called her. "Hijiri, Martin's right. Don't get discouraged."

"I'm not," she said, even as her mouth ran dry. "This challenge had nothing to do with love *charms*. There's no reason for me to be upset."

The words poured out of her, but she felt their falseness as easily as she saw it on her friends' faces. They didn't believe her.

The sound of canal water lapping at the bank could be calming. Sometimes. Hijiri rested her elbows on the ledge as she peered down at the water. She chose a bridge with a rough ledge, the rocks uneven and catching her sleeves. Behind her, bicyclists whizzed by. Leaves parachuted to the ground.

The hurt of losing the challenge was a barb lodged in her heart, unfamiliar and unwelcome. She hated how mangled she felt inside.

When the rebellion had found out that she was a love charm-maker, Hijiri felt validated. Her knowledge aided Nico in negating Camille's hold on Martin. The twins asked her for advice. They used the charms she created. Nothing made her prouder. Once cracked open, her secret became her way of making real friends.

Back home, she shared her love charm creations with her neighbors, if she shared them at all. Privacy was key to her crafting, so hiding her talent when she came to Grimbaud for her freshman year had come naturally. She had no reason to assume she was a good love charm-maker. After all, she only had herself, her parents, and her friends to attest to her skills.

Love *believed* in her. Love had even offered her Zita's old position, had she wanted it. That counted for something, right?

"But other people exist in the world," Hijiri muttered, resting her chin on the ledge. "And they have opinions too. I better get used to it."

This competition gave her a new perspective. Showed her that maybe she wasn't as good as she had thought.

Since the bridge was close to the Barnes Canal Cruises main booth, Hijiri walked the short distance to see if Nico was inside. A line of people waited to book cruises for the day. The booth was striped white and pink, with an old statue of a mermaid squeezing a heart in each hand. Hijiri thought the mermaid looked a little too happy holding those hearts. No one in the Barnes family remembered the significance of the mermaid, so she fell into the habit of theorizing each time she passed the booth. Did the hearts belong to a pair of lovers who threw themselves into a canal? Not that mermaids had ever lived in the canals, not even in Grimbaud's mythology.

One of the cruise boats returned. As the tourists disembarked, Hijiri spotted Nico behind the wheel with his father. He wore his trademark windbreaker, his damp hair sticking on end. No matter what kinds of plans her friends made, Nico always had to go running back to the canal cruises afterward; his parents expected him to use his free time working the booths or helping on the boats. Only a few hours before, Nico had been with the rest of the club at the challenge.

Seeing him back at work made her sad but also comforted. This was normal. Losing the challenge hadn't changed everything.

Nico waved at her when he saw her. *Hold on*, he mouthed, before turning back to his father.

Hijiri sat on a bench overlooking the canal while she waited.

"Did you shake off the second-place blues?" Nico asked, warming his hands with a cup of coffee from the booth.

"I think I'm beginning to," she admitted. "It's not easy."

Nico sipped his coffee. "You're pretty competitive."

"A trait I didn't know I had."

He stared thoughtfully at his feet. "You know, I never thought of myself as competitive either. I didn't have time to, keeping up with learning the ins and outs of the family business. As an only child, I don't have any rivals for inheriting the business someday. But then, I've been competing with myself the whole time, with my father as judge. It gets exhausting."

Hijiri competed with herself too. No one else had served as her judge before. Her parents hadn't evaluated her love charms. As a sophomore without an apprenticeship lined up with a love charm-maker, and no plans to choose one, she was lost. Only her heart and head could guide her.

"We were all worried about you after the challenge. You didn't have to run off."

"Sorry."

"Ken even went looking for you."

Her heart jumped. "I didn't see him."

"Must have gotten lost." Nico tapped on the lid of the coffee cup. "Martin's coming over tonight to study."

Grateful for the subject change, Hijiri said, "So you *do* have time to spare for him."

"My dad and I argued about it during the summer, but he's okay with me being a normal teenager sometimes," Nico said with a laugh. "Especially after he and Mom met Martin. They both like him."

"That's good."

"It won't last though."

His morose response startled her. Hijiri looked up. "What do you mean?"

"This is our last year together. Martin graduates in May," Nico said, fiddling with his coffee lid. "He should be going away to college."

"Should?"

"I don't know. He hasn't told me anything." Nico sighed. "I've tried asking him, but Martin refuses to talk about it. Says he'd rather focus on me than think about post-graduation."

"That's flattering." Hijiri frowned. "Kind of."

"Not really. He's thrown himself into student government, now more than ever. I wonder what he's trying to run from." He shook his head. "It seems like only yesterday that we saved him from Camille. But come May, I might have to say good-bye to him."

Hijiri buried her hands in her shirt, twisting the hem. She wanted to devise a charm for Nico and Martin. Her fingers itched. A communication love charm. But neither boy would accept her charm, no matter how well-meant. "What did Fallon tell you?"

"To keep chipping away at Martin until he caves."

"Well, there you go."

Nico finished his coffee. "It's not that easy. Martin clams up whenever I mention the subject. I don't want . . . I don't want to lose him, just because I'm curious."

"You have a right to be curious. He's your boyfriend. You need to know what's going to happen after May." Hijiri fought the itch to craft by rising to her feet. She circled the bench, pacing. *I wish they would accept a love charm. I don't know how else to help.* After the challenge, she wasn't sure if her instincts alone were good enough to rely on.

"Oh, look who's here," Nico said with a smile.

Hijiri looked to her left, seeing a familiar boy leading a couple across a bridge. Ken was walking backward, talking excitedly to the couple—Sofie and Lars. Her heart thumped with a startling mix of fear and surprise. What was Ken doing with them?

Ken whipped around as they came close. "Hijiri, you wouldn't believe the luck I had, running into Sofie and Lars on their first date."

"First date already?" Hijiri asked without thinking.

"Why wait?" Sofie said. She was holding hands with Lars, her energy positively glowing.

"The first of many, I hope," Lars said, his eyes soft behind his gold-rimmed glasses.

Hijiri wished she could have felt happy for them, but her eyes burned with unshed tears. *Sanders's question brought them together. I didn't do anything.* Seeing the happy couple only made her hurt worse.

Nico asked them if they were considering Sunday's romantic night cruise. The couple exchanged glances and said yes at the same time.

A second date, Hijiri thought, sinking back down on the bench.

If anyone noticed her discomfort, they didn't give any indication. As Nico led Lars to the Barnes booth, Sofie took a seat next to Hijiri. "I'm sorry about how the challenge turned out," Sofie said.

"There's only one winner," Hijiri said, sniffing.

"No matter how the voting turned out, I want you to know that your question was the one that helped me figure out which man I was interested in," Sofie said firmly.

Hijiri's lungs stopped working.

"That's not to say the other questions *weren't* helpful," Sofie said, "but none of those questions were ones I would have asked if I'd had the choice. The museum question was just . . . perfect. I *needed* to know how the men would answer. I just applied for a volunteer position at Grimbaud's art museum. I know the experience will make me a better teacher. I never thought that meeting a man who shared my love of the museum was something I ever expected or looked for when dating."

Lars returned with cruise tickets, catching the end of Sofie's response. "My parents used to take me to the museum every weekend when I was a boy," he added, smiling at Hijiri. "I got bored by the new exhibits, and my parents never figured out why."

"Maybe they didn't realize how attached you became to ancient clay pots and watercolors," Sofie said.

Lars sobered. "I hated anything that went away. The more permanent a thing was, the better."

"Your parents . . ." Sofie ventured.

"They struggled," Lars said, forcing the smile back on his face. "The permanent exhibits gave me hope. If they could last thousands of years relatively in one piece for people to admire and enjoy, then I could be just as strong as they were. I know it's an odd thought, but—"

"It's beautiful," Sofie insisted.

"We're on our way to the museum now," Lars said.

Hijiri stood up. Her cheeks burned and her heart felt

ready to cry. She couldn't believe what she was hearing. "Then it's true? My question really helped you like this?" she asked.

"We're so glad your friend Ken found us so that we had the chance to tell you." Sofie touched Hijiri's shoulder with her charcoal-stained hand. "I—no, *we*—wanted you to know how thankful we are that your question allowed us to find each other."

"You've earned our votes, Hijiri," Lars said.

Hijiri choked back a sob. She covered her mouth with her hand and squeezed her eyes shut. "Thank you," she whispered.

As the couple went on their way, Nico beamed from where he stood outside the booth.

Ken ruffled his hair, failing to hide his high-beam smile. "See what I mean, Hijiri? You made a difference. You brought two people together using your instincts. And the club's help. You shouldn't ever doubt your abilities."

Sofie's words echoed in her head. The woman who *actually* fell in love thanked her. The town's opinion on the matter suddenly felt less important. Hijiri started shaking as tears slid down her cheeks.

Her heart broke out of its box and took control. Hijiri threw her arms around Ken, startling him as he stumbled backward. Her forehead bumped his chin, and her cheek rubbed against the scratchy fabric of his sweater.

He said her name, probably a few times. When she didn't move, Ken gingerly drew her close. His hands were warm on her back. She breathed in his cool, evergreen scent.

Using his sweater as a tissue, Hijiri softly cried. She couldn't put into words how she felt. Little by little, her faith in herself came trickling back.

The *thump-thumping* of Ken's heart betrayed him; he was nervous, or maybe just startled, though his voice remained gentle. "What's the matter? Aren't you happy?"

The simple questions made her want to laugh, but it came out more as a strange sob. "I forgot," she said.

Ken waited.

"I forgot that it's about the person using the love charm." Love charms weren't supposed to be the stuff of popularity contests. Contests were fun and necessary sometimes, but the power of a love charm was personal. As long as the person or couple using it was satisfied, the love charm-maker did his or her job. She couldn't afford to forget that, no matter how immersed she became in Grimbaud's contest.

Feeling came rushing back into her fingertips. Her skin heated up as she realized how inappropriate her hug was. Hijiri stepped back. "I shouldn't have done that," she said.

Hurt flashed in his eyes. "Don't apologize for hugging me. I'm glad you did."

She sniffed.

"You look better already."

Nico jogged up to them, a curious look on his face.

"I'm *fine*," she stressed. The tears on her face had dried

thanks to Ken's sweater. "I'm just not used to . . ." *Being exposed. Hugging boys because I needed it. Crying. Definitely crying.* She had never considered herself a crier until coming to Grimbaud.

"Sure you won't drink coffee? It always makes me feel better," Nico offered.

"She doesn't drink coffee?" Ken asked.

"Gives her headaches."

Ken rubbed his chin. "With that extra caffeine, she'd be a love charm-making machine. We'd blink and her apartment would be crammed with new charms."

"You're right." Nico deadpanned, "It could be the worst crisis Grimbaud has faced in ages."

Hijiri managed a laugh, even though her body felt leaden. "It's not worth suffering through that drink. Tastes like mud."

The boys couldn't argue with that, though Ken insisted that using unhealthy amounts of sugar and milk could help. "It's an option," he said, after letting Nico get back to work. "In case you run out of energy."

September had already proved that she would be working long and hard this semester. The month had only just begun and yet she'd already failed one challenge by losing the popular vote and was not any closer to solving Ken. *So how am I doing, Love?* Hijiri thought grimly. She wasn't sure if she wanted the answer.

Chapter 7

THE UNFORTUNATE ACCIDENT

The charm theory club met in the same science room as last year, this time on Wednesdays after school. Stepping into the classroom again, Hijiri was hit with memories from the first time the rebellion, under the guise of the club, met one another. Since the science rooms were in the basement, shadows splashed the walls and the lightbulbs alone couldn't dispel them. Jars of animal parts lined the shelves in the back.

Ken unsnapped his chest strap and dropped his backpack on a desk. He examined the room, drinking in the details. He picked up the jar of eyeballs and weighed it in his hands. Flipping it over, he ran a finger over the glass underside. His mouth twitched into a smile. "Watch this," he said. He twisted the jar.

"Don't open it," Hijiri said. She braced herself for a pickled, vinegary scent.

Fallon and Sebastian came into the room, and Fallon gasped when she saw Ken pop the lid off. Sebastian grinned and asked Ken to toss him an eye.

But when Ken reached inside, he pulled out a rubber bouncy ball. And another. And three more. There was no liquid inside. The bouncy balls themselves came in different colors.

Sebastian caught the bouncy ball Ken threw at him. "Where are the eyes?"

"It's just a trick," Ken said, pleased. The outside of the jar still showed eyes floating in preservatives.

"How did you know that?" Hijiri asked.

Ken shrugged. "Just a guess."

"It's a charm," Hijiri insisted. "But I don't know what kind would create an illusion like that."

Ken put the jar back. "I bet it's a hearth charm," he said quietly.

"Did Love teach you about other charms?"

Ken stared at the jars. "All charms are interesting, but hearth charms are my favorite."

He dodged my question. Why does he keep doing that? Hijiri pressed a hand to her forehead, flattening her bangs. "If Love only created you days ago, how can you possibly know enough to have a favorite type of charm?"

Ken's eyes flickered over her face. "Sometimes you know what you like. It's called trusting your heart."

Hijiri's cheeks burned under his gaze. She looked

down. "So your totally fake charm-heart told you that you love me and you love hearth charms."

Ken's jaw tightened. "That's right," he said, a little too harshly, and brushed past her to sit next to Sebastian.

Hijiri raised her eyebrows. She was just trying to solve him. Had she said something wrong? If anyone should lose a temper, it should be *her*. She was getting tired of having her questions unanswered.

"I guess that means dissection isn't in our future," Sebastian said, bouncing a ball on the tile.

"I wouldn't say that," Mirthe said, overhearing the conversation. She rushed into the room to claim the teacher's desk. Instead of making room for her twin, she dumped her textbooks across the free space. "Senior biology is scheduled to dissect a pig in November."

Hijiri leaned forward in her chair, hoping to sneak a peek at Ken. See if he still looked frustrated. With her. Before she could get a good view over Fallon's shoulder, Femke arrived, creating an entrance that left Mirthe sputtering.

Curls of fog rolled into the room like a carpet. Only the top of Femke's head and green eyes showed. The fog dampened the room. Hijiri smelled feathers and raindrops.

"What are you *doing?*" Mirthe shouted, using her folder as a fan. "Don't bring clouds in here. We won't be able to see."

"I wanted to show everyone what I made," Femke said in her quiet, composed voice.

Mirthe's fingers went white on her folder.

Femke closed her eyes and the fog shifted, returning to her in frothy waves. The gray fog formed the shape of a dense fur coat. When she walked to the teacher's desk, the fog left a smoky trail behind her.

"That's amazing," Fallon said carefully, her eyes flickering between the twins.

Hijiri wasn't sure if she should clap or not. Since when did they *not* celebrate the twins' inventive weather charms? But Mirthe's reaction confused her.

"Dad's been teaching me some new skills," Femke said to Mirthe, calmly pushing her twin's textbooks aside so she could hop up on the desk. Somewhere underneath the fog-coat was her bag; she opened her notebook to a clean page and waited.

"Did Dad tell you to use charms in school? You know that's not allowed," Mirthe bristled.

"Since when did you care about the rules?" Femke said coolly.

Hijiri exchanged a stunned look with Fallon. Femke and Mirthe *never* fought. This was a first, and it made the usually cheerful club meeting oddly tense.

Luckily, the moment was interrupted by Nico and Martin's arrival. The minute he saw the fog-coat, Martin's eyebrows nearly shot into his hairline. He was about to say something when Nico grabbed him by the arm.

"Let it go today," he said firmly.

"The hazards," Martin argued. "There's a reason we don't use charms in the building."

Femke apologized to Martin and said she'd take care of it. She played with the tortoiseshell barrette in her hair—Mirthe wasn't wearing a matching one—until something clicked. A latch.

The barrette pulled the fog in like a magnet. Within seconds, the fog swirled its way inside the barrette until nothing was left but the faint taste of rain on their tongues.

Mirthe refused to stay sitting on the desk with her sister. Instead, she paced the front of the room and asked everyone to take their seats.

They arranged their desks in a U shape, careful to leave enough space so that Mirthe could continue burning off her agitation. Hijiri pressed her palms flat against her desk, waiting to see what would happen next.

Femke asked the first question, unperturbed by her sister. "Who's going to be representing our club at the student government meetings this year?"

Fallon and Sebastian said they'd be serving again.

"We don't have to make our club sound as boring this year," Nico said.

"Yes, we do," Femke said lightly. "New members are strongly discouraged."

Hijiri smiled at that. At least someone felt the same way as she did about keeping their group small and private. With new people, the memories of the rebellion would fade faster. She knew she was being selfish, but she didn't want to let go. They had the rest of the school year together before the twins and Martin graduated. And one more mission: winning the love charm-making competition.

"Ken managed to sneak past our defenses," Sebastian said, smirking. "He must love charm theory."

"Or a certain someone," Fallon added.

Hijiri rolled her eyes.

"Thank you for letting me be here," Ken said with amusement, "however debatable my motives are."

"Next order of business," Mirthe said, clapping her hands. "The first challenge should be a wake-up call for us. We need to be prepared for the next challenge."

"I don't think *anyone* could have prepared for this one," Fallon said.

"There has to be something we can do," Mirthe insisted.

"Not cheating, I hope?" Femke said flatly.

"We've been sneaky before."

"This time it's different," Fallon said. Her expression turned serious. "Detective Archambault is not like the other police officers in town. She's keeping a close watch on us. If any of us are suspected of cheating, Hijiri's chances of winning the competition are over."

"We're not used to playing by the rules," Sebastian said,

making everyone laugh. The tension eased, and even Mirthe slowed her pacing.

"Then let's brainstorm love charm ideas for the end of the competition," Mirthe said.

"We've only been in a school a week," Sebastian said, slouching.

"And already lost one challenge," Hijiri said. The admittance hurt less now, but it still stung.

"This is Hijiri's specialty. Maybe she should tell us what *she* has in mind," Femke said.

Mirthe stopped her pacing to glare at her twin.

The room was thick with tension. Hijiri wanted to crawl under her desk.

Ken leaned forward, elbows on his desk. "Why don't we start with the love charm's purpose? Should it be practical or showy?"

Hijiri scooted up in her chair too, so she could see him.

"What do you mean?" Mirthe said.

"I mean, what kind of charm would steal the show? Something flashy or shocking to grab the audience, or a practical charm that people would actually use?"

"Showy won the first challenge," Nico said. "Sanders's question was so random, it caught everyone's attention."

"Practical is always best," Fallon said. "A charm that's needed. No one can resist what they think they're missing."

"That may be true," Mirthe said, "but Hijiri can't sell

charms yet anyway, so why create something in demand? Better to entertain people instead."

Hijiri gripped the corners of her desk. "Both," she said softly. Then louder: "The perfect love charm should have a little of both to win the competition."

"Have you come up with anything?" Mirthe asked.

"A few ideas. Nothing stands out yet." *Not when Nico and Martin are having problems, and so are you and Femke,* she thought, frowning. How could she concentrate on winning when her friends needed her help?

The twins pulled Hijiri aside after the meeting. Mirthe waited until everyone had left the room before grabbing Hijiri's shoulders and asking about Ken. "So what have you discovered about him so far?"

Hijiri's forehead wrinkled. "He still stubbornly believes he'll win me over. He smiles too much. And he's too nice."

"None of that sounds magical," Mirthe said.

"I disagree." Femke crossed her arms. "Niceness *is* magic, but no one thinks of it that way since it's quiet and constant."

Mirthe ignored her. "But what about the charms? What's he made out of?"

"I haven't figured that out yet."

"You're kidding me."

"Look, he won't answer any of my questions." Hijiri brushed Mirthe's hands off her shoulders. "I've tried to see if he knows anything—he *has* to—but he's been dodging my questions. Or conveniently has coughing fits."

Femke gasped softly. "The coughing. Does he really do that only when you ask him questions?"

"I guess so?" She hadn't paid that much attention.

"Try to test that. If he doesn't have a cold," she said, "maybe it's some sort of defense. Like, Love built him to keep his secrets, so Ken can't tell you anything that would help you solve him."

Hijiri's pulse quickened. *Could that be true?*

"Love wouldn't make it easy for you," Femke said, smiling. "You have to be cleverer."

"That's why we're here! The De Keyser twins, at your service. Tell us what we need to do, and we'll have that charm-boy solved by the end of the week," Mirthe boasted.

"Such a short time frame," Femke muttered.

"Maybe not a week, then. But soonish."

Hijiri sighed. "Thank you for the help. I'll keep that in mind."

"We've given her a lot of think about," Femke said to her sister. "We should go."

"You just want to get home faster," Mirthe said. "Dad's going to give you another fog charm lesson, right? Go ahead. I don't want to be there."

Femke's green eyes flashed, but she said nothing.

After she left, Mirthe hopped back up on the teacher's desk and pretended, very badly, to not care that her sister was gone.

Hijiri huffed in exasperation. "What's going on with you two? I've never seen you fight."

Mirthe tapped her fingers on the desk, the hollow sound filling the room. She looked ready to burst. "Femke and I need to make a big decision when we graduate, since we're weather charm-makers," she said in a rush. "Our discipline is so broad that we're required to claim a specialty. What we choose determines our apprenticeships for the next few years."

"How could you possibly decide? There's no way I could with love charms."

"Love is love," Mirthe said, "but weather is snow, fog, clouds, wind, heat, volcanoes, hurricanes, tornados, sun, and moonlight . . . I could keep going."

"Is that why you're upset? You can't make a choice?"

"That's part of it," Mirthe said, squirming in her seat. "But the bigger problem is my sister. She's engrossed in studying clouds, kind of like my dad with his wind. But clouds are *boring*. What could she do with them? I've tried to tell Femke she needs to choose something more exciting. She won't listen."

Hijiri waited. She knew there had to be more.

"We're supposed to do everything together. We're

twins. I'm scared we'll go our separate ways unless we pick the same specialty."

They wouldn't be twins anymore. Out in the world, under different apprenticeships, Femke and Mirthe would be individuals. For the first time, it sounded like. Hijiri didn't have siblings, but she tried to show some sympathy. "Being alone isn't so bad," she said.

Mirthe gasped. "That's a lie."

"I'm happy."

"You don't always *look* happy. Content, maybe. But there's a difference."

Hijiri's heart rattled in its box. She mentally sat on the lid. "If it's that bad, you should learn to love clouds."

"Not gonna happen."

"Then what?"

"I'm going to make her fall in love with another specialty."

Hijiri balked. "I'm *not* making a love charm for this."

Mirthe burst into laughter. "No way! Even if I was tempted, seeing what happened to Zita is enough of a warning. I'm glad that weather charms don't often infect a person's insides like love charms do."

"So what's the plan, then?"

"I just have to show her how much fun other weather elements are. She'll see."

Hijiri wasn't convinced. More than that, she was worried. *The twins probably do need a love charm for this,* she admitted to herself. *Not manipulation, but there must be some way to help them.* Another charm to make.

She needed to start crafting.

When Hijiri returned to her apartment, she dove into her love charm supplies. Her cramped bedroom was still a problem. She inched past the shoji screen to root through her open suitcase, tossing wrinkled clothes on the bed in her search for materials. "Candles, candles," she muttered, finding a packet of dried hollyhock petals and a few loose red strings instead. Orange candles would be best for the charm she had in mind for Nico and Martin. Orange candles felt lively, like sunrise waking a sleepy couple with its bright rays, a comfortable touch that opened the lines of communication.

Balanced on her heels, she clung to the sides of the suitcase to keep herself steady. She thought she saw orange underneath her sweaters. When she reached for it, her foot slipped and she fell backward, knocking into the shoji screen.

The screen crashed into the table it hid. Everything else happened in slow motion.

With so many materials and experiments piled on her table, Hijiri had failed to notice the table's dying creaks and groans. The impact from the screen caused the table leg to break, sending glass bottles and open containers tumbling to the floor. Her heart jumped into her throat. She was scared to look behind her; her hand landed in rosewater from a spilt bottle.

A feeling worse than dread settled in her stomach. When she finally peeked over her shoulder, she couldn't breathe. Most, if not all, of the glass bottles had shattered on the wood floor. If she had left any dry materials open, they were now soaked and useless. Tears burned the back of Hijiri's eyes, but she forced herself to her feet and wiped her hand on her shirt.

The materials are replaceable, she reminded herself. *Nothing was too expensive. It's okay.* Anything to take away the numbness spreading through her body.

Then she heard a knock on the door.

Hijiri rubbed her eyes and gingerly stepped around the broken glass.

She opened the door while Fallon was in the middle of talking to someone—Ken. "Ms. Ward still can't believe the school paid for new card catalogs," she said, "and I can't either. The library's seen better days. If the carpets could be replaced too, I'd call that an improvement."

Hijiri croaked out a hello.

Before Fallon could respond, Ken shoved himself through the doorway and cupped her face. "Your eyes are red," he said, his brow furrowed. "What's wrong?"

His hands were warm on her face. She tried to smother

her tears, to push them down with her other buried feelings, but the hurt was too real. Too soon. Tears ran down her cheeks and wet his fingers. "My charms," she managed.

Ken dug a tissue out of his pocket and wiped away her tears.

Fallon sniffed the air. "Something smells . . . strange. Like candy and flowers mixed together."

"I knocked them over," Hijiri said.

"Oh no," Fallon said.

They entered her apartment and headed straight for the chaos in her bedroom. Fallon gasped when she saw the shattered materials. "Can you find anything to salvage?" she asked.

Hijiri couldn't speak, but she nodded.

"There's too much broken glass. Just tell me what you want and I'll get it," Ken said.

While Fallon ran back to her apartment to get a broom, pail, and cleaning supplies, Ken picked through the mess for Hijiri. She pointed to everything that could be wiped clean, that hadn't lost potency being mixed with the liquids. Ken handed her golden buttons, cinnamon sticks still sealed, rose quartz, and a few sentimental items that made her charms stronger when she held them while crafting.

"How do you use these?" Ken asked, tossing her a teddy bear missing an eye.

Hijiri wiped her nose with the tissue. "If I tell you, you'll steal my ideas." She was only half-kidding.

"I don't know the first thing about crafting love charms," he said.

"You're lying."

"That's not something Love felt was necessary for me to know."

"But you're—"

Ken turned his face away from her, intent on brushing more glass out of the way with a towel. "There are other subjects, other parts of life, that interest me."

Hijiri sank down on her bed. Clearly, he hadn't forgotten their earlier conversation at the club meeting. Neither had she. Love made him for her, so logically he'd have to be a love charm-maker himself, or at least have the aptitude for it. What was the point in making him otherwise? She couldn't let it go. "What else could you possibly like?"

Ken balled up the towel. When he looked back at her, his eyes flashed with bitterness. "I am more than you think."

Chapter 8

CHANGE OF PLANS

Hijiri stared at her feet. Another pain flared up, worse than seeing her supplies break. Maybe he wasn't real. His heart might be iron, his blood made of charms, but he obviously thought different of himself.

"Anything else?" Ken asked tightly.

"No."

He stood up and inspected his wet knees from kneeling in the spilled liquids. He let out a ragged sigh and said, more softly, "It's okay to think of me as a person, you know."

Hijiri's heart wiggled up her throat and stayed there. To think of him as human would mean she had given up on trying to solve him. She couldn't indulge in that kind of thinking, could she? "I'm not giving up," she said.

"I know that," Ken said. "You could pretend sometimes. See how it feels."

Hijiri turned inward, mentally poking her heart for feedback. Maybe she could try. Charm or no charm, he was asking for respect, and she had to find a balance between that and her own desire to solve Love's riddle.

"Sorry," she said.

"I'm sorry too," he said. He plucked the tissue from her hand and gave her a new one.

"If you don't want to craft love charms," she ventured, "what do you want to do?"

Ken was about to answer when Fallon came back.

Fallon held up her broom like a sword. "Leave the cleaning to me."

Ken turned back to Fallon. "I think everything else here is beyond saving."

"That's fine." Fallon grinned. "After this, your room is going to be the cleanest it's ever been."

Hijiri had no doubt of that.

Between the three of them, cleaning the bedroom took about an hour. Hijiri moved her suitcase out into the living room, along with the shoji screen, and Fallon generously dusted the inside of the closet when they were done.

"The leg snapped," Ken said, inspecting the table. "Bad structure."

"Someone had left the table out for recycling last year. Seemed like a waste to leave it when it worked," Hijiri said.

"It lived a good life," Ken said.

Hijiri let out a laugh. The tension between them had eased with Fallon's presence and a task to focus on.

"How are you going to craft your charms now?" Fallon

asked. "Please don't move it into the kitchen. That's unsanitary."

"I need a safer place to store my materials," Hijiri said. Once she put them back in order, she would be able to start experimenting with her competition charm ideas.

Ken brightened. "Fallon, you were talking about the library before. What happened to the old card catalogs?"

"Ms. Ward said she couldn't bear to get rid of them. Too many memories."

Ken clapped his hands. "Would she give one to Hijiri?"

Fallon matched his excitement. "I don't see why not. Hijiri, can I use your phone? I'll ask her right now."

"That would be perfect," Hijiri said quietly. All those deep compartments. Most of her materials were small. She could fit almost everything into the catalog drawers.

Fallon went to the phone and dialed Ms. Ward's new number. After the Spinster Villas were shut down, Grimbaud High's head librarian found an apartment close to the school. Fallon worked in the school library as part of the office-experience program; she and Ms. Ward had formed an alliance, then a friendship, all because they had shared love fortunes declaring them spinsters from Zita's shop.

"I didn't want to say anything before," Ken said, "but you could use more furniture."

Hijiri sighed. "It just never seemed important before."

Decorating had been so far from her mind last year. She hadn't given up on the idea of transferring to a Lejeune high school back home after seeing how tight Zita's grip on Grimbaud had been. She was thankful now that she stuck it out in this town, but that meant she needed to treat her apartment as a home away from home. Add some of her personality and make it look like she was really living there. That also included fixing her love charm-making situation. She'd have to have all her materials safely stowed and at hand.

Fallon returned with good news: Ms. Ward would be happy to give one of the card catalogs to Hijiri. They could go see the catalog right away at Ms. Ward's apartment, just to make sure it would fit in Hijiri's place.

"I've never seen so many books," Ken said as soon as he entered Ms. Ward's apartment.

Hijiri smiled at that. Of course he hadn't. Still, Ms. Ward *did* have an excessive collection of books. With so many books, mostly hardcovers, the librarian had to find inventive ways to make space for them. Books were stacked behind the front door, next to the shoe rack, and Ms. Ward had installed small shelves above the door to accommodate magazines. The living room had floor-to-ceiling book-shelves. Some books were shoved between couch cushions. Others were piled underneath the coffee table.

"How did you organize them this time?" Fallon asked.

"By height," Ms. Ward said.

Hijiri looked at the shelves again. One side of the room had tiny books, gradually growing in size as she turned to look at them down the hallway.

Ms. Ward had soft features hidden by the cat-eye glasses that swallowed her face. In her twenties, she had been the youngest of the spinsters, and took to wearing skirts with cat prints, though she didn't have pets. "You couldn't have come at a better time," she said, leading them through the kitchen. One cabinet was open, revealing numerous cookbooks crammed inside. "I have a few books still in storage, but with the catalogs, I have no room to bring them home."

Ms. Ward had both card catalog cabinets in her bedroom; Hijiri could see that losing one of them would give her some breathing room—or more likely another bookshelf. The drawers were too small for her to fit books inside. The card catalog was made of oak, with brass handles and frames around the labels.

Imagining all her materials inside each little drawer was easy. Her heart thudded as she ran her fingers over the labels. "I'd love it."

"Great." Ms. Ward said they'd need to arrange movers since the catalog was heavy even when empty.

They sat down at the kitchen table, calling a few companies in Grimbaud's directory until they found one that offered a reasonable price and speedy service. Ms. Ward brewed some green tea and unearthed a half-eaten choco-late cake from the fridge to celebrate. Fallon wouldn't try the cake, but Hijiri didn't hesitate to take a slice. Neither did Ken. The frosting was fluffy and sweet, a perfect match with the dark chocolate inside.

Ms. Ward welcomed Ken as quickly as the others had, asking him a few questions, but nothing too invasive. She seemed preoccupied with another matter. "Fallon, we have to talk about throwing some events at the library this year. Something fun for students to do besides just using the space for studying."

Fallon frowned. "About that . . . I've been meaning to tell you . . . everyone . . . that I secured an internship at the police department."

Hijiri gasped. "Is this about Sanders?"

Fallon's jaw tightened. "Not exactly. After what hap-pened with Zita, I wanted to see if I was interested in using my inspecting skills to catch other charm criminals. With a new detective at the helm in Grimbaud, I have hope that we'll see changes. I want to be there helping in any way I can." She shrugged. "Of course, while I'm there, I'm going to make sure Sanders is not overlooked. That man needs to be stopped."

Ms. Ward smiled fondly. "That means you're going to be busy."

"After school, yes. I know you have big plans this year; I'm sorry I can't help."

"That *is* a problem," Ms. Ward said. "I can check with Mr. Drummond if there are any students willing to switch jobs in the program. I've tried before, of course, but they just love working in the front office."

Fallon brightened. "What about you, Ken?"

Ken pointed at himself, bemused.

"You were telling me that you got the last open position in the program."

"Working in the copy room," he said.

"The library is more exciting than being crammed in a tiny room, getting paper cuts," Fallon said.

"We have windows. With sunlight," Ms. Ward said.

Hijiri didn't know whether to laugh or feel mystified. She hadn't known he had signed up for the office-experience program. Then again, she never asked him about orientation.

Ken sat back in his chair, his eyes crinkling with his smile. "Okay, okay. Save me from the copy room."

Ms. Ward and Fallon exchanged victorious grins.

Hijiri asked him, "Why the copy room?"

"As much as I'm enjoying school, I can't stand sitting all day," Ken said, sobering. Something sad flickered across his face. "Getting a little relief by helping around the school sounded like the perfect solution. Obviously, I'll get more exercise in the library."

"Gotta keep that heart pumping," Ms. Ward said.

Ken's hand leapt to his chest, as if he had forgotten the

organ beating under his skin. He paled and said, "Yes. Very important."

Hijiri narrowed her eyes. She mentally shelved his reaction in her head. The charm-boy was definitely suspicious sometimes.

While cleaning up, Ms. Ward pulled Ken off to the side. Hijiri pretended to keep busy drying the plates; she strained her ears to catch every word.

"Love made you," Ms. Ward said, "so you must know what you're about. But just . . . take care of her, okay?"

Ken's expression softened. "My heart already belongs to her."

"Love wouldn't have it any other way," Ms. Ward said.

"*I* wouldn't either," he stressed.

Ms. Ward ruffled his hair and grinned. "Yes, you *are* a storybook boy. Just checking. It's my duty as the adult around here."

Hijiri's cheeks burned.

"That plate's already dry," Fallon whispered.

Flustered, she handed the plate to Fallon and grabbed another. "I knew that."

❧→

Hijiri hadn't heard from her parents all week, so she decided to call both of them Sunday night. Weekends weren't really vacations for the Kitamuras. Calling home would have been a waste of time. She tried her mother's work number first, twirling the phone cord around her wrist while she waited. Went straight to voicemail. She tried three more times, just in case her mother was at her desk, but she heard nothing. She didn't leave a message.

Her father picked up the second time she called him. "Hijiri, it's late. Is something wrong?"

"Nothing," Hijiri mumbled, tugging on the phone cord. "Just wanted to let you know I'm okay. At school. School is fine."

"Of course you are. You've done this before, remember?" Mr. Kitamura said with a laugh.

She couldn't tell if he was joking or not, so she laughed anyway.

"Grimbaud hasn't changed?"

It has, in more ways than you can imagine, she thought. The town was free. Chaotic and a little confused by the freedom, but it was a huge step forward. She doubted her parents would be able to tell if they came to visit though. "Same old hearts and chocolates," she said.

The conversation ground to a halt then, silence punctuated by the typical office sounds of keyboards clicking, phones ringing, and wrappers crinkling and breaking— dinner for some of the employees. Probably from the snack machines.

"How is work?" Hijiri asked, tired of the quiet. Ever since she was a child, that question always worked in getting her parents to talk. Asking was like turning the key in windup dolls.

Her father launched into a full account of his day. He was an actuary, which meant he spent all day and occasionally late nights making predictions based on the data the company collected. Hijiri used to imagine him as a fortune-teller not unlike Zita, but in his case, he made predictions about mortality and accidents, rates and risk. It sounded like a morbid job to her, but Mr. Kitamura loved it. Her father's voice could be soothing when he wasn't stressed. She focused on the pitch of it rather than the words.

"What do you think I should do?" Mr. Kitamura asked.

"About what?"

His heavy sigh made static on the phone. "Weren't you listening?"

How many times had she wished she could ask him the same question? Hijiri worked at unraveling the phone cord. "Tell me again."

Back when her parents had time to notice her behavior, Mr. and Mrs. Kitamura scolded Hijiri for her inattentiveness.

"Look at me when I'm speaking to you," Mrs. Kitamura had said after catching her daughter reading a charm theory book at six years old. She had to pry the book from Hijiri's hands before getting her attention.

Hijiri didn't learn how to navigate her own city until middle school, when she was responsible for filling the empty fridge with food and running other errands for her parents when she came home from school. Before then, she had used her time in the backseat of the family car absorbed in her own brainstorming.

One night when Hijiri had woken thirsty, she tiptoed down the stairs and stopped when she heard her parents talking in the kitchen. Their voices were low but hardly hushed.

"She's oblivious," Mr. Kitamura said. His back was to the hallway as he dried the dishes dripping in the rack. "Her teachers say she doesn't participate in group work and can't remember her classmates' names when asked. Do you think it's a memory problem?"

"Of course not," came Mrs. Kitamura's tired voice. "She just can't be bothered to learn their names. You know Hijiri."

Do they? Hijiri had thought, squeezing the railing's bars. *Do they really know me?*

As she grew, her memories of spending time with them faded, and sometimes she wasn't sure if her parents had actually taken her to the park or out for pizza until she consulted the family photo albums: a sad collection of thin books sharing space with her father's old business textbooks from college.

If her parents could put their jobs before her every day,

why shouldn't she do the same with her passion for love charm-making?

After Hijiri finished talking (listening, really) to her father, she hung up the phone and sighed. Her hands itched to start crafting like she always did, but with her supplies in shambles and no surface to work on, she didn't have that option.

She tossed and turned in her bed. Kicked the sheets off. Drank three glasses of water. Her mind was a restless machine, begging her to make charms. She counted her friends like sheep. Over and over.

The card catalog was scheduled to arrive on Thursday. "Four days," Hijiri muttered, crawling out of bed on Monday morning.

No love charm-making until then.

Hijiri tossed two slices of bread into the toaster and spilled a few drops of orange juice on the kitchen counter. *When was the last time I couldn't make charms?* she asked herself, tapping her fingers on the counter.

She couldn't remember.

By the time Hijiri had entered first grade, she had taken over the guest room with love charms. Her own little laboratory where she made messes her parents had no time to notice. She taught herself the fundamentals of love charm-making there. Just her mind, heart, library books, and the silent house.

The memory warmed her somewhat as she buttoned her blouse and gave an extra tug on her knee-high socks.

Since she hadn't slept well, and therefore woke before dawn, Hijiri decided to be productive with her extra time. When the card catalog arrived, she wanted to be ready to stock it with her materials. Hijiri tore a sheet of paper out of her history notebook and made a list of everything she had to replace.

Of the broken bottles, Hijiri needed to buy rosewater, powdered milk, and a few specialty items like love letters melted down into a papery perfume and good intentions that smelled like cherry-flavored medicine when uncorked. Luckily she had kept putting off unpacking her suitcase; all the materials in there were still okay.

Hijiri sat cross-legged in front of her suitcase and checked each item. The one she'd spent the most money on that summer was a swan-shaped glass vial of tears. She gingerly turned it in her hands, watching the light catch on the swan's elegant neck.

When she was young, she thought that good love charms were comprised of happy thoughts and syrupy ingredients. But then she learned that love had a darker side. To ignore it would mean limiting yourself as a love charm-maker. *To change lives and get to the root of love, there must be tears. There must be anger, jealousy, and hope-lessness*, she thought. *Use them sparingly, but use them. Those are the feelings that invite change, whether we like them or not.*

During an art fair in Lejeune, Hijiri had found a sharp-dressed man selling preserved tears. After searching the shelves, she chose the swan one since it held a woman's tears that she had cried for months after a breakup. Tears of a broken heart.

At the time, she had been working on a charm that would help someone give advice to a broken-hearted friend. When she included two drops of the tears into the mix, it finally worked: her neighbor, Yumi, had never been skilled at soothing her sensitive niece, but after wearing Hijiri's locket sealed with the tears, good intentions, and flecks of silver for smoothness, she was able to speak from her heart.

Like sought like sometimes.

Her best charm to date was True Love's Kiss, but that had only worked with Love's direct help. She had made some changes to the charm's formula but hadn't gotten a chance yet to see if it worked on its own. The charm had the consistency of lip balm, hopefully providing a miraculous spark once the wearer's lips touched his or her beloved. Just like in fairy tales. Using the True Love's Kiss charm in the competition would have been tempting if she had figured out how to make it work again. But for now, it was another puzzle to solve, just like Ken.

Love gave her Ken. He was another challenge. If she couldn't work on her charms, she would spend the next few days focused on him.

Chapter 9

SKIN AND SIGNATURES

Hijiri peppered Ken with questions on the walk to school—anything she could think of. She fired them quickly, disappointed when he gave her answers each time.

"Favorite color?" she asked.

"Brown," he said, "like wood."

"Favorite food?"

"Probably the waffles," Ken said, smiling. "Drizzled with chocolate *and* caramel sauce. The vendors always look at me sideways when I ask for that, as if I were ruining the chocolate."

"Favorite sport?"

"Archery. Haven't gotten to do that yet in gym class though."

Then she thought about what the twins had said about Ken's coughing. Changing her tactic, she asked, "When did you first realize you loved archery?"

Ken hesitated. The streets were crowded that morning,

fellow Grimbaud High students waiting with them on the corner to cross the street. His eyes flickered to hers, his eyebrows furrowed. But the moment he tried to answer, his throat failed him. His voice turned into a wheeze. He covered his mouth with his hand and coughed.

Hijiri wanted to pat him on the back, to dislodge whatever he'd swallowed. But there was nothing. "Come on, tell me," she pressed.

He coughed harder. His shoulders slumped and he sighed after catching his breath. "I'm good at it, naturally."

"How did you know you were good at it?"

"I hit the targets."

"That's only a piece of the truth," she said, grabbing his sweater sleeve as they crossed traffic. "You're not telling me everything."

Ken peeled her fingers off his sleeve, only to wrap his own hand around her wrist when they reached the sidewalk. His skin was clammy, but that could have been from the sweltering morning heat. He was the only person in town wearing a sweater, after all.

"Love didn't want to make it easy on you," he said, keeping his voice low. His grip on her wrist tightened. "Before he sent me to Grimbaud, Love planted a kind of silencing charm in my throat. If you ask me something that could possibly help you solve me, my throat closes up. I can't answer you. I wish I could, Hijiri."

Hijiri groaned. "Why didn't you tell me this from the beginning? It would have saved us both so much time!"

"It's kind of embarrassing," Ken admitted, blushing. "Besides, I'm serious about wanting you to treat me like a person. I want to *feel real*, Hijiri, and a charmed throat isn't doing me any favors."

"Doesn't mean I'm going to stop asking you questions," Hijiri said after a moment. "I need to test the boundaries." *A crude silencing charm won't stop me.* It *was* a crude charm. Obviously, Love couldn't trust his charm-boy to keep secrets. If Ken was really in love with her, he'd want to tell her everything. The silencing charm solved that problem.

Ken squeezed her hand. "Look at that."

Across the street, they saw a familiar face: Ryker from Heartwrench. Far from his store, the young man drew a crowd.

What was the strange love charm-maker doing out so early in the morning? She needed a closer look. Ken obliged her, curiosity written all over his face, as they joined the crowd.

Ryker wore overalls and gloves, his hair especially oily and smooth against his skull. He told the crowd that Heartwrench was offering evening classes in mechanical love charm-making—discounted price for high school students. "Who knows? If you take enough classes, you just may learn how to make something as impressive as this."

Hijiri shoved through the crowd to the very front, just in time to see Ryker grab two tin contraptions from his battered suitcase: a tin angel and a tin devil, hollow-looking and small. The angel was an unfriendly, solemn thing with dull eyes. The devil's long face and pointy whiskers glinted. Neither could stand up since their feet had been engineered into clips. "Can anyone tell me what these are?" Ryker asked.

"They sit on your shoulders," Hijiri said without thinking. "Angel and devil, both sides of a person's conscience. How is that a love charm?"

Ryker's electric-blue eyes widened behind his glasses. "Should I tell you? You might be here to steal Heartwrench's ideas."

Hijiri's skin burned when she felt everyone's eyes on her. "Not my intention," she said through gritted teeth. "But if you're so worried, maybe you better put them away."

Ken squeezed her hand again.

Ryker laughed. "Just a joke, Hijiri."

"Then please continue."

Ryker clipped the angel to his left shoulder, then the devil on his right shoulder. The clips were strong enough to keep the angel and devil upright, like parakeets sitting on either shoulder. They sprang to life. The angel's wings flapped. The devil whipped his tail back and forth. "My uncle and I created this love charm for people who need help in making smarter decisions in their dating lives. They give you two choices, but you must learn to listen to the right one. Let me show you how it works."

Ryker stroked his chin. "I wonder what I should do," he said, "with the pretty young girl here. Should I kiss Hijiri?"

Hijiri paled. What was he saying?

The devil had a deep, cackling tin voice. *"Go for it. She'll be swooning in your arms in no time."*

The angel crossed its arms, its tinny voice high and frantic. *"Don't you dare! She's underage! Step away from the girl now."*

"Uncle Gage was thinking of installing a small electrical jolt in the angel," he said, laughing, unclipping them both, "just in case someone actually listened to the devil."

"That sounds dangerous," Hijiri said.

"I agree. I had to talk him out of trying." Ryker sighed. "He thinks that we should enter these in the competition, but they're not ready yet. I wouldn't know how to market them. They're more like nagging tin toys than the valuable resources we hoped for."

"How did you make them talk?" she asked. The voices were off, but the angel's and devil's sentences had formed naturally.

"Too many all-nighters with recordings of talk shows," he confessed. He rubbed his eyes as if the memory fatigued him. "We were able to load them with magazine advice too. They only have room for advice regarding love, of course."

A few onlookers jumped in too, asking him questions. Some even asked if they could touch the creepy tin charms. Ryker showed a curious girl the back of the tin angel, explaining that he loaded the data through wiring underneath the angel's tin robe.

"We're going to be late," Ken said, reminding her that they had been on their way to school only moments before.

Hijiri nodded, but her mind turned. The image of Ryker opening the back of the tin angel stuck with her. If she had wanted to know how Heartwrench's charm worked and had a head for mechanics, she would only have to pry the back open and look inside.

Unlike electronic devices, charms didn't have obvious openings. But if a seasoned charm-maker knew where to look, some charms could be unraveled by finding a kind of keyhole or crack in the crafting. Sometimes charm-makers even left behind signatures, marking each charm as their own creations.

Kentaro Oshiro was sophisticated. Love had to have woven hundreds of charms to make him, interlaced and endlessly functioning with each blink and breath from the boy. *Maybe there's an opening on Ken. Some kind of keyhole for me to peer through, to see the charms that make him tick.*

If not a keyhole, than a signature. Love's proud enough to have left one.

Her heart bumped against the cage of her ribs, both scared and excited by the prospect.

Mrs. Smedt had left Hijiri her first odd job of the semester: trimming the potted plants on the patio. She stopped by the aging caretaker's house to pick up the key to the shed and share a cup of bitter tea. Hijiri had worked for her last year, but it wasn't a steady job. The Student Housing Complex required very little upkeep since the inside of each apartment was the responsibility of the student staying there. Raking leaves in the fall. Pruning. Making sure the wooden gate wasn't creaking. Hijiri had never found the jobs hard; they usually gave her mental space to brainstorm and ponder over her latest charm experiments while exercising her body.

When she got home from school on Tuesday, Hijiri unlocked the shed to retrieve the pruning shears. She clipped dead leaves while students sat on the patio, chatting about their classes.

How can I see Ken without his clothes? she thought, her cheeks reddening. No matter how she phrased it in her head, her skin reacted badly. It felt shame for her, perhaps, in thinking about divesting a boy of his clothing. *Another girl might want to peel the clothes off the boy she loved, but my intentions are purely scientific.*

Her heart had other ideas.

The minute she examined her heart, trying to follow Fallon's directions, the tiny, beating thing overwhelmed her with images of Ken: Ken with his shirt unbuttoned, his ankles bare, his forearms seeing Grimbaud's sunshine for the first time. And with the images came an unsettling realization.

She was torn between wanting to look for the signature and wanting to . . . just touch his skin.

It's not funny, she thought, mentally scolding her heart. *Cut it out, now!* Her hand slipped. She clipped a perfectly healthy branch by accident.

The options were grim. Maybe she could find ways to get him to take off his socks, or even his sweater if she turned up the thermostat in her apartment. But getting flashes and glimpses of his skin would take a long time. She didn't think she had the patience.

"Hijiri," Fallon said, carrying textbooks in the crook of her arm. "Are you busy?"

Hijiri welcomed the distraction. "Almost done here."

"Have you been . . . handling not being able to craft love charms okay?"

"I've been distracted," she said, thinking of Ken, "and haven't been sleeping well. Thursday's too far away."

"Well, I have an idea." Fallon smiled brightly. "How

about you and I do something fun in town? I know a place you can work out your frustrations."

"I don't need a punching bag," Hijiri said. Maybe she did.

Fallon shook her head. "You'll see. Ready in an hour?"

Hijiri's curiosity flared. She couldn't wait to see what her friend had in mind.

✎→

"Only two?" the woman at the counter asked, her eyes flickering between Hijiri and Fallon. "Do you have a couple's discount coupon?"

"Oh no, we're just friends," Fallon said.

"Right this way."

Crafty Cupids was a favorite Grimbaud destination for those easily amused by glue sticks and paint splatters. The back of the store had numerous tables occupied by fidgety children and anxious parents. Balloons pressing against the ceiling tickled the tops of people's heads with their strings.

"Consider this room your craft haven," the woman said, gesturing to the rows of plates, mugs, cute animals, and cupids lining the walls, just waiting to be painted and covered unceremoniously with glitter. "Nothing is off-limits. But remember that the bigger the item you're painting, the higher the price."

"So what do you think?" Fallon asked, wandering over to the shelves.

"You're wearing the wrong outfit for this place," Hijiri said. "If you think your skirt is going to survive this place unstained, you're naive."

Fallon only laughed. Then she leaned close to whisper, "The truth is that I bought the shirt and skirt when I was out with Sebastian last week. *Off the sale rack.* The second button on the skirt was even missing."

Hijiri snorted. "No way."

"I'm trying," Fallon said, shuddering. "What are you going to paint?"

Hijiri considered the choices. Choosing a plate or mug would help fill her empty kitchen cabinets, but the cupids drew her attention in the end. She chose one with little wings, one dimpled cheek creased with the beginning of a mischievous grin.

She and Fallon took a corner table away from the giggling children and party hats. Fallon neatly squeezed different paint colors in her dish, each one safely separate from mixing with the others, and started to paint her mug right away.

Hijiri opened the drawers underneath the shelves; they were stuffed with supplies she would have considered using for her own charms. Seeing the fake gemstones, stickers, felt, and neon pipe cleaners brought back the itch to craft love charms. She took a deep breath. "Have fun," she ordered herself under her breath. *Don't think about charm-making.*

Hijiri dipped a fat brush in sparkling gold paint, tickling under the cupid's armpits and rubbing the bristles across its belly.

"Did you try what I suggested? Listening to your heart?"

Hijiri poked the cupid in the eye with gold paint.

"Are you okay?"

"Fine," she said, dunking her brush in the paint. "I did try. A little."

Fallon's expression turned serious. "What happened?"

"It's not easy," Hijiri blurted. "My heart does strange things. It doesn't want to stay put. It likes to dance and send feelings shooting up and down my spine."

"When Ken's around?"

Hijiri rubbed her chin. "Yes."

Fallon's mouth twitched. "What do you think your heart's saying?"

"I don't know. It confuses me too much."

"Try harder," Fallon said. "Promise me."

"Other people's hearts are so much simpler," Hijiri mumbled.

"It does seem that way, doesn't it?" Fallon said lightly.

"Regardless of what my heart's doing, the fact remains that Ken must be solved," Hijiri said, eager to change the subject, however slight. "I've come up with a new plan."

She told Fallon about keyholes and signatures, and how she needed to find ways to search Ken for such signs. Weakness. A way to see what he was made of.

Fallon painted the lip of her mug with neat strokes. "Hmm."

"It's a good plan, right?"

"It'll be tricky." Fallon covered her mouth with her hand. "I just can't see you trying to rip his clothes off."

Hijiri's face was a burning coal. "I'd never!"

"Then where do you think Love would leave a signature on Ken?"

"It could be anywhere."

"Maybe . . . maybe it's in the most obvious spot," Fallon said.

Hijiri gasped. "His heart."

"When Zita's charm activated, it spread over Sebastian's heart," Fallon said quietly. Physical proof of the attack on his life with each swirling cursive letter of his love fortune written into his skin.

The heart would be key. It was as much Love's symbol as the storks and cupids. If Love left anything behind on Ken, it would have to be there.

Chapter 10
WATERWORKS

Hijiri's Crafty Cupids creation gained a few additions after it had been sealed and fired in the kiln. She had wrapped neon pink and blue pipe cleaners around the neck as a scarf. Gold tinsel glued down like hair gel for added dimension to the cupid's curls. And a felt heart, cut as tiny as Hijiri could manage with her scissors, glued on its chest.

"Hello, tiny heart," she whispered. In a way, she felt like she was speaking to her own heart.

When Hijiri returned home, she placed the cupid on her kitchen table with the wilting begonias, realizing that the cupid was probably the most striking feature now inhabiting her dull apartment.

Then she called the twins and told them about her plan to get Ken's shirt off.

"You're letting us help?" Mirthe said.

"You offered," Hijiri reminded her. Besides, Fallon had been right: she'd have a difficult time managing the feat on her own, especially when the idea alone made her turn cherry red.

Femke must have pried the phone out of her twin's hand. "Mirthe and I need time to form a mutual plan. . . ."

"Why wait?" Mirthe said, tugging back. "We're not going to agree. I'll show you how much better *my* weather charms are, Femke. Your fog and clouds won't get Ken to take off his shirt. I'll use much stronger charms."

"Where are you going to get those?" Femke asked testily.

"I have my ways."

"Ways that Mom and Dad wouldn't approve of, no doubt."

"Don't worry, Hijiri. Ken will be naked from the waist up before you even blink!"

Hijiri listened to the *beep-beep-beep* of the call being dropped before realizing that the twins were already gone. She opened her fridge and pressed the orange juice carton to her burning skin.

Wednesday was a small victory. Hijiri managed to make it through the school day without fidgeting too much, but her heart throbbed when she walked between classes wondering if she'd see one of the twins' plans in action. Mirthe gave her a thumbs-up in the hall between Hijiri's algebra and literature classes.

Hijiri returned the gesture, puzzled.

Meanwhile, she did her best to examine snatches of Ken's skin that she *could* see.

The curve of his neck, sticking out of his bulky sweater.

His unremarkable wrists.

The backs of his ears. Hijiri had never noticed that his ears were naturally pink. It wasn't a blush.

By the time Thursday rolled around, she felt she had stared down every exposed sliver of skin. Love hadn't left a signature where Ken's jaw met his ear. That would have been clever.

Her card catalog was supposed to arrive today, but the sky didn't think it was worth celebrating. Overcast and humid, unusual for a September day in Grimbaud. Hijiri eyed the gray clouds warily on her walk with Ken to school.

"You must hate the rain," Ken said.

Hijiri grumbled. Her skin was damp, her hair sticking to the back of her neck.

Ken's compact umbrella fit the front pocket of his backpack. He never took it out, not once, even when the clouds breathed mist on their heads. "Are you worried about your hair? Will your face melt if you get wet?"

Hijiri let out a surprised laugh. "Those are strange questions."

"Really?"

"Well, I don't wear makeup," she said. "So no face-melting." But he was a charm-boy, so maybe *his* face would melt. Somehow. Unknown charms were unpredictable.

A group of girls passed, fanning themselves with folded notebook paper. Vendors sold frozen yogurt topped with blueberries still glittering with ice crystals.

"There's something romantic about rain," Ken said softly.

"Says the boy who claims he knows nothing about love charms."

Ken smiled. "I think it's the eyelash dripping that does it."

Hijiri stopped, causing a harried tourist to bump right into her. She didn't care.

Ken shoved his hands into his pockets; despite wearing a thick sweater, he seemed unbothered by the heat. "Have you ever looked at someone's eyelashes when they're caught in the rain? The beads of water that pool on their eyelashes. It's mesmerizing."

A question burned her tongue: when, in his short life, did he stare at someone's eyelashes in the rain? Maybe Love made him watch some movies before he came to Grimbaud. She took a breath, and suddenly that question didn't seem as important. Ken's eyelashes were thin; she didn't know how they would hold droplets. *Not that I want to see it*, she thought.

Ken raised his eyebrows. "What? No questions?"

"Just this once."

They started walking again, and Ken kept his face turned away from her. But she could still see another smile tugging at his lips.

Grimbaud High's air-conditioning systems broke in both wings. The rate of paper fans and folders being used grew exponentially. Teachers unlocked and opened their classroom windows, but the humidity crawling inside did little to help ease the discomfort.

After homeroom, Hijiri saw the twins being chased through the hallway by students begging them for wind charms. Mirthe jumped over a boy who had kneeled to tie his shoe. Femke stuck out her tongue and followed Mirthe around the corner.

Principal Bemelmans tried to instill some order by announcing over the loudspeaker that a repair crew was on its way. No one believed him.

"Even if the repair crew arrives, how will they fix the entire school before the day's over?" Anais said at lunch. "We'd battle one another over which wing gets fixed first. I'd have the upper hand with Bear."

Bear tucked into his second plate of meat loaf. He looked at his girlfriend adoringly. "You could climb on my back as I throw our enemies to the ground."

Anais loved the idea. "And I could defend you from my height!"

Fallon hid her laughter with her napkin. She was almost crying. "Look," she said, taking a few breaths, "I don't think it'll come to that. If anything, Grimbaud High should purchase some charms from the twins' shop."

Hijiri tugged at her blouse; it stuck to her like a second skin. She didn't have much of an appetite.

"But then again, Martin would say it isn't in the budget if they haven't done it already," Fallon added.

Anais's fluffy blond hair clung to her flushed cheeks. She tapped her fingers on the table and drank her lukewarm bottle of water. "On a day like this, no one will be able to concentrate."

Already, the students in the cafeteria picked at their too-warm food. Some even raided the salad bar since the greens were cooler than the meat loaf and steamy pasta.

Hijiri tried to focus on the exciting evening ahead: she'd have her card catalog around dinnertime. Spending the night putting her charm supplies away in the numerous drawers would be fantastic—but she was missing one more piece. "I need to find a table," she said.

Fallon looked at her. "For your apartment?"

"I'll need a reliable one this time. I don't want to lose my supplies again."

Instead of suggesting some shops, Fallon asked, "Did you tell Ken that you're looking for one?"

Hijiri blinked. "Why?"

"Seems like he knows some things about furniture," Fallon said. "I mean, he came up with the idea of using the card catalog for your supplies. And he knew why your old table broke."

"Anyone could know that," Hijiri said. Just because she didn't know, it didn't mean Ken was some kind of secret furniture genius.

"Maybe you're right." Fallon folded her used napkin. "But you should ask him anyway. I'm sure he wants to spend more time with you."

"I want more time with my charms."

"Charms can't hold conversations." Fallon held up her hand. "*Unless* we're talking about a boy made of charms. In which case, you should be talking to Ken all the time."

Hijiri thought she was spending enough time with Ken as it was. But she knew that look on her friend's face so she sighed and said, "Fine. I'll ask him about the table."

⊱⟶

With no repairs and the temperature rising, Hijiri suffered through her classes as best she could. She lost the desire to pay attention in her literature class, even though her teacher forced them to read from the textbook. Ink came off on her fingers when she turned the pages.

She grew sleepy. The words swam on the page. Hijiri was close to closing her eyes and letting the heat snuggle her into a nap when rain slammed against the classroom door.

Hijiri sat straight up, puzzled. Why was it raining inside?

Her fellow students didn't share her confusion. All they saw was relief. Bursting out of their chairs and leaving their textbooks behind, the teens ran into the hallway. Hijiri stood in the doorway with her teacher, observing the chaos in the hall. Puddles had already started forming. Students splashed and opened their mouths as the rain poured in. Sweet respite from the pressing heat. Hijiri looked up and saw thin, snakelike clouds crawling along the ceiling, releasing rain with factory precision.

"The twins," Hijiri whispered. Then she ran into the rain.

The rain wasn't just cold. It was chilling. Her teeth chattered from the shock of it as she dashed through clumps of soaked students and teachers. Everyone smiled, laughed, screeched. But she was looking for someone in particular.

Her class had been on the second floor, but she knew that Ken was taking biology at the same time on the third floor. Once she reached the staircase, she fought against the tide of students on the stairs and climbed, anticipation drumming through her bones. Her bangs stuck to her forehead as she ran, blinking back water and calling Ken's name over the sound of the rain.

Ken was in the middle of the hallway, his hair sticking up in tufts and his sweater hanging heavy and wet. He was looking up at the charmed clouds, entranced.

And completely unaware that the De Keysers were sneaking up on him.

Femke gestured sharply at Mirthe, warning her off, but Mirthe deliberately ignored her sister. Mirthe withdrew a bottle from her bag. It had a cork in it, plugging up what looked like fierce winds.

Hijiri's heart stopped.

When Mirthe uncorked the bottle, she flew backward as the wind came charging out. Right at Ken.

She couldn't warn him, not loud enough. Never loud enough. The winds hit the clouds and mixed badly, spiraling rain through the hall and slamming into lockers and students alike. Hijiri covered her eyes and sank to the floor. The rain lashed at her face. She heard Femke yelling at her sister, felt the murky heat of fog pour along the floor. Then she forced herself to get up and find Ken.

He was lying on his side in the middle of the hallway. His knees were curled to his chest.

Her heart tumbled out of its box and flopped around somewhere near her stomach. She was by his side in seconds, her hands hovering over his face. She checked the back of his head for bumps or bruising. Then smoothed back his hair. *Now's your chance*, a little voice inside her head whispered. *Lift his shirt up. Check his heart.*

Ken's eyes fluttered open. He caught her wrist just as she was about to tug his sweater up. "Hijiri?" he croaked.

Disappointment and relief rubbed together inside her chest. The twins had failed badly. What were they thinking? "You're okay?" she asked, her voice trembling in the cold.

"Looks like I fell," Ken said, sitting up on his elbows.

Hijiri hovered above him. "Are you hurt anywhere?"

Ken's eyes narrowed. A small smile tugged at his lips. He stared at her with such warmth. "Look at that," he said softly. "Your eyelashes are catching water. It's beautiful."

Her cheeks did that burning thing again. "Are you listening to me?"

Principal Bemelmans turned the corner with three teachers. He had kept relatively dry with a twisted umbrella in his grip. "Standard evacuation," he yelled. "Head toward the nearest exit."

One of the teachers opened a window, letting the wind out.

"Hey, don't do that!" Mirthe said. "That wind's worth a lot of money. You can't just—"

Femke slapped her own forehead and grimaced.

"The De Keysers," Principal Bemelmans said dryly. "You couldn't help disturbing the school with your charms, could you? I thought we were doing so well, too."

"This was an exception," Mirthe argued. "The AC was broken. That's human suffering. Femke and I were just cooling everyone off."

"And possibly damaging property in the lockers," he said, "as well as releasing hurricane winds. Which, I'm sure, has nothing to do with lowering body temperatures. You two follow me to my office. We're going to call your parents."

"Oh no," Mirthe groaned.

"You won't be allowed to stay after school for the rest of the year," he told the twins. "That means you'll need to hold your charm theory club meetings elsewhere."

Femke gasped.

"Why?" Mirthe asked.

"I don't relish the possibility of further damage to school property."

Hijiri got to her feet, then helped pull Ken up with her. As much as she felt for the twins and for the club, speaking up would only endanger her participation in the love charm competition. Plus, Principal Bemelmans wasn't wrong. The twins went overboard this time. She knew it wasn't about Ken. *Far from it*, she thought, watching the twins scowl at each other as the teachers escorted them out of the hall.

After much debate, Principal Bemelmans decided to send Grimbaud High's students home. Forcing damp, sweaty students to spend two more hours in school felt cruel to both teachers and students alike. The hallways needed mopping up, at any rate.

Hijiri grabbed Ken by the back of his sweater. "Where are you going?"

"We don't walk home together," he said.

Hijiri didn't let go. "We don't usually get released early either."

"Aren't you getting your card catalog today?"

"Kentaro!"

His eyes crinkled when he laughed. He glanced up at the sky and said, "Looks like rain."

Halfway back to the complex, a light drizzle rained down on the town. Hijiri didn't care anymore about getting wet. The wooden gate creaked when Ken opened it. They were so close to their apartments now that she didn't feel the need to rush.

Ken stopped at the staircase. "Will you come upstairs?" he asked.

"Your apartment?" Hijiri stared at the staircase as if the steps had holes.

"Come on," he said. "There's nothing to be afraid of."

"I'm not scared of an apartment," she said, frowning.

Ken laughed again, though she didn't see what was so funny. "No, you shouldn't be. I would never have designed it that way."

His strange words made her feet move. She followed

him up the stairs. She passed Fallon's apartment and turned the corner, finding a few apartments nestled away. When Ken unlocked the door, Hijiri felt a wave of peace wash over her. The tension in her shoulders eased. She took off her shoes and looked around.

His apartment shared the same plain walls and wood floors as the others in the complex, but he had somehow made it cozy and personalized. A plush, dark green rug covered most of the living area; Hijiri felt the softness through her damp socks. The couch pillows had been fluffed, perhaps even washed, because they looked like new. He had a desk with cubbyholes and a tea canister holding his pens and pencils. The semester's major dates and flyers from around town had been tacked on his corkboard.

She stopped in front of a canvas photograph taken from one of Grimbaud's bridges. The black-and-white photo showed the gentle swell of canal water and a tour boat cutting through it—one of the Barneses' boats, to be precise. Hijiri felt a prickling at her elbows. The water began to move in the photograph. She smelled the dampness of the canal and heard the faint sounds of cameras flashing from the boat.

"Come see my bedroom," he said.

Hijiri frowned, but she didn't object when he gently tugged her hand. On the way, she noticed that the kitchen was the least decorated. Still, he had used colorful plaid

tape to frame each cabinet. The tape continued in his bedroom; he had used it to frame his small bookshelf. His
bedroom was a boyish green-and-brown plaid.

"I made the headboard last night," he said proudly.
"Plywood and quilt batting. It was the best I could do on
short notice."

Hijiri felt strangely at home. She wanted to curl up on
his couch with a mug of tea, or maybe even sprawl out
on the rug and dream up love charms.

"Love has been generous. He sends me an allowance,
and I was able to buy this." Ken reached into his closet
and pulled out a staple gun. "It's a brand-new one. I can
work on so many projects with this."

Stunned, Hijiri wandered over to his bed and sat on it.
The mattress sank under her weight. The comforter was
so downy she had to fight falling asleep right there. "Don't
tell me you have a glue gun."

"It's in my desk," he said, grinning. Ken put the staple gun away. "I hope this is proof enough that you can
trust me with your card catalog. Or anything else you
need."

"There's something odd about your apartment," she
said faintly.

They went back to the living area. As soon as she was
settled on the couch, Ken kneeled on the rug in front of
her. He didn't have any backpack straps to grab this time,
but he flexed his fingers anyway. "So what do you think?"

he asked. "I know they aren't love charms, but this is my passion."

"The mood, the photograph, the furniture," she whispered, snapping out of her catlike comfort. The pieces added up. Hijiri gasped. "These are hearth charms."

Ken nodded. "I can craft them."

Simply put, hearth charms were charms crafted for the home. Hijiri's parents never bothered purchasing hearth charms, relying on a recommended interior designer for their house instead. But hearth charms worked in a way regular furnishings didn't: they affected mood, atmosphere, and functionality. *Not as exciting as love charms,* Hijiri thought. *Why did Love give Ken this talent?*

Disappointment flooded Ken's eyes. "You're studying me again."

"I can't help it."

"I know."

The flatness in his voice stung. Hijiri rubbed her face.

"Hearth charms and love charms have a lot in common," he said gently. "Romantic love isn't the only love there is. Hearth charms come from love of home and family. A couple is happy if their *home* is a happy place."

Hijiri shook her head. "That's not true. A couple is happy only when they are in love with each other. A house reflects their feelings."

"Spoken like a love charm-maker," he said, amused.

"Think of it this way. If a couple is struggling—with each other, with money problems, with rowdy, unruly children—hearth charms help dull the aches and pains. It's a valuable discipline. I mean, just look at you. I've never seen you so relaxed before, even though you're completely baffled right now."

Hijiri raised her eyebrows.

"I love your baffled face," he added.

"How can you know these things? How can you even argue with me about love charms and hearth charms?" Hijiri asked.

"I could try answering," he said softly. "But you know what'll happen."

Hijiri sighed into her hands. Each time she felt like she was getting closer to understanding Ken, she hit a wall. He wouldn't even take off his sweater. It was drying already, stiff and wrinkled, but he didn't seem bothered in the least by it.

Ken leaned forward, pulling her hands away from her face. He rubbed her clammy hands, warming them. His voice was so gentle, so sorry, that she felt her heart start to thaw too. "Keep asking me questions. I'm the best source for Kentaro Oshiro facts."

"I'm *always* asking you questions." Hijiri's gaze dropped to their hands. His fingers slid over hers. Her skin tingled.

"Sometimes I worry what will happen when you stop asking."

She looked up sharply.

"I know your dedication to love charms is immense," he said, "but would you be interested in trying a hearth charm? I'll walk you through it."

"Yes," she breathed.

Chapter 11

THE RIGHT KIND OF MOOD

When she had said yes, Ken stumbled to his feet to fetch what he needed for the hearth charm. He came back carrying a stethoscope.

"What's that for?" Hijiri asked. And why hadn't she thought of purchasing one for herself? Maybe it could be a good tool for measuring her heart.

"Patience," he said. After returning to his spot on the rug, he asked Hijiri to join him and lie on her side, facing him. "This charm works best with direct contact," he said, patting the wood, "but it's also really uncomfortable. So we'll stick with the rug."

Hijiri slipped off the couch and onto the rug. Her hair was still damp and clothes stiff from the twins' charms, but she settled easily. Treating him like a mirror, she curved her legs like his and copied the way he tucked both hands against his chest. *We must look like two halves of a heart,* she thought.

They were close to each other. His body heat radiated

between them. If she stretched a little farther, she could brush her toes against his.

Ken handed her the stethoscope. "Put this on. Since you're not practiced in hearth charm-making, you won't see what the charm does on your own."

Hijiri put the earpieces in.

Ken pressed the stethoscope's bell against the wooden floor above their heads. Then he closed his eyes and said something under his breath.

She squeezed her eyes shut and breathed deeply. At first, nothing happened. She felt the soft rug against her body, smelled the damp, evergreen scent that was only Ken.

Then, like an orchestra tuning up, she heard other sounds through her earpieces: creaking footsteps, radios tuning, pipes humming, furniture shifting, and undefinable creaking from the belly of the Student Housing Complex.

"Focus," he said. "Soon you'll *see* the complex too."

Hijiri shoved the sounds aside, save for a few ghostly creaks and footsteps, when color flashed behind her eyelids. The colors became blue and white, forming lines, dimensions, angles. A blueprint of Ken's apartment. Just as it came to her, the blueprint slithered away. Other apartments drew themselves across her eyelids, white lines and frosty blue backgrounds.

"Hold on," he said.

She flew through the pipes and walls, her own apartment a playground of abstract lines, before traveling deeper into the building. Finding leaky faucets and jammed windows. They flashed red, easy to spot amid the whites and blues.

"This charm is running a diagnostic of the complex," he said softly. "I can see the very fabric of the building and pinpoint its flaws. People just assume that hearth charmmaking is all about making rooms inviting. But it's more than that."

Slowly, the colors and sounds began to fade. When she opened her eyes, she found Ken smiling at her. Hijiri pushed herself up and stretched her arms. "I don't know what to do with you."

"That's okay. I'll be here when you do."

Her breath hitched. "Promise?"

Ken sat up, looking tousled and content and solid. Like he wouldn't go away. "I promise I won't leave. Do what you need to do to solve me. I can weather anything."

Hijiri wanted to laugh at his wording. He *did* survive a full-on attack from the twins. Maybe he wasn't as delicate as she thought. Some kind of pressure left her.

Ken stood and offered his hand, pulling her up with him. They were both stiff from air drying, with disheveled hair and wrinkled uniforms. "We better get cleaned up," he said. "Don't want to scare the movers when the catalog arrives."

She walked to the door on wobbly legs. After shoving her feet into her shoes, she turned back to him. "You'll be there later?"

"Sure."

She squared her shoulders. "I need a table. Will you help me find one?"

Ken smiled wide enough to hurt. "Absolutely."

⊶⟶

Hijiri took a shower hot enough for steam to fog the mirrors. She stayed under the showerhead until her hair flattened against her back. Catching a cold would be a terrible setback. She hoped she burned it out of her skin with hot water and pear-scented scrub.

The shower made her feel drowsy for only a few minutes before the anticipation of receiving her card catalog brought back the fidgets. She threw on a T-shirt and jeans, tried attacking her homework, but mostly paced her apartment.

By the time the movers arrived, her bare feet slapped against the floor in a messy rhythm.

"Wait," Ken yelled, running past the movers as they unloaded the catalog.

"What's the matter?" Hijiri asked. She had opened the door as wide as it would go, hoping the catalog would fit.

"Have you decided where it's going?"

"Wherever the movers put it should be fine."

Ken huffed. He entered the apartment and turned in a circle, his eyes flickering over every piece of the room. "It's not going in your bedroom."

"It could, if I want the privacy," she said.

"Not if you want to use the rest of your bedroom. It's too big, Hijiri." He gestured at the stretch of wall between the living area and the kitchen. "How about having your work area here? It's wasted space. You don't even have a picture hanging over here."

Hijiri thought about it. In Fallon's apartment, she used that space for her corkboard and desk area, as did Ken. But Hijiri had shoved her standard-issue desk near the door, unused, since she preferred wide worktables or doing her homework on her bed. No matter how she thought about it, that space would work best. "I could still use my shoji screen to hide it," she admitted.

"A little privacy and a little mystery," he said. "And there'll still be room for your table."

With a few grunts and adjusting in the doorway, the movers wheeled the card catalog inside. The catalog had more drawers than she remembered and she loved how the natural sunlight illuminated the messages scratched into the wood.

Ken debated with the movers over the placement of the catalog, insisting they shift it to the left, then a pinch to the right, while the two men said they couldn't see a difference in the shifting.

Hijiri perched on the armrest of her couch, relieved to let Ken take over. If it had just been her, she would have had them put the catalog anywhere, desperate as she was to give her supplies a new home. Then she got an idea. "Why don't we use the card catalog as a wall?" she said.

The movers shook out their arms and sighed.

Ken brightened. "I didn't think of that."

"It's like building a little room for myself," she said, excited. If they moved the catalog so that it was adjacent to the wall, with its back toward the front door, she'd be able to hide behind it to do her work. Even more room for her future worktable, since she would be using some of the living area space.

By the time the movers left, Hijiri was humming with anticipation. Charm ideas popped and fizzed inside her head, just waiting to come out. For the last time, she hoped, she pushed the feeling back. "I need that table."

"Today?" Ken asked.

"You can't expect me to wait any longer to start crafting," she said.

"But the shops are closing now. It's almost dinnertime."

"Ken," she whined. She hated herself for begging, but she needed to start crafting. Now. That very night.

He scratched the back of his head, ruffling his hair. "Okay. Let's see if anything's open."

Hijiri snatched her bag and keys. After locking the door, she told Ken to run. They both dashed through the complex gate and onto the sidewalk. Ken breathed harshly behind her; looking over her shoulder, she saw that his cheeks were flushed and he was trying hard not to laugh.

"What's so funny?" she asked.

"Us, trying to beat the clock," he replied.

"Just you watch. We'll find that table!"

Hijiri wasn't familiar with the shops like her friends were since she spent her walks daydreaming, but Grimbaud had a fair share of antique and thrift stores. Her worktable *had* to be there. They came upon an antique shop with twinkle lights still blinking in the windows. Hijiri stopped abruptly. Ken bumped into her from behind; she stumbled forward, her hand on the doorknob.

"Here?" he asked, his breath on her neck.

Hijiri's skin tingled. "I hope so."

The shop was narrow and cramped. Hijiri sucked in her stomach as she walked through the rows of piled, dusty items. She couldn't tell one piece of furniture from the next, covered as they were, but Ken had an easier time.

"What kind of table do you need?" he asked softly. "Because I can see if there's anything here that meets your requirements."

"Using a hearth charm?"

He nodded.

Hijiri lowered her voice so that the shop owner at the counter couldn't hear them. "A big, wide table that doesn't wobble. It won't break under the weight of my bottles and supplies, because I tend to use so many at once."

"Anything else?"

"Not really."

Ken whispered a few words under his breath. The air shifted, and she felt herself being tugged this way and that. The wind chimes hanging from the ceiling sang a haunting song.

Hijiri felt the presence of the table before she saw it. It was a deep feeling of *right*, as if no other piece of furniture could meet her needs like this one. The feeling was foreign to her; she never thought much about such things.

Ken met her questioning gaze with a smile. "Come on. It's this way."

They squirmed through the rest of the row, stepping over a pile of fallen children's books and toward the back wall. Ken unearthed a creamy-brown table, very small and dirty from having shouldered a basket of clown dolls and an open packet of sidewalk chalk.

"It's not big enough," she said. "I can't work on that."

Ken's eyes glimmered like a little boy's. "Don't count it out yet."

After carefully picking up the table and moving it to a spot with a little space, he showed her that this was no ordinary table: it was a gateleg table. The table surface could be made larger by lifting the leaves and using the hinged legs as support to keep them in place. "Since it's a wide table, you have a few options. Put down one leaf or both—however much you need to shrink it."

"And it won't break?"

"Not at all. This one looks well-made. Just don't lean too heavily on the edges."

Hijiri couldn't imagine putting the leaves down—she needed as much table space as possible—but at least it would make carrying the table back to the complex easier. "Okay," she said. "This could be the perfect table for me."

After she paid for the table, Hijiri and Ken each took one end of it. The table creaked as the leaves bounced. Her arms shook under the weight, but she knew that Ken had a firm grip on his end. They'd make it back to her apartment just fine.

The gateleg table went against the wall next to the card catalog, but Hijiri would probably move it out when she needed to walk around both ends of the table. She felt cocooned with the two pieces of furniture, as if she could craft her best love charms with them to support her. "I've never thought about furniture this way," she confessed after telling Ken about how pleased she was with the new furnishings. "It's like they're people."

"You're not turning into a hearth charm-maker, are you?" Ken asked, raising his eyebrows.

"I'm not that easily swayed."

Ken took a damp cloth and wiped the table. "Well,

what you're feeling is a side effect from using hearth charms. Objects are very important to the craft, so they often feel like people or animals. Vases, bedside tables, rugs—they need homes too. Or rather, they want to make your house a home."

If objects had personalities, how snarky would my golden cupid be? she thought. Hijiri snatched the cupid she had painted with Fallon off the kitchen table to show Ken. On her way back, her still-damp socks slid on the wood floors. She stumbled, about to knock into the card catalog.

Ken dropped the cloth and grabbed her around the waist.

Ken adjusted his grip, cupping the back of her head. His palm felt good there, buffering her from the hard, knobby drawers inches away from her head. Hijiri's breath came short and quiet. Her cheeks were twin flames. "Thank you," she whispered.

Ken seemed to have trouble breathing himself, and it had nothing to do with his charmed throat. He reluctantly let go of her waist. When he withdrew his hand, threads of her hair trailed through his fingers.

Hijiri couldn't feel her heart. It fell somewhere by her feet. So she hugged the golden cupid. "Now I can get back to the competition," she said. "Three months."

"Three months," he echoed breathlessly.

"Look what I made," she said, instantly feeling like a little girl.

Ken looked down at the cupid. "Nice scarf."

"I thought it was cold with only a diaper and a bow and arrow."

Ken took the cupid from her and examined it, touching the cupid's dimple and running a finger over the tiny felt heart. "Whose heart is this?"

"His heart."

"Not yours?"

"Mine is smaller."

Ken's eyes pinned her. "I don't believe it."

Hijiri shrugged. "One day I'll figure out how to measure my heart, but I'll probably need a microscope to start with."

"Another love charm?" He sounded tired.

"Hopefully."

"Don't let me keep you, then. You've got everything you need now to start charm-making again." Ken walked to the door, his hand on the knob. "I'm happy for you. I know how hard it's been this past week."

"Good night?" Why did she say it as a question?

"See you tomorrow," Ken said. He shut the door behind him.

Hijiri stared at nothing, her hands clutching the golden cupid. Its wings dug into her palms.

Chapter 12

THE BELLS OF GRIMBAUD

The De Keyser incident seemed to have inspired a change in the weather; September cooled the town. Leaves browned, cardigans came out of closets, and chocolatiers added ginger and cinnamon to warm the insides of their pralines. Hijiri spent most nights crafting love charms, just the way she preferred. She kept the windows cracked in her apartment to let in the soothing breezes.

Project Find Love's Signature took an unfortunate hiatus while the twins suffered through another grounding by their furious parents. Hijiri managed to find small ways for seeing more of Ken—his calves and knees, when she dragged him through a field that muddied his pants, and his forearms when she tugged his sleeves up for him to avoid getting lead pencil smudges. Nothing charm-worthy. This assured her that Love's signature had to be over Ken's heart.

Ken stuck close by her. He smiled more, if that were possible, especially with his eyes. Hijiri had to wonder if there was a timing mechanism that Love added to the charm-boy: as time passed, he'd grow to love her more.

Rather than less. There was always a chance of that.

"How convenient," Hijiri muttered, crossing campus to get to her next class.

She managed to get through the day without her teachers calling on her. Using yellow roses to craft a rejection love charm was an idea she toyed with in the margins of her notebooks. *Soften the blow if you're rejecting someone's love confession,* she wrote underneath one of her algebra problems. *No one deserves to be ashamed for speaking their feelings, reciprocated or not.* Then she drew two stick figures; the crying one had just gotten rejected. Hijiri drew flower petals around the figure, wondering if adding a whimsical flourish would further lighten the blow.

As she thought about how to bottle the charm—should it be in potion form, or was there a way to make it verbal only—her final class of the day ended. Hijiri shoved her textbook in her bag and followed her classmates out of the room. She walked over to the library.

The school library had been slightly renovated over the summer, the biggest change being the new card catalogs. Everything else was more or less the same. Corny inspirational posters hung on the walls, urging students to read. The carpet that Fallon despised hadn't been pulled up yet, though it was certainly time; faded patches and ancient food stains did not make the library enchanting.

There was, however, a kind of coziness about the library that went beyond the facilities. Tables were lined up against the windows, providing strong light and a view for study groups. The books were covered in plastic and still reasonably well taken care of. Ms. Ward took pride in running the place as smoothly as she could.

"Getting ready for the next challenge?" Ms. Ward said when Hijiri approached the circulation desk. "The love charm books are in the back, over there, if you came for inspiration."

Hijiri had just heard the news during lunch. The second challenge would take place on October first. Only a few days away.

"How would she prepare?" Ken said, pushing a cart of to-be-shelved books. "Bram hasn't given any hints."

"The town council is keeping an eye on him," Ms. Ward said.

Hijiri leaned on the circulation counter and cocked her head. "Have you been spending time with Bram?" She'd been meaning to ask her about the bachelor.

Thanks to Fallon, she knew that Bram used to have a massive crush on Ms. Ward in high school, but it became a source of grief when she had unknowingly rejected him. With Zita gone and the Bachelor and Spinster Villas destroyed, she thought that maybe, just maybe, Bram and Ms. Ward stood a chance at finding happiness together.

Ms. Ward shrugged and tapped a few letters on the

keyboard. Her eyes didn't leave the computer screen. "We see each other sometimes, just to check on how our friends are doing."

"He's your friend?" Hijiri pushed.

"Oh, I don't know. We were victims of circumstance before, at the villas," she said dismissively. "If Fallon hadn't drawn us into the rebellion, we may never have spoken."

Hijiri tried to hide her disappointment. Clearly, Ms. Ward hadn't grown any closer to Bram. Maybe she shouldn't have felt as disappointed as she did, but as a love charm-maker, she liked looking for happy endings. And making them.

She wandered over to the new love charms section, reading the spines. Books and magazines that printed love charms had been banned from Grimbaud while Zita was in charge. Putting the books in the library was a major step forward, but Hijiri didn't want to feel like she was cheating by reading them.

"I've been talking to Ms. Ward about the posters," Ken said, joining her. "They could use some updating."

Hijiri looked at him sidelong. "Are you thinking of adding some hearth charms here?"

"Something like that. I think this library needs more love."

"Hmm."

Ken pulled a book off the shelf and flipped through the

pages. "You seemed awfully curious about Bram and Ms. Ward. Are you going to make a love charm for them?"

Hijiri sighed and lowered her voice. "This is one situation I can't interfere with. Bram likes her, but he won't do anything about it. Worse than that, Ms. Ward doesn't seem to have feelings for him. It's a stalemate."

"You could change that."

"I could, but at least one of them has to want that." Hijiri frowned. "I'm not a matchmaker. People decide who they fall for first. Then they come to me for help."

"What do your instincts say?" Ken asked.

Hijiri took the book from his hands and put it back on the shelf. "They could be good for each other."

"No hesitation with your answer," Ken said proudly. "You must be practicing for the next challenge."

Her stomach twisted. "I want to do better this time."

"How do you feel?"

"Mostly scared," she whispered. "But a little excited."

Ken smiled. His eyes crinkled. "Now," he whispered back, "I don't know anything about anything, but my own instincts say your feelings are normal."

"I shouldn't be scared," Hijiri said, swallowing thickly. Her fear went beyond being stared at by hundreds of eyes while onstage. She didn't want to fail. She wanted to be as good as her friends believed. As good as Love believed.

Ken said nothing. He squeezed both her hands and

smiled until her own lips tried to mimic his. She probably grimaced again. That only made his smile wider.

❦➤

When the calendar flipped to October, Hijiri found herself onstage once again with her fellow love charm-makers. She stood with her hands interlaced, squeezing hard.

Bram's amiable voice reverberated through the square. "Grimbaud, I won't be keeping you in suspense any longer. You're going to see love charms today."

The audience stamped its feet and waved heart-shaped banners. Hijiri wondered if the banners had been distributed or if people had taken the time to make them. Either way, it made her feel like smiling.

"The fires of healthy competition are indeed burning here, but don't forget that we're all human beings. Humans with our own romantic pasts." Bram stepped aside and gestured at the love charm-makers. "So today's challenge is simply this: how well do you know your competition?"

Hijiri flinched and drew in a sharp breath. There was the twist.

"Our charming charm-makers will have two hours to craft a love charm for one of their opponents. Now, because we're springing this on them, they didn't come with any supplies. That's okay. They can run around Grimbaud collecting what they need for their charms, just so long as

♥ 183 ♥

they come back here to craft their charms in front of the audience. So I ask you, Grimbaudians, who will make charms for whom?"

The audience shouted their preferences, but Bram had other ideas. He made each love charm-maker pick a name from his fedora.

Hijiri closed her eyes and stuck her hand in the hat. She grabbed a slip of paper and gasped when she saw Metamorphosis on it.

Clea and Mandy must have pulled her name too, since they started whispering to each other and staring at her.

Volunteers carried four tables onto the stage. One little boy handed Bram a heavy hourglass. "Two hours," Bram said, raising the hourglass. Then, with a flourish, he turned the hourglass upside down and planted it onstage. "The challenge starts now!"

Ryker and his uncle stumbled off the stage and pushed through the crowd, probably on their way to their shop to gather supplies. Sanders whistled for his employees standing in the audience and told them to collect some materials from Love For All.

Hijiri followed suit, leaving the stage to join her friends. A handful of love charms came to mind, but she needed one that would fit Clea and Mandy. *Love charms are about individuals*, she thought, remembering the last challenge.

"What's the plan?" Mirthe said. "What do you need us to do?"

Hijiri shook her head, searching. Maybe she got off easy by getting the Metamorphosis owners since they were a couple. She didn't need to pick their brains for a proper charm. What did all couples need help with from time to time?

Communication.

The knots in her stomach eased. She had a charm for that: the honest communication love charm for Nico and Martin. For weeks she had been drafting the charm and slowly gathering the right ingredients. She hadn't made it yet . . . but it was ready to be made now. It would work.

"There's a charm I've been working on," she said, eyeing Nico and Martin, "and I think it'll be perfect. I'm going to need your help in getting the supplies for it."

She made a list using a page from Femke's notebook of what she needed from her apartment. She gave her key to Fallon. "Take Nico and Martin with you. With the catalog, you should have an easy time finding everything."

"Leave it to us," Fallon said, nodding. She gave Sebastian a quick good-bye kiss before heading on her way with Nico and Martin.

"Sebastian, I'm going to need your help securing two missing ingredients for my charm," Hijiri said. "You have your recorder?"

"Always," he said, pulling the tape recorder out of his pocket.

"Great. Make sure you have a new cassette in there."

"And Ken," she said, "you have your slingshot?"

His mouth dropped open. "I'm coming with you?"

"Why do you look so surprised?"

He ducked his head. "I don't know this town very well. I just assumed I'd be staying behind."

"That's *our* job," Femke said firmly, much to her sister's distress. She pointed out her parents in the back of the crowd. Mr. and Mrs. De Keyser wore matching stern expressions. "We're lucky our parents let us watch."

"Keep an eye on the other competitors," Hijiri said. Even with Detective Archambault scrutinizing the challenge, she felt better knowing her friends were looking out for her too.

Sebastian shoved his hands in his pockets, a lazy smirk on his face. "So where are we going, Kitamura?"

"The first thing I need," she said, "is 'silence in a clamor.' This is a huge component in crafting a love charm about communication. An arguing couple can't hear each other unless we wedge silence between the noises, to show them how listening goes again. Do you know of a place?"

Sebastian's eyebrows scrunched in thought. Just then, the belfry struck eleven in the morning, covering the town with its sober, beautiful tones. His smirk returned. "*That's* where we're going."

Her legs burned as they ran down the street, over a cobblestone bridge, and through a neighborhood that was the shortest route to the belfry. Sebastian led the way, skidding around street corners and shouting directions as they came closer.

Grimbaud's belfry towered over the town, a narrow brown brick structure that housed forty-eight carillon bells. The bells were said to have rung since the town's birth.

"We don't have time to wait in line," Ken said, eyeing the people waiting to buy their tickets to climb the belfry's 355 steps.

Hijiri realized the same problem. She hoped that the entire town knew about the competition. That would be enough to get them through.

One of the belfry workers guarding the narrow side staircase saw her and waved them over.

Hijiri, Ken, and Sebastian ran through the tower's halls and found the main staircase up. Of course, tourists were already struggling their way up the belfry.

"We're in the middle of a challenge," Sebastian yelled, cupping his hands over his mouth. "Not trying to cut on purpose. Please make way."

Tourists grumbled and pressed themselves against the old brick walls of the narrow spiral staircase as Sebastian continued his message. A few people clapped—they must have been locals—and cheered Hijiri as she passed.

"We don't have to go all the way to the top," Sebastian reminded them. They needed the bells.

The carillon room was underneath the stone parapet where most of the tourists shot their panoramic photographs. Hijiri, Ken, and Sebastian squeezed themselves into the room just in time to catch a performance. The bells hung like grave, ancient creatures. Each bell was attached to a manual keyboard, controlled by the carillonist's musical whims.

The carillonist, a weathered man with knotted knuckles and rheumy eyes, bowed before taking his seat at the keyboard. Hijiri had expected the playing to be delicate and precise, so she gasped when the man used his feet and fists to play the chords. The roughness of his playing translated into a familiar love song. Tourists mouthed the words. No one could compete with the deep vibrancy of the big bells and the fairylike chiming of the small ones.

Fallon once told Hijiri that her older brother, Robbie, and his girlfriend had snuck into the belfry to take photos with the bells. She wondered how they had done it since the bells were well-protected from harm, suspended over their heads. The corners of the room were decorated with retired bells, lovingly polished but still old and regal-looking. Some bells were behind glass. Others had been suspended by sturdy rope.

Sebastian took out his recorder. "How do you need it captured?"

Hijiri asked him to repeat his question twice before answering; the sound bordered on deafening in its beauty. "Catch some of the bells," she yelled, "and then the silence, and bells again." The silence would be worthless to her charm without the noise framing it.

They stared at the bells. One second. Then five. The man's fist hit the key destined for the largest bell. Drowning in the bell's voice, so deep she felt the vibrations to her bones, Hijiri knew that this was the moment to strike.

Sebastian hit the record button. Ken stilled next to her.

When the vibrations ended, the carillonist raised his hands to begin the next line of music. In the few precious seconds between, there was silence. No screaming children. No chatter. No cameras flashing.

Hijiri dared not move. She stared at the red light on Sebastian's tape recorder. Time slowed.

The bells sang again.

Hijiri was out of the room in seconds, murmuring apologies if she stepped on someone's feet or elbowed them too hard. They didn't have time to stay listening. Sebastian and Ken weren't far behind. By the time they reached the bottom of the belfry again, the air was deliciously sweet and Hijiri happily pocketed the cassette tape. Her ears throbbed from the vibrations of the carillon room.

Sebastian shook his head like a dog trying to dispel water. "Should have brought earplugs," he said. "Ouch."

If Ken's ears hurt, he didn't mention it. "What's the other item you need?"

"This one's going to be harder," Hijiri said. She didn't know if they could pull it off quickly. "I need a bird's nest."

Sebastian didn't question the request. He thought hard.

Ken, however, ruffled his hair and asked, "Why a nest?"

"It's symbolic of the home a couple builds together," Hijiri said. "My charm needs a foundation of comfort and trust. It's the only way the truth can come out comfortably."

"I like that," Ken said, his eyes gentle. "Building a home."

"You would."

"What does our home look like?" he asked.

"It's made of charms. Not very sturdy."

"Ah, so we *are* building one together," Ken said, his eyes crinkling. "And here I thought I was the only one working at this relationship."

Hijiri sputtered. "The only relationship we have is puzzle and solver."

"Stop flirting, you two," Sebastian said. "Let's go find some nests."

Sebastian had taken them to a private garden only minutes away from the belfry. The garden, functioning as a backyard to three large houses, was almost completely shaded by bowing oaks. A careless gardener had left the gate open so they slipped inside and searched the trees for a nest. They found one that looked empty, but they couldn't reach it without low-enough branches to climb.

"This is where you come in," Sebastian said, nodding at Ken.

Ken grabbed a pebble from the soil and notched it in his slingshot.

"Careful," Hijiri warned. "Don't want to break it."

"I'll hit the corner. You'll have to catch it before it hits the ground," he said, closing one eye and aiming.

True to his word, he knocked the corner of the nest, sending it tumbling into Hijiri's hands.

By the time they returned to Verbeke Square, the other love charm-makers were back onstage, crafting. Hijiri ran through the cheering crowd and up the stage's stairs to her table. Fallon, Nico, and Martin were waiting for her up there with her materials.

"Is everything here?" Fallon asked.

Hijiri scanned the table. She dropped the cassette tape and nest with her other ingredients and double-checked that nothing was missing. "Yes. Thank you."

"You can do this," Nico said.

Hijiri wanted to tell him that if everything worked with the charm, she'd love for him to use it too. That was, of course, stepping on the no-love-charms decision he and Martin had made together, but she could still hope.

She had crafted a few communication-based love charms in her time, but this was the first that centered on repairing a lovers' quarrel with honesty. Hijiri placed the bird's nest in the center of the table and shifted her supplies around. She felt the townspeople watching her. The sensation was like hundreds of ants crawling on her skin. She pressed her lips together and lowered her gaze to the table. *As long as I don't look up, I can do this. It's just me and my charm.*

Slowly, Verbeke Square and its distractions began to dull. She started crafting.

Chapter 13

KISSABLE

The beauty of charm-making was that the process always varied. Each charm-maker, no matter the discipline they studied, had a different way of creating charms. Hijiri discovered that her way had everything to do with symbolism.

Materials she collected for love charms had some kind of meaning to them—whether she gave them meaning or they came with the connotations already. If she combined certain items in certain ways, she made a functioning love charm. Most of the time.

Hijiri lit the orange candles that Fallon, Nico, and Martin brought back for her. The relaxing scent of zested orange wafted, evoking exactly the kind of lively date-night feeling she had wanted when she first searched for them (and subsequently broke her old table). When the wax melted, she tipped the candles over and drizzled the nest with wax. *Orange candles for approachability and loosening the tongue*, she thought. Pressing her symbols into the action.

Fallon hadn't had trouble finding the twin stainless steel forks Hijiri had bought at a thrift store ages ago; they were small and had three prongs, used for dainty desserts rather than meals. She wiped both forks on her shirt before securing them on opposite sides of the nest, prongs facing out. "This is about eating truths," she muttered, "and digesting them with courage."

The nest began to hum underneath her fingers.

After sprinkling the nest with sugar—to dull the sting of truth—she picked up Sebastian's cassette tape. She opened the cassette gingerly, gently pulling out the tape so it spilled like a ribbon on the table. She closed her eyes and felt for the short recording. The pads of her fingers thrummed with the bells' ghostly vibrations when she found it. After snipping the excess tape ribbon, she wove the tape through the nest, over and under the dried orange wax and forks. "Even if the world is watching, even if you argue again and again, you will stop and listen. The space is there, waiting within the noise," she whispered.

"Five minutes left," Bram said, checking his watch rather than the dwindling hourglass.

Hijiri checked her love charm, touching each area to make sure every piece interlaced with the others. One piece unconnected, and the charm didn't stand a chance of working. She looked over at the other love charm-makers.

Sanders had somehow made his table into a makeshift

kitchen, with a hot plate (extension cord disappearing into the crowd) and eggs carefully wrapped in cloth. An omelet filled the edges of his saucepan. Periodically, he scooped castor sugar out of a paper bag and dripped a jewel-like liquid—*rum*, she read, squinting at the bottle—onto the delicious-looking creation. But what kind of charm would that dessert carry?

Ryker and Gage tinkered with what looked like a broken vacuum cleaner. Gage stuffed its insides with magazine pages of sharply dressed men and beautiful women. Clea and Mandy surrounded themselves with a palette of powders and liquids. They kept staring at her, sizing Hijiri up, as they picked their lineup of charms. Hijiri turned away, her stomach clenching.

Bram dramatically counted down the seconds. The top of the hourglass emptied. "Time's up," he said. "Stand back from your tables."

Hijiri wiped her hands on her jeans.

"This is the exciting part," he said. "What have our love charm-makers created for each other?"

Detective Archambault stepped onto the stage and took the microphone. "One moment," she said sternly. "I must examine the love charms first."

Hijiri reminded herself to look the detective in the eye when she came to her table. She was nervous, unsure of what the detective was expecting to find.

Detective Archambault lifted the nest, sniffed it, and

closed one eye while turning it this way and that. "Clear," she said, moving on to Sanders's edible love charm.

The audience waited respectfully, though some of the younger children were restless and tugged on their parents' hands. When the detective finished her examination, Bram asked the paired love charm-makers to stand on opposite sides of the stage with their charms.

Sanders handed his sugared omelet to Ryker and Gage, while Hijiri stepped right into giving her charm to the Metamorphosis owners.

"This is a love charm that improves communication," she said, loud enough for the audience to hear. They'd find out soon enough what it would do. Sanders hadn't bothered with an explanation; he just handed out forks and knives and told the Heartwrench owners to eat.

"Cup your hands around the nest," she said, helping position Mandy's and Clea's hands so that they stood facing each other, the nest held between them. Then she stood back, waiting.

The air around Clea and Mandy smoothed, becoming silky and warm like sunrise on a cold morning. The audience's curious murmurs dulled. Hijiri knew they would have felt the change too. Clea and Mandy seemed to forget about the audience. Where they were. They stared into each other's eyes. Then the truth came.

"Clea," Mandy said, leaning closer, "I've been meaning to tell you something."

"I'm listening," Clea said easily.

A crease formed between Mandy's eyebrows. "It's just . . . I miss your face. Your real face."

"This *is* my real face," Clea said, laughing uncomfortably. "Just enhanced by our products."

"But you shimmer all the time, and your cheeks are always smooth and warm and I know it's because you're so good at applying our products. What happened to the girl I fell for years ago? Why haven't I seen her in such a long time?"

Clea dug her nails into the nest. "Where is this coming from? I thought you liked my face like this."

"I like *all* your faces," Mandy said simply. "But I think it's getting extreme now that you even wear your makeup to bed. Can't be good for your skin, anyway, no matter how well-charmed the products are."

"So what are you asking me to do?"

"Watch your temper," Mandy said with some annoyance. "I'm just speaking my mind."

Hijiri winced while listening, but she expected as much. *No one ever said that speaking the truth would be painless. Words drenched in feelings could tangle, cut, and sting. But my charm is supposed to soothe those feelings somewhat, allowing room for couples to solve their problems.*

Supposed to. Hijiri could tell that Clea was fighting the charm. She shouldn't have been able to, but maybe . . . maybe the charm had a weak point that didn't account for

Clea's personality. She had, after all, made her charm with Nico and Martin in mind. *Their problem has to do with the need for a little honesty. But Clea and Mandy's problem is much more complicated.*

Hijiri's heart sank. *I should have chosen something larger than a nest. And maybe a mirror, to reflect all of Clea's faces back at her.*

"We'll talk about this later," Clea insisted.

"Now," Mandy said.

Clea gritted her teeth and let go of the nest. Mandy still hung on, but the charm lost its hold on the couple. "Very clever," Clea said gamely. "But not a pleasant charm, is it?"

"Wasn't supposed to be," Hijiri said, standing taller. She took her love charm from Mandy and adjusted one of the forks.

Mandy rubbed her temples, squeezing her eyes shut.

Hijiri looked over her shoulder at the crowd, determined to gauge their reactions. She wished for more than the crowd's confusion and disappointment, but the love charm didn't exactly show how well it worked with Clea's stubbornness bleeding through.

Sanders's sweet rum omelet had Gage and Ryker scrambling for writing tools—chalk, pens, markers. Both uncle and nephew drew hearts wherever they could—anatomically correct hearts, since both men were scientific-minded, but nonetheless. Their hands moved of their own accord, drawing hearts in the air when they ran out of paper. After getting a few laughs, Sanders made Ryker and Gage drink lemon water to stop the love charm.

"Rein it in, rein it in," Bram said, patting Ryker and Gage on their backs. "We've got two more love charms to see!"

"Just wait until I get my hands on you," Clea said, lifting Hijiri's chin. "We're going to make you beautiful."

Hijiri tugged her chin away. Her knees trembled.

Hijiri sat on her hands to keep from squirming in her chair while Mandy and Clea buzzed around her with their powders and brushes. She lost count of the layers of product they put on her face. The first layers were probably meant to feel cool and cleansing, making her skin tingle, but Hijiri only sensed the love charms at work. *I don't feel different*, she thought, constantly assessing herself as the minutes ticked by. No sudden burgeoning of confidence. Nothing tearing at her sense of dignity.

The audience sighed and murmured like forlorn lovers.

Not good.

Clea rubbed the apples of her cheeks with liquid blush. Used three different colors to highlight the dips and shadows of Hijiri's eyelids. Not that she *could* see—her eyes were closed for most of it, and Clea had asked Bram to keep the mirror faced away. Mandy held her still to line her eyes and plump her eyelashes with mascara. Clea put three different charmed products on Hijiri's lips as the finishing touch.

"Faces are unfinished paintings," Clea said, addressing the crowd. "Metamorphosis's love charms are masterstrokes, bringing out the best in everyone who uses them. Answering their desires. Bringing the beauty of the inside to the outside and allowing love to flourish. Hijiri Kitamura is no different."

Clea and Mandy took her by the arms and lifted her out of the chair. Delighted gasps erupted all around her, but she wouldn't dare open her eyes. Her heart rattled in her chest and tried to find an escape route. She wasn't ready for this.

She heard the wheels of the mirror grow louder. Then it stopped.

"Open your eyes," Mandy and Clea said at once.

Hijiri forced herself to get it over with. When she saw her reflection, she felt sick.

The girl in the mirror was beautiful. Her skin was unnaturally even and shimmered when the light caressed it. Mandy must have glued fake eyelashes on because the thick, dark lashes made her eyes look more intense and dramatic. Her lips were the worst; Clea hadn't forgotten what she had promised to do to Hijiri's lips when they had first met.

My lips are three times bigger, she thought with growing horror. *Like a swarm of bees all stung me at the same time and left my lips looking purple and bruised. They looked like they've kissed and been kissed. These are kissable lips to the extreme.*

Her face was a lie. A giant, beautiful lie. Hijiri Kitamura was somewhere underneath it, but her face had been tampered with to attract people and make them love her for what they saw with their eyes.

She hated charms like this. Hijiri wanted to cover her face and run for the nearest sink.

The townspeople sighed with longing when they saw her face. Men and women alike reacted to the charmed makeup. The crowd pressed against the stage. Binoculars were whipped out of bags. When some men tried climbing the stage, intent on stealing a kiss or two, Detective Archambault ordered the police to step in and restrain the crowd.

Hijiri shot a pleading glance at Bram. "Just announce the winner, please," she whispered. *So that I can get this gunk off my face. So that the entire town won't hunt me down for kisses.*

"Ryker! Gage! Your love charm was no competition for Metamorphosis," he said, jogging to the other side of the stage where Heartwrench's love charm for Sanders had gone largely unnoticed. The broken vacuum had been repaired and charmed into acting like a doting mother, pinching and prodding Sanders into "first date" material.

The vacuum had pulled off his stained baking apron, steamed his wrinkled shirt collar, and taken a comb to his scraggly hair.

But when it came to makeovers, Hijiri's combination of charmed makeup had the town in a frenzy.

Bram shielded Hijiri with his body when some of the men broke through the police's grip. "I think you'd better leave the stage," he said.

Hijiri nodded and ran for the back of the stage. The platform was tall enough to hide her when she slid to the ground, covering her face and breathing through her nose.

The audience slowly began to settle down again on the other side. She heard footsteps and her name being softly called by Ken. "Found you," he said, breathless.

She gingerly took her hands away from her face. "Don't look," she said.

Ken's eyes darkened with desire; he struggled to tear his gaze away from her lips. "I can't pretend I'm immune to Metamorphosis's charms," he said thickly. "I want to kiss you so bad right now, but I know that's the last thing you want." He dug through his pockets. "What you want," he said, "are these." Damp makeup remover pads.

"Where did you get those?"

"Fallon."

Hijiri shook her head. "Always prepared."

"Hold still," he said, leaning in close. Ken cupped her

face with his left hand, then rubbed the first makeup remover pad against her lips.

Hijiri held her breath while he worked, trying not to think about the firm pressure of the remover pad and how it made her feel too warm for a chilly October morning.

"How many layers did she put on?" Ken muttered, rubbing harder. When the purple gloss stained every inch of the remover pad, he returned to her lips with a fresh one. Gradually, the smoldering behind his eyes faded. "*There's* Hijiri," he said with a sweet smile. "Hi."

Her heart wanted to say hi back, bumping against her rib cage to meet him, but she held it back. Hijiri took the remaining remover pads and wiped off the rest of the makeup until she was sure her whole face was red and shiny clean.

Just in time to hear the audience decide that Metamorphosis earned its win for the second challenge.

"Well-deserved," Bram said thinly, "if not a terrifying experience for all of us. I thought I was going to get trampled."

Hijiri curled her hands into fists and sighed.

Fallon and Sebastian chose Café Gisteren as the location of the next charm theory club meeting on Wednesday. The café was well-known in town for preserving a sense of artificial poshness with crystal-dripping chandeliers, mahogany furnishings, and portraits of turn-of-the-century Grimbaudians in hunting gear and hearts stitched over the breasts of their coats. The menu was ironically a homage to greasy, messy food.

After securing a large round table in the corner of the second floor, Sebastian bragged about how he had gotten Fallon to eat there last April by using the lure of the café's appearance. "She even shared a basket of onion rings with me," he said.

"It wasn't so hard to do when I peeked in the kitchen," Fallon said, nudging him. "The chef was gracious enough to let me look. Everything is fresh and homegrown, even if most everything on the menu is fried by the time it reaches your plate. We're all safe from food poisoning here."

Hijiri couldn't focus on her menu. The weight of her second loss in the competition sat heavily on her heart. She knew her love charm worked. Had Nico and Martin been the ones using it, the charm would have shown well. *But it wasn't them*, she thought miserably, *and my charm just wasn't strong enough for Clea and Mandy's problem. It failed to capture the town's attention.* If the competition continued to be a popularity contest, she wasn't sure if she had what it took to truly win Grimbaud over. Ken couldn't bring her another Sofie and Lars. This time, she had to deal with her failure on her own. Somehow.

"The tuna melt looks good," Ken said, pointing at the line on her menu. "I'm sure it's dripping with cheese."

Hijiri frowned.

"Cheese is good," he insisted.

After ordering food (Hijiri did end up choosing the tuna melt), Mirthe wanted to rehash the second challenge.

"Why is Sanders even in the competition?" Martin asked, crushing his silk napkin. "My sisters are still buying his candy. They ate chunks of dark chocolate that had them blurting out 'I love you' to strangers on the street. To anyone who made eye contact with them, really."

"Did they say it to you?" Nico asked.

Martin shrugged. "It was sweet until I figured out why."

"I've tried bringing it up to Detective Archambault," Fallon said, weary, "but apparently I have to work my way up to get her attention. Believe me, I've tried. She's barely in her office. I guess she prefers working her cases on the streets."

"Sanders should be one of her cases. The most important one," Martin said.

"I agree," Fallon said. "I'll keep trying."

"At least he didn't win this time," Mirthe said. "His love charm was childish."

"Hijiri's charm worked too well," Femke said with admiration. "I couldn't believe how easily they started talking about their problems. Well, Mandy did. I wasn't expecting that."

"The quiet ones sometimes have the most to say," Hijiri said.

"Says the quiet one," Mirthe teased.

Martin's knuckles turned white. "He needs to be stopped. Soon. I don't want . . . if I'm not here for my sisters . . ."

Nico's gaze sharpened. " 'Not here'? Are you talking about graduation?"

"It's nothing," Martin said, pushing Nico away. "Forget it."

"You can't ask me to do that," Nico said.

Martin took off his glasses and cleaned the lenses with his napkin. He wouldn't look at Nico.

After getting no response, Nico pressed his fist against his lips, his eyes watery.

Hijiri wanted to grab her losing love charm and shove it at Nico and Martin. Anything to make things right again.

Femke tapped her knife against her glass. "I bet there's going to be another challenge in early November just to keep the charm-makers on their toes before the thirtieth."

"We haven't won a challenge yet, but that's okay," Mirthe said. "None of the challenges matter in the end."

"How can you say that?" Femke argued. "The townspeople are judging us with each challenge. The final love charm we present in November won't matter if the townspeople have already decided who they will vote for."

"They can change their minds at any time," Mirthe said.

"Hijiri's love charm *will* be the best," Ken said softly. "Let's give her some time to work on it."

The twins hadn't heard him. They glared at each other from across the table. Once again, neither sister dressed alike. Mirthe had worn a puffy orange coat while Femke managed the cold in a sweater with a begonia pattern on the collar.

The waiter delivered the entrees, much to everyone's relief. Hijiri tucked into her tuna melt, the cheese and salty tuna drowning out the sour taste in her mouth.

When Mirthe bent to get something out of her bag, a glass bottle tumbled out and rolled under the table. The cork popped out when it hit the table leg.

The floor began to shake.

Chapter 14

NEW HEART, OLD HEART,
REAL HEART, FAKE HEART?

Hijiri had never experienced an earthquake, but she knew the signs. What other weather charm could make the world shake so bad she felt trapped in a snow globe, colors and faces swirling as the ground jumped beneath her feet?

Femke cursed and dove for the bottle.

The table fell over, spilling food everywhere. Nico covered Martin's body with his when Mirthe's hamburger flew. Lettuce wet with ketchup stuck to his hair, the back of his windbreaker greasy with hamburger meat. Sebastian and Fallon had both managed to keep the table off them when it tumbled over. The front of Ken's sweater caught a splatter of spaghetti sauce. Hijiri had ended up on the floor, her tuna melt only inches away from her ear.

Mirthe grabbed the cork just as Femke had the bottle. They fumbled between themselves, arguing over who would do the honors of stopping the tremors.

"Hurry up," Sebastian yelled, "before we get kicked out of here too!"

Femke took the cork and shoved it in the bottle. The tremors ceased. Some of the portraits on the walls had tilted and the other tables, thankfully empty, had shifted positions with some fallen chairs.

"Not so bad," Mirthe said, looking around with a grin. "It wasn't that potent."

"Tell that to the café owners." Femke grabbed her sister by her coat. "What were you thinking, carrying that charm around?"

"But it was exciting," Mirthe said. "Just think of the charms we could come up with using something this powerful."

Femke tightened her grip. Her words came dangerously quiet. "Do you mean to tell me that you've been carrying around a bottle of earthquake tremors to entice me into changing my specialty?"

"Clouds *aren't* your specialty," Mirthe said, close to crying.

"You can't change my mind," Femke said, "because we've never shared the same brain. Quit bothering me and decide what *your* specialty is. Alone." She got up, picked up her bag, and left the room without looking back.

Nico broke the silence, rolling away so that Martin could sit up. "Did anything land on you?"

Martin peeled the slimy lettuce off Nico's head. "I think you caught it all."

"Victory," Nico said.

The others laughed, if only as an outlet for the shock of what they'd witnessed.

Hijiri felt like the world was still shaking.

When they returned to the Student Housing Complex, Hijiri said good night to Fallon and Sebastian and promptly grabbed Ken's arm. The spaghetti splatter had only gotten worse after drying on his sweater. "Use my sink," she said, tugging him toward her door.

"My apartment is just upstairs," he said.

"Every second counts," Hijiri said, cringing at the desperation in her voice.

She knew her excuse was flimsy, but the meeting had rattled her in more ways than one. Her friends were breaking down. Nico and Martin still had their difficulties. The twins would not compromise either of their ideals. Her failures in the competitions haunted her, no matter how hard she pushed them away. So she saw an opportunity. *My plan is going to succeed*, she told herself. *I'm going to find Love's signature tonight. All I have to do is get his shirt off. Then we'll see if Fallon was right about his heart.*

If Ken had guessed her intentions, he didn't say a word about it. "Okay, then. I'd like to wear this sweater again. The spaghetti sauce looks like a bloodstain, doesn't it?"

"Too much," she agreed, unlocking the door.

When Ken went to the bathroom, Hijiri checked under the kitchen sink for anything stronger than soap. She didn't have as many cleaning supplies as Fallon, but she did find laundry detergent. Good enough. After pouring the detergent into a small cup, Hijiri walked over to the bathroom door and twisted the knob.

She burned with embarrassment, knowing that strolling into the bathroom without knocking was beyond rude, but she had to catch him unawares. "This should help," she said loudly after pushing the door open. When her eyes flickered to him, she found exactly what she wanted.

Ken was standing over the sink with his sweater bunched like a wet cat in his hands. All the bulky layers he wore hid a lean body underneath. His waist was narrow, pants hung low over his hips. Hijiri's heart stirred and her legs felt like jelly. She dragged her eyes up. His waist and chest lacked definition. He was arrow-thin and almost as fragile.

Ken looked up from the sink and gasped, his hands scrambling to cover his chest. Not chest. The stripe of pink she saw fleetingly over his heart.

A scar.

Love's signature.

Hijiri leapt forward, determined to catch his hands. "I saw it," she said. "Tell me what it is."

Ken's back brushed the shower curtain. He slowly lowered his hands.

Hijiri leaned forward, her breath ghosting over his skin. "Can I?" she asked.

He nodded.

She ran her thumb along the pink line of scar tissue. A neat, precise cut. Her thumb lingered and his scar began to glow.

"Sorry," he said softly. "It does that sometimes."

The glow wasn't dramatic. It was soft and rosy, spreading from his scar across his chest. Kind of like . . . "A blush?"

Ken ruffled his hair. "Yeah."

Hijiri felt her own cheeks heat. But when she looked at him, he wasn't blushing, despite his obvious bashfulness. "Is that why you look so calm all the time? Because you're actually blushing here."

"My heart blushes," he said, "whenever I'm around you."

Hijiri forgot words.

"If it helps you," he said after a minute, "I think Love decided to redirect my blushes to keep me looking incredibly confident at all times."

Her heart pounded. She had always thought exactly that. Kentaro Oshiro had been the picture of certainty around her. Always sure he loved her. Always saying the right things. He was a rock, steady against the tides of her emotions.

"I don't know what I'm doing," he whispered, smiling sadly. "I don't know if you're falling in love with me or just the puzzle of me. I don't know if you'll ever believe that I could be real. I'm just trying."

"The scar isn't working in your favor," Hijiri said, pressing her trembling hand flat over his scar. "I knew you had to have one. Love left behind a mark. Charm-makers usually call it a signature."

"Then what do you think?"

"Love made everything else first. Your eyelashes, lips, nails, ankles, toes," she said, testing her theory, "and what's inside you. Blood, veins, bones. But Love saved your heart for last. It's the most important part."

Ken's mouth lifted at the corner. "What would I be without a heart?"

"Not as convincing," she said, smiling too. "So that heart. Where did it come from?"

"From someone else who couldn't use it anymore," Ken said quietly.

Hijiri frowned. "Is that really true? Are you recycled?"

A laugh seemed to force its way up Ken's throat. "When you put it that way . . ."

Hijiri leaned closer.

". . . it sounds like having a secondhand heart is a bad thing."

"I didn't say that," Hijiri insisted. She loved old things. Her supplies were rarely new. She needed ingredients with history. An old heart could be more powerful than a new one. "Am I looking at a recycled boy, or is your heart made of something else entirely?"

Ken shrugged. "You could go with my theory about having a recycled heart."

"I find it hard to believe because you didn't have a coughing fit when you told me."

He laughed. "Well, then. Keep guessing."

Hijiri hadn't realized she still had her hand pressed against his heart until she *felt* his laughter under her palm. She let go, flexing her fingers, still warm from the heat of his blushing scar. *He said I could keep guessing,* she thought, *so I wonder if hearing his heart will give me any clues.*

The idea sounded so good that she didn't think anything of pressing her ear against his chest. Until she was there. His skin was almost feverish and his heart rapidly drummed against her ear. Hijiri reached out to steady herself, fingers sliding against his bare forearm. *Bare. Forearm. Bare. Chest. Hold on.*

"You're not . . ." she said, looking up at him. "Your heart doesn't sound weird. You feel . . . normal." *Too* normal. Normal enough to make her second-guess how easily she had laid her hands and face all over his naked chest.

"Normal, huh?" he said softly. He gently gripped her elbows to steady her. His hands were warm too, everything about him was, and she didn't understand how he would ever feel cold enough to wear sweaters every day.

If he had been a real boy, Hijiri would have been

mortified by her actions. *But he's not real*, she thought. *He's not real and yet I can't quite breathe.*

Hijiri stared at the scar, the boy, and the scar again. The back of her neck burned. Real or not, she needed to get some air. Now. "I'll ask Sebastian if he'll let me borrow a shirt for you," she said. "It's too cold for you to run upstairs in that sweater."

"Thank you," he said.

Hijiri nodded before heading for the door.

October grew colder by the day. Students started wearing scarves around their necks. Leaves drummed the sidewalks. Sometimes the sound of leaves and wind made her dream of love charms, but not in a useful way. Potions grew legs and ran up and down staircases. Paper hearts glued themselves to doors, spreading cinnamon dust on doorknobs. Hijiri started eating stews rich with pumpkin and squash. Her nose always went numb when the temperature dropped.

Her homework had kept her from the school library over the past few weeks; she had piles of essays and reading to do and concentrated better in the privacy of her apartment. However, her algebra homework gave her some trouble.

Staying after school to go over some practice problems

with Mr. De Pelsmaeker, Hijiri had simplification on the brain. She had never been good at simplifying, whether it came to math rules or her own charms.

Her feet took her to the library. Fallon had already left to go to her internship, but Ken was there, stacking the shelves with a cart full of books. Ms. Ward tried to hide the romance novel she was reading at the circulation desk, but it was obvious that she was reading rather than keeping watch over the study groups.

Hijiri paused. Something was different about the library. She looked around. Same musty book-smell. Same plastic sleeves. The inspirational posters were gone. In their place, large vertical photos with abstract, school-supply-themed patterns added warmth to the room. One photo was a magnified close-up of a yellowing page, the words artfully blurred. Another was a pile of freshly sharpened pencils.

Ms. Ward put down her paperback and said hello. "What do you think of the replacement posters?"

"I love them." The library felt a little more modern.

Ms. Ward beamed. "Ken suggested the change. We ordered them from a hearth charms shop in Lejeune. Our humble budget allowed it. They're supposed to smell like what was photographed if you stand close enough. I'm guilty of lingering too long near the pencils one."

Now Hijiri was curious to stand near each photo and have a sniff. "The library feels more welcoming already."

"I completely agree. Students are spending more time here. With a few more improvements, it could really be something. I want this library to look as beautiful to Grimbaud High's students as it always has to me."

"I think we can handle that," Ken said, rolling the cart up to the desk. "What brings you here, Hijiri?"

She couldn't say for sure. Her eyes drifted to his chest. Since seeing his scar, she couldn't stop wondering if it was blushing when they spent time together. If *he* was blushing. So distracting. "Just got some help with my algebra. I didn't feel like going back to the complex yet."

"I was talking with Yasmine and Helena about our high school days," Ms. Ward said, resting her chin in her hands. "The carpets were nicer then."

Hijiri hadn't been sure what happened to the old residents of the Spinster and Bachelor Villas beyond Ms. Ward and Bram. A few of them left town, while others relocated in the neighborhoods making up the outskirts of town. No more labels. As far as she knew, they were back to taking their own romantic fates in their own hands. "But you still talk about Love?"

"Sometimes," Ms. Ward said, laughing. "Actually, we were sharing our latest missed connections over dessert last weekend."

"Missed connections?" Ken frowned. "What is that?"

Ms. Ward had a dreamy, sad look in her eyes. "It's when you feel the spark of attraction with a stranger—someone you've just met or spotted in the crowd. You want to get to know him. It feels like the beginning of something. Like a thousand possibilities crammed into seconds. But for whatever reason, you never connect. Maybe you're too shy to talk to this person, or the timing is all wrong. And if you shared a moment, you didn't exchange contact information."

"So you never see them again?" Ken asked softly.

"That's usually how it goes." Ms. Ward toyed with a dog-eared page in her paperback. "And you keep wondering, what if? What if I had stayed to talk to him? What if I hadn't forgotten my pen to write down his number? I've had so many missed connections myself. They still haunt me. I wish I could have pursued those relationships. Had the chance to see what would happen."

Ken nodded, his expression grave. "I understand."

Hijiri didn't see how.

"Have you ever had a missed connection?" he asked her.

Up until last year, boys didn't even notice her. Her heart never once skipped a beat when spying a cute guy from across a crowded room. Probably because she stayed away from crowded rooms on principle. "Never," she said.

Ken had moved to pick up a few books from the cart. When she answered, his hands twitched. The books scattered like startled pigeons from his grip.

Hijiri bent to pick up some of the books.

He smiled weakly. "Sorry. It's just that . . . it's sad."

"It's not an experience I need," she said. "Don't be upset on my part. We have something in common. You haven't had a missed connection either."

Ken smoothed the pages of a bent turnip cookbook. He didn't say anything.

"Don't worry," she said, babbling. "A missed connection can happen any second."

Ken stood up and placed the book with its fallen brethren on the circulation desk. "I've been too busy looking at you. How could I notice another girl like that?"

Stop saying those things, she thought, pressing a hand over her loud heart. *Charm-boy. Puzzle-boy, Fake-boy.* The nicknames did nothing to soften the sound of her heartbeat.

Ms. Ward watched the exchange with growing interest. She hadn't even bothered to help pick up her poor books. "Wouldn't it be nice," she said, "if there was a way to surmount that problem?"

"That's why love charm-making is so intriguing to me," Hijiri said. "Most of the time, romance doesn't work out. It's just a fact of life. But I want to fight for other people's happy endings. I want to help them get there, instead of . . ."

"Missing them?" A smile ghosted Ken's lips.

Hijiri nodded.

"I wish there was something we could do," he said. "Second chances don't come easily."

Her heart thumped harder, a wild beat that flooded her ears. She didn't have time to think about his words because they triggered something.

An idea.

A love charm idea.

"What if I could?" Hijiri whispered.

Ken looked at her sharply.

Hijiri stared at him in wonder. Did he realize how important this moment was? *Did he?* Her mouth wouldn't echo the exhilaration in her veins.

"What's going on in there?" he said, gently tapping her temple with his finger.

She grabbed his wrist and held on tight. "A charm. *The* charm."

➷─▷

"Watch me, Love," Hijiri said, rolling up her sleeves. She opened her gateleg table all the way and began sketching her idea on a piece of drafting paper that Ken had given her. The paper was thin, almost like a cloud pressed into solid form, and Hijiri thought of the twins as she scribbled over every inch of the paper. The duality of the charm would be difficult to marry, but once she did it . . .

She worked long into the night, drawing charts and

sifting through her collection of glass bottles to find the shape she liked best. When her stomach whined, she stood at the kitchen counter and ate trail mix with salty cashews and raisins. Around midnight, her hair got in the way, so she pulled it into a loose bun that started coming apart seconds after she made it.

At three in the morning, she heard a knock on her door. Hijiri rubbed her eyes with her knuckles and answered the door.

Standing unabashedly in his pajamas, Ken gave a drowsy hello. "Figured you were awake."

Hijiri opened the door wider. "Could you hear me all the way from your room?"

"I didn't need to. The look on your face when we left the library was enough," Ken said. "Show me what you've done."

Fatigue melted off her bones when his eyes met hers. *He's serious. He really wants to know*, she thought. Her heart hummed. Her toes curled.

"The love charm is going to be a communication device made of memories and wishes. It's beautifully complicated, and if I can pull it off, I can give people more than just hope. They might find their almost-loves again."

"Almost-loves." He squeezed her hand, his voice breathless. "I know you can do it."

Her faith in herself had been crumbly at best these past few weeks. This was the first night in weeks she felt grounded, full of purpose. "When Zita controlled the town, she had that loom that everyone's hearts were attached to. And it makes me believe that our hearts can be tangled and tied to each other, no matter how far apart we are. If I can tap into those threads, I can access a line of communication between hearts. My charm will connect missed connections."

The simpler she could make the love charm, the better. She showed Ken the green glass bottles she had collected over the years and how they would be the items she'd craft the charm around. "Like throwing a message in a bottle into the sea," she explained.

Ken picked a bottle and closed one eye to look inside it. "Where's the letter going to go?"

"I'm thinking of including a standard message saying 'Hello Again' and instructions on how to respond. When they uncork the bottle, what's going to hit them first is the heart's memory."

"So the person who receives the bottle will be able to see the missed connection?"

"Just like experiencing a daydream from the sender's point of view. With the sender's feelings."

Ken smiled softly. "Sounds brilliant. Where do you start?"

Hijiri turned back to the table to hide another blush. Why was her skin reacting like that? It wasn't like Ken had never complimented her before. In fact, he did it too much.

"I need to dissect some long-distance-relationship love charms to get the mechanics of my own charm right. I believe they usually work by using an invisible bond. If I tweak that, I can probably reach the heart's thread."

"How will you test it?"

"I need a volunteer," she said. "Do you think Ms. Ward would be agreeable? She has more missed connections than anyone I know."

"Sure," Ken said.

"I hope she wants to know what happened to her almost-loves."

Ken's smile fell away. He lowered his lashes, reaching for her hand. He rubbed his thumb against the inside of her wrist. "Anyone would."

Hijiri watched his thumb, barely breathing. Fallon had told her to listen to her heart and her heart had been talking a lot lately. In thumps and rattles and electric shocks that set her cheeks aflame. It was saying one thing: *I think I could love this boy if he was real.*

If he was real.

That was a problem her tiny heart hated.

Chapter 15

THEY SAY LOVESICKNESS IS INCURABLE

Hijiri needed to talk with Love. She didn't sleep at all, crafting her prized charm, and left the complex at dawn that Sunday. There was only one place she could think of going.

Many of Grimbaud's parks were small, nook-like escapes, but the largest park held the famous statue *Love Being Cherished*. After Zita had tried to remove it last year, the statue grew in popularity, rivaling even the Tunnel of Love. The rest of the park had been refurbished after the return of the statue. Cobblestone paths led to weeping willows and rose-covered arbor hideaways, while heart-shaped bushes and trees looked on. Coins glittered in the fountain.

Hijiri approached the statue, craning her neck to admire the details. Made of marble, the statue featured three figures. In the center was Love, a naked, curvy woman with a waterfall of hair. The teenagers on either side of Love had different stories to tell. The girl kissed Love's cheek, unafraid of loving, wanting whatever blessings she could hold in her outstretched hands. The boy on the left was meek and sorrowful, carrying a poetry book and roses speckled with his marble tears.

The girl's bravery was admirable, but not as interesting as the boy. "You're more inspiring," she told the marble boy, reaching to touch the roses. "There's something in you to fix. The girl's okay already."

She wished the statue would give her more ideas.

Love's marble eyes stared back at her.

"Where are you?" she whispered.

Where was Love now? Snoring in the last train car? Hitchhiking the highways of the world? Taking inventory, wherever it was. She wondered how Love measured its success. The amount of couples, perhaps, or maybe broken hearts.

"Will you count me as a success?" Hijiri asked. No one was around, so she raised her voice at the statue. "You haven't won yet. Ken is still a puzzle I'm going to solve. Thank you for the challenge, but I don't intend to lose my heart in the process." *Not completely.*

Leaves rattled like laughter against the cobblestones. Hijiri flushed with shame. She knew she was lying, but to say it out loud? She rubbed her arms to dispel the chill.

Hijiri had gotten comfortable with thinking her heart

had no room for more love. Of course her heart was too small; that explained why she never had nor wanted a second date and why she was always so bored with the boys who were interested in her—until Ken came along. The box she always shoved her heart into wasn't holding it anymore.

So she tried pleading one more time.

"Make him give me my heart back," she said brokenly.

A sense of unease rippled through her. Goose pimples covered her skin. Her insides felt colder than the wind tossing her hair. Hijiri looked around her, expecting to see a sign: maybe a stone cupid pointing its arrow at her, or a stork strutting through the grass.

Instead, something slapped the back of her head. Hijiri flinched and grabbed at whatever it was, feeling the crunch of paper between her fingers. A flyer. It had only one sentence, printed in typewriter font:

STOFFEL'S HUGS HEAL HEARTS

The flyer made her skin crawl. Hijiri shoved it in her coat pocket rather than tossing it back on the ground for someone else to find. She rubbed her hands on her jeans. The park was as empty as it was seconds ago, but she still felt *something* there. Watching her.

Hijiri heard her own shallow breathing as she backed

away from the statue. The wind picked up, blowing her hair to the side and stinging her exposed neck with cold.

Something creaked behind her.

When she turned, she saw four trees covering a path with shadows. Three of the trees were heart-shaped, but the other . . .

It was *not* a tree.

Hijiri squinted into the shadows. What she saw made her tremble.

Tall as the laurel trees it stood with, the thing had a wide chest and a heart for a head. From the waist down, its endoskeleton was exposed.

"A robot?" she whispered. A very poor one.

Whoever designed the robot had attempted to go for a child-friendly look. The robot's head was a big heart with rosy cheeks, tiny, electric-red eyes, and a red mouth opened in delight. The hands were covered with white gloves, its chest in squishy-soft material. The endoskeleton was a nightmare; tears and rips along the surface of the robot's upper body gave her a clue that it was capable of moving.

"Stoffel," she said, inching backward. Was *that* its name?

Stoffel walked toward her with a fluidity that didn't make sense coming from a broken-looking robot. Hijiri felt a familiar tingle on her skin. A complicated charm had to be behind the robot's ability to move. *Move?* she thought, panic rising. *It probably does more than that.*

She finally found her legs and started running.

Stoffel chased after her. It creaked and sparked, metal feet crushing the grass.

Hijiri pumped her legs faster and crossed the cobblestones, leaping over a row of shrubs to lose the robot in the heavily gardened corners of the park. Rough leaves scraped her jeans. She didn't care if she was trampling flowers or bending the love-themed topiaries.

Behind her, Stoffel snapped the topiaries into pieces to reach her.

Think. Can I use anything on me? Hijiri thought, mentally searching through her pockets. She had the flyer, a compact mirror . . . did she have glitter? Hijiri slowed down long enough to feel around in her coat pockets, mistaking a tin of lip balm for her silver glitter. Just for a second.

"Yes," she hissed, palming the compact mirror and opening the lid of the glitter with her thumb. Carrying the ingredients for her Blinded by Love charm with her had become almost compulsory. She never thought about it.

Hijiri sprinted to the fountain, her lungs screaming for air. At the last minute, she spun to the right, spraying the surface of her mirror with glitter, and blew. The love charm worked as it always had, blinding anything in its path with light.

Stoffel tried to grab her, but its arms came just short of her. Those little red eyes were unaffected by the glare of the charm. Its mouth widened, spilling hundreds of flyers: *STOFFEL'S HUGS HEAL HEARTS. STOFFEL'S HUGS HEAL HEARTS. STOFFEL'S HUGS HEAL HEARTS.*

Hijiri raised her arm to shield herself from the on-slaught of flyers. Stoffel's hand clamped down on her forearm; she gasped and tried to pry her arm away, but its grip was too strong. "Let go," she cried. Her mind franti-cally scrambled for names to call.

"Ken," she screamed, kicking at its knee, exposed wir-ing and all. A knee that was attached to a leg that should not, under logical circumstances, have been able to move on its own.

Stoffel's other hand gripped her waist; it pulled her off her feet and muffled her scream when her cheek con-nected with the robot's chest. Stoffel's arms wrapped around her in a hug.

The hug only lasted a few seconds, but the charm attached to the robot flowed into her. Every nerve end-ing felt on fire. Hijiri's tiny heart started to ache—small pangs of hurt, growing bigger and bigger until she started crying. When Stoffel set her back down, she couldn't stand.

Hijiri tumbled to her knees, then slid against the lip of the fountain until her hair tangled with the leaves.

Stoffel loomed over her, staring.

"Heartache," Hijiri whispered, struggling to keep her

eyes open. Waves of foreign emotion washed over her. It seemed to come from nowhere.

Or, more specifically, the robot. Stoffel cocked its head.

"What have you done to me?" Hijiri asked.

Stoffel spit another flyer at her and stepped back. She heard it walking away; a few more branches snapped, and then the sounds were gone.

Hijiri lay where she was, tears streaking down her cheeks as the effects of the charm made her sick. Love-sickness. She was lovesick. The blue sky above her dimmed until she lost consciousness.

$$\mathrel{\vartheta\!\!\!-\!\!\!\triangleright}$$

When Hijiri surfaced again, waves of longing and sorrow followed her. She wanted to curl into a ball. The sensation was close to feeling nauseated, but it was coming from her heart rather than her stomach.

She knew the feelings weren't her own.

Hijiri heard the faint murmur of voices, beeping, and shoes shuffling on tile. Slowly, Hijiri opened her eyes, taking in the pale purple walls and the thick blanket covering her from neck to feet. She shared a room with another woman whose bed was screened off. The woman cried, moaning and thrashing.

I'm in the hospital, Hijiri thought thickly. Heaviness made her want to shut her eyes again.

The door opened and a doctor came in, followed by two nurses. "Miss Kitamura, good to see you awake," said the doctor, introducing himself as Dr. Vermeulen. He was a short man with a receding hairline and three red pens in his front pocket.

Hijiri blinked and squinted. Her vision was strange too. She saw everything slightly pink, as if the twins had slipped rose-colored glasses on her while she was sleeping.

"You're the fourth one today," Dr. Vermeulen said. "Same symptoms. Heart palpitations, stress, depression, stomach pains, excessive longing, the urge to write bad poetry, and shortness of breath. In short, lovesickness. I've never seen cases this extreme in Grimbaud."

One of the nurses muttered something about lovesickness not being real. The other nurse elbowed her in the ribs.

"Don't tell me there's an incredibly handsome stranger running around making men and women swoon until they're lying in the hospital," the doctor said.

"Not a stranger," said a rough, familiar voice. Detective Archambault leaned against the doorway, radiating an intensity Hijiri could feel even through her sickness. "A runaway love charm."

"Love charm?" Dr. Vermeulen echoed.

Detective Archambault's expression hardened. She crossed the room to Hijiri's bedside and asked her to tell her what she saw. "I know you're in pain right now, but I need all the information I can get to catch this love charm and the person who made it."

Hijiri swallowed thickly and nodded. Her arms felt like noodles, but she managed to sit up. Her eyes swam with tears, and longing made her achy. Still, she spoke as clearly as she could about Stoffel. The flyers. The endoskeleton. Its impossible motion. The hug that infected her with this sickness.

The detective held her hand, her touch surprisingly gentle. When Hijiri finished, Archambault said, "Thank you. The other three victims had fainted early on. They couldn't tell me anything about how they got sick."

"I tried to run away," Hijiri whispered.

"Good girl," the detective said. "And so you should have. I would have done the same."

"The culprit is obvious, isn't it?" said another familiar, welcome voice. Fallon marched into the room, her chin lifted and her eyes trained on the detective.

Hijiri raised her head and smiled through the heartache. Behind Fallon, a few of her friends gathered in the doorway. Ken was in front, looking pale and worried. He squeezed his hands into fists over and over.

"Think about the suspects we have. Hijiri said a charmed robot attacked her. A *robot*. Which of the love charm-makers works with technology?" Fallon said.

Detective Archambault's mouth twitched. "Yes, I've noticed the connection too."

"I'm sorry. It's just that my friend's hurt and I can't sit here while the town is in danger." Fallon gestured to the ex-rebels. "*We* can't just sit here."

"I appreciate your concern and quick thinking," the detective said, not unkindly, "but you are high school students. This is not your responsibility. Care for Miss Kitamura and focus on your studies. I will apprehend whoever is behind this."

Fallon's cheeks flushed, but she didn't argue.

The twins exchanged a look. No way were they going to wait this one out. Hijiri sensed a plan brewing between them. Which, considering the fight they had at the café, was a miracle in and of itself.

The nurses insisted on ushering everyone out of the room—too many people, not good for the patients' health—but Detective Archambault silenced them with a deep frown. "Let them stay," she said, "just this once."

"Ten minutes," Dr. Vermeulen said, compromising. "Miss Kitamura needs her rest. We must run some tests to figure out how to treat her. So far, the cure eludes us."

Hijiri took a few shallow breaths. She had school. Her missed-connections charm needed to be crafted. Her heart stirred with anxiety, making her double over in pain.

"Easy now," Dr. Vermeulen said. "You'll be excused from school. I've already notified your parents."

"My parents?"

"Well, I left messages through their emergency contact numbers," he said with irritation. "They can't be reached."

Hijiri shook her head. Typical.

The more cheerful of the two nurses moved to fluff her pillows. "Don't you worry. As soon as we cure you, you can go home."

A cure? How? This is not a medical illness. It's a charm. Hijiri wanted to say something, but her throat felt dry and her tongue too thick. She sank back into the pillows as the doctor and nurses left the room.

Within seconds, Ken was by her side, covering her hand with his. "I'm so sorry," he said. "I didn't make it in time." He had been the first person to find her collapsed near the fountain. After carrying her to the nearest shop, he had the manager call an ambulance.

"How did you know where to find her?" Sebastian asked.

"Love," he said.

"Love's too busy," Hijiri muttered.

"Who else could have made the stone cupids point their arrows in the direction of the park?" Ken said, his eyes shining. "They changed their poses right before my eyes. If that's not Love, I don't know what is."

And you couldn't help me? Hijiri thought bitterly to Love. Now she was stuck in a hospital bed for who knows how long. Only another charm could overpower this one.

Fallon's gaze slid from Ken to Hijiri. After hesitating

for a moment, she said, "What about the True Love's Kiss charm?"

Hijiri's eyes flew open.

The twins gasped. Mirthe rubbed her hands together. Femke raised her eyebrows.

Nico, who'd been quiet up until then, almost whooped at the idea. "It should work, right? We can get Hijiri out of here by tonight!"

"It's not that easy," Hijiri said. Three tears slipped down her cheeks. Some uninfected part of her heart warmed to the idea, but hanging on to the feeling was too hard. As she stared up at Ken, the charm amplified the ache in her chest. Part of her wanted his kiss. She just didn't know what part. Not that it mattered. "That charm hasn't worked since Love helped me. It's useless."

"Even if it *did* work . . . she's not a boy," Sebastian said bluntly.

Hijiri wished she could have laughed. He had a point. As a girl, her heart was in a precarious location for kissing. No, they needed another option. A charm that would get her out of here. "Okay," she said. "I think I have a love charm for this."

The charm was an old one that she had crafted in middle school, back when her anxiety made her jittery and sick. She had bought a ton of ingredients and spent weeks working on the right combinations to craft tea that could calm her heart and ease her nerves. She called it Heart's

Ease. It was one of the only charms her parents had taken notice of, though Hijiri wished she hadn't been so adamant to share it with them. Mr. and Mrs. Kitamura had signed her up for multiple summer programs to help her "socialize more," and Hijiri ended up sharing her charmed tea with rowdy campers and hospital patients alike. Her memories of those summers were tainted with painful awkwardness—a big reason why she didn't think often of the useful tea she kept in a tin in her kitchen.

Heart's Ease was more than useful in this case. The tea was infused with a special brand of love she had squeezed from watching touching family movies and researching comfort desserts. Anything to make the heart feel snuggled and warm. Secure.

When she told her friends about the tea, Ken's grip on her hand tightened. Hijiri stared at him under her lashes, curious about his tight-lipped smile, like he was suppressing a full one. The lovesickness tugged her concentration away.

"Tell us where you keep the charm," Fallon said. "Sebastian and I will go get it."

"The kitchen cabinet above the stove," she said. A filigree spice box held the charmed loose tea.

Hijiri leaned back into the pillows after her friends left. Ken stayed behind, pulling a chair next to her bed. He held her hand so long that she forgot where hers ended and his began.

Chapter 16
SABOTAGE

S toffel's charm affected her dreams too. She paddled her way through a pink sea, unable to find up or down. The sea tasted bitter like biting into dark chocolate when you expected milk. Hijiri pressed her mouth closed and kicked toward the surface—*Was that the surface?*—but the water pushed her down.

Her heart had somehow escaped her chest; even in her dreams, it was smaller than a fist. It carried a rope for Hijiri to grab on to. As it passed, she reached for the rope with both hands but her fingers missed.

Her heart left her behind.

Hijiri woke three times to the sound of the woman in the bed next to her sobbing. Hijiri reined in her symptoms as much as she could, but she cried too. Silent tears. Sniffles. A longing so deep it drowned her even in her dreams. Ken was there each time she woke up. "You don't have to stay," she murmured.

Ken frowned and wiped away the tear tracks on

Hijiri's face. "Is the lovesickness worse with me here?" he asked.

Hijiri shook her head. "The terrible part," she said, "is that the aches and pains are abstract. No one's causing me this heartache. It's got a life of its own, all the symptoms without a beloved to feel sick over."

"Is there anything I can do?"

"I want a notebook," she groaned, "so I can write bad love poetry."

Ken chuckled softly. "They should be back with the tea soon. Rest."

"Some people don't like hospitals," she said, pressing her cheek to the pillow.

"I'm not one of them," he said, threading his fingers through her hair.

Hijiri leaned into his touch; it was a welcome distraction and she didn't want him to stop. The sickness wasn't real. It was just a charm.

When she woke again, she overheard Dr. Vermeulen saying that another victim had been found in Verbeke Square: a lace shop employee taking out the trash at the back door.

"Grimbaud can't fall into panic," came the detective's voice. "I need to make an arrest soon."

"And we need to stop the sickness," the doctor said.

"The *charm*," the detective corrected. "Take care of the victims. With any luck, we'll have this case solved soon." The detective's footsteps echoed down the hallway.

Hijiri felt someone gently shaking her shoulder.

"We're here," Fallon said. She held the filigree spice box with reverence. Sebastian was by her side.

"What day is it?" Hijiri asked, struggling to sit up in bed. Ken handed her a cup of water. She drank it slowly, careful not to cry into the cup. She hated the crying.

"It's still Sunday," Sebastian said. "A little after seven."

Hijiri opened the spice box. The loose leaf tea smelled delicious—strongly of hibiscus, with vanilla and caramel undertones. One of the nurses came in with a mug of hot water. Fallon provided an infuser shaped like a lounging cupid, its silicone arms resting on the lip of the mug. The water turned a rich, ruby-red color. Everyone gathered around the bed while Hijiri blew on the hot tea.

The first sip burned the back of her throat as it went down. Fire spread through her veins, clashing with the lovesickness charm residing there. Hijiri kept drinking. Normally, the tea brought warmth to loosen muscles and relax the body, but it was fighting another charm and re-acting strongly. One charm had to overpower the other and she hoped that her charm would win.

Her heart trembled between the two charms for what felt like ages. Then, slowly, the Heart's Ease tea gained the upper hand. But *only* the upper hand. Stoffel's charm stayed put. Her vision cleared with only the slight flickering of a pink tint and her tears dried, though she still felt on the cusp of crying. *The longing is manageable,* she thought. *I just have to keep drinking the tea.*

Dr. Vermeulen burst through the door, his stethoscope hanging from his neck. His eyes widened when he saw Hijiri push back the covers and slip out of bed. "What's going on here?"

"I'm fine," Hijiri said. Her body still felt weak, as if she hadn't slept in weeks.

"If this is a trick . . ." Dr. Vermeulen said, wagging his finger. Then he sighed and used his stethoscope to listen to her heart. "No more palpitations," he said with wonder. "No more tears. No heartache? How could this be when the other victims are only getting worse?"

Hijiri pursed her lips. She could play dumb—it would get her out of the hospital quicker. The other victims were safe enough in the hospital, even if they wouldn't heal without the aid of charms. But that wouldn't be right. Hijiri took the spice box from Fallon and pinned the doctor with a solemn look. "Thanks to this love charm I made. It's only a temporary solution, but it will take away the worst of the symptoms if they keep drinking it."

She spent the next hour explaining to the doctor and a few nurses how to use the charm, reluctantly having to part with half of her loose leaf tea. She promised she'd make more when she returned to her apartment. She had to. Heart's Ease was not meant to be a powerful charm, but the town needed it nonetheless.

Fallon turned to the detective. "What if Stoffel is drawn to people who are already suffering from love problems?"

"How do you figure?" one of the nurses asked.

Fallon shrugged. "The flyers. 'Stoffel's Hugs Heal Hearts.' It wouldn't be chasing people with happy love lives if those words are true."

Hijiri flashed Fallon a tired grin. That made sense. Her own heart had been troubled when Stoffel appeared.

Ken took the empty mug of tea. He breathed in the lingering scent, his gaze soft.

"What is it?" she asked, remembering his reaction to her love charm earlier.

He looked up sharply. The beginnings of a cough bubbled up in his throat. "I love tea," he whispered.

Hijiri raised her eyebrows. "More than waffles?" His proclaimed favorite food.

"More than I can say," he said, his smile fragile and fleeting.

Monday brought news of more victims. Hijiri tried not to burst into tears or cover her notes with poetry during her classes. She carried a heavy thermos of Heart's Ease tea with her. Whenever her vision started to darken to pink, she knew it was time for another cup. Grimbaud High couldn't get enough of talking about the charmed robot.

Detective Archambault must have felt that releasing information on Stoffel would help keep Grimbaudians safe, so the local paper had printed a front-page article.

The entire town knew about the robot now. They also knew that Hijiri's love charm was making a difference in healing the victims.

Hijiri was surprised to see her name in the article, already wishing she could hide in the shadows of the tunnel until the news blew over. Students who had never spoken to her before came up to her to talk about the tea.

"This is really good for you," Nico said as he played bodyguard between her second- and third-period classes.

"Yeah, being bombarded by strangers," Hijiri said, dabbing her wet eyes with a tissue. "If I knew that Dr. Vermeulen couldn't be discreet, I never would have given him my charm to use."

Nico snorted. "Uh-huh."

A headache bloomed that had nothing to do with the pop quiz she had taken. "Look, I didn't expect the news to get out so quickly. I was only just in the hospital myself yesterday. This is happening too fast."

"You should have stayed home and gotten some sleep," Nico said with some concern.

"I'll sleep when the competition is over."

Nico rolled his eyes.

She drifted through the rest of her classes and made it to lunch. Crumpled newspapers doubled as tumbleweeds by then; all the paper reminded her of the flurry of flyers Stoffel had spit at her. Hijiri shivered and pushed the thought away. She sat down at the lunch table with vegetable soup and her tea.

"Doing okay?" Fallon asked Hijiri.

"Surviving." Hijiri dipped her spoon in the soup. Anais and Bear looked as happy as ever, sharing their lunches and talking about the shared elective class they had together. Still, she couldn't stop the warning that fell from her lips. "Be careful walking home," Hijiri said, looking at both Anais and Bear. If their hearts were even remotely troubled, they could be targets for Stoffel.

"I heard the news." Anais said with a huff, "If any robot tries to get me, I'll snap its arms in half."

"You're not quite there yet," Bear said fondly.

"That robot is just a bully," Anais insisted. "It makes me so mad to think that it's hurting so many people."

Hijiri drank deeply from her tea and looked around at the students occupying tables and the lines for food. Any of them could be attacked by Stoffel. Just thinking about it gave her the chills.

"Who are you looking for?" Anais asked.

"Not Ken," Fallon said, concerned. "You know he's not in our lunch period."

Hijiri blushed and gripped the table as a wave of dizziness washed over her. "I may be lovesick, but not *that* way. My memory's fine."

Anais perked up. "So where's this new boy I've been hearing so much about? I'm beginning to think he's imaginary."

Imaginary. Hijiri flinched. *He just might be. A bundle of charms in human form.*

"He was at the first two challenges," Fallon said.

"Well, Bear and I weren't introduced," Anais said, pouting.

Hijiri squirmed and waited for Fallon to smooth over Anais's hurt. They weren't her friends, even though they seemed nice enough. She felt the smallness of her heart in moments like these. A tightness that made her reluctant to share. She took another gulp of tea and tucked her hands under her legs to keep herself from writing bad poetry on her napkins. The school day couldn't end fast enough.

❧—▷

Tuesday followed in much the same way: Hijiri ripped up pages of her terrible poetry and drank so much tea her stomach felt bloated. She spent the night working on her missed-connections love charm for the competition, but it was hard to focus when her heart pounded and longing slowed her movements. Her parents still hadn't called. She wondered when they'd schedule in a time to see if their daughter was still breathing.

Ken was a quiet presence beside her on their morning

walks to school. He'd seemed lost in his own thoughts since Sunday.

He came by her locker after school. "Do you mind the company?"

She shook her head. "With Stoffel around, company is a good idea."

"Is your heart in peril again?" he asked with a twist to his smile.

"I don't know. Is yours?"

Ken hesitated. "Perhaps we're not safe with each other."

"Let's go," she said, grabbing his sweater sleeve.

Walks provided her with brainstorming time. Usually. They had only walked a few blocks when Hijiri heard someone angrily call her name. Hijiri turned around to see Clea striding toward them—or a woman who looked kind of *like* Clea. Her pixie cut was in disarray, all the shine and glitter from her charmed eye shadow smeared like a paint stain across her face. One of the crystal butterflies always pinned to her smock had lost a wing.

"I know what you're up to," Clea said, stabbing the air with her finger. "Very clever of you to take advantage of this runaway charm to steal votes."

Hijiri gasped. *Is that why Clea chased me down?*

"Who's to say *you* didn't craft Stoffel?" Clea said.

Hijiri didn't acknowledge the accusation. Something had upset Clea badly. "Where's Mandy?"

Clea's bottom lip trembled. "She's in the hospital. Stoffel got her. *Right in front of me.*"

"I'm sorry," Hijiri said. No wonder the poor woman was upset. "Then you should be there with her. My Heart's Ease tea will lessen the lovesickness symptoms, but not for long."

"This is all because of you," Clea said. "Ever since you made Mandy and me use that charm in the second challenge, she's been ridiculously upset with me about my makeup habits. *It made her a target for Stoffel.* None of this would have happened if you hadn't meddled in our relationship."

Ken's jaw tightened. "Hijiri's charms would never create problems that aren't there."

Hijiri swallowed down a wave of longing and sorrow from the lovesickness. Her head throbbed from the effort. "Thank you," she whispered.

Ken smiled at her.

Clea wiped her eyes, spreading more glittery makeup. "I'm going to win the competition, I swear."

"Best of luck to you," Hijiri said with a fake smile plastered on her lips.

Clea growled and turned on her heel. They watched her walk away.

"Stoffel's turning this town upside down," Ken said, sighing.

Hijiri couldn't agree more. She took a sip of her tea

and tried to push Clea's angry face out of her mind. They fell into step again, heading toward the Student Housing Complex, when she noticed the townspeople gossiping in small groups on the street. When she and Ken waited to cross the street, what they were saying became clear.

"Archambault's making her move," said a man with a briefcase.

"Oh really? Where is she headed?" said a woman wearing a headscarf against the wind. "I bet money on Love For All's owner."

The man with the briefcase chuckled. "Then I'm sorry for you. The detective is at Heartwrench."

Hijiri exchanged a quick look with Ken. No words were needed. They both broke into a run and raced to Heartwrench. Her thermos thumped painfully against her thigh through her bag. Running was good. She could pretend that her eyes were watery because of the sharp wind rather than Stoffel's charm.

A small crowd of people gathered outside of Heartwrench, blocking the car repair shop next door. Two police cars were parked out front, lights spinning. Hijiri stood on her toes and found a pocket of space between two men's shoulders to see the front door open.

Detective Archambault's satisfied expression met flashes from cameras—the newspaper reporters had gotten there too. She wore a sleek black coat with a matching black fedora; she had probably anticipated being photographed after securing this arrest. After all, word always spread fast in Grimbaud.

Behind her, Gage appeared in handcuffs. The man had terrible bags under his eyes and looked as if he hadn't taken a shower in a few days. Ryker trailed his uncle, hands covered in grease, his eyes worriedly flickering between Gage and the police officers flanking him.

A reporter rushed forward with her microphone, asking for details about the arrest.

Archambault sighed and held up her hand for silence. "Gage Chappelle is the creator of the runaway charm known as Stoffel. As such, he must take responsibility for the havoc this charm is causing our town and its people."

Gage's pale face turned red as he lunged for the microphone. The reporter was all too glad to hear his side of the story. "Stoffel *is* mine," he said breathlessly, "but it's been tampered with. Someone's sabotaged me."

Detective Archambault shot Gage an irritated glare, but the reporter inched closer.

"Stoffel was my love charm for the contest. He's supposed to heal anyone ailing from a broken heart with his hugs. But someone had broken into my workshop and perverted the charm so that it infects people with lovesickness instead. You've got to believe me! I wouldn't have created a charm that hurts people!"

"All charms can go wrong," Detective Archambault

said coldly. "Whether an accident or not, people are suffering."

"Sabotage!" Gage bellowed.

The police officers took him by the arms and led him into the backseat of one of the police cars.

"What do you have to say about this, Ryker?" The reporter shoved the microphone at him. "How do you feel now that your uncle has been arrested for his love charm?"

Ryker took off his glasses and rubbed his eyes with his clean knuckles. "My uncle is a good man. He would not have done this on purpose. But he's always been a little careless with his crafting. I wish he had shared Stoffel with me so I could have helped prevent this from happening."

"You weren't working on it with him?" asked the reporter.

He shook his head. "Said it was a surprise."

Hijiri snapped out of her trance once the police cars drove off, leaving Ryker behind with a slew of reporters and questions. Gage was pathetic. He didn't look like a criminal. Her gut told her that something was wrong. She liked listening to her gut better than her heart.

Despite having Gage behind bars, the police hadn't come any closer to ending Stoffel's stealthy attacks on the town. The number of victims grew. Hijiri couldn't keep up with their consumption. By Thursday, she said good-bye to the last of her tea.

"No more hibiscus petals," the florist told her, wringing her hands. "We'll special order them, but it could take a few days."

The petals were her key ingredient. Without it, the other pieces of the tea wouldn't work.

Hijiri drank the last drops of her tea and tried so hard not to think of the lovesickness coming back full force in a matter of hours.

"I can do this," she whispered before heading to her algebra class.

She survived two class periods before the lovesickness pulled her under again. Stoffel's charm knew it had been tampered with by the tea; as if seeking revenge, it made Hijiri's vision turn opaque pastel pink for a few heart-thundering minutes. She smashed face-first into a locker, blind and grasping for anything to hold.

Students shouted for help. Familiar hands grabbed her shoulders. Fallon's hands. Her voice demanded everyone to step back.

Then Nico's horrified gasp. "I'll get the nurse," he said.

When Hijiri's sight came back, it was still tinted pink and blurry with fresh tears. Her cheeks felt raw from the crying, her throat harsh and raspy.

Ken knelt before her, his hands on his knees. "Where's the tea?"

"Gone," she choked. "Nothing left."

Ken cupped her face, forcing her to look at him. "Focus on me, then. Don't let the charm win. You're not suffering from lovesickness. You've got me. The boy who loves you."

Her fingers tightened around his wrists. Hijiri's heart felt like it was splitting, jagged and sharp as the words came flying from her mouth. "You can't help me, *charm-boy*."

Ken swallowed back his hurt.

"You and Love are playing a game with me. Love thinks it's funny, huh? That he's let you infiltrate my life? You're both liars."

"When have I lied?"

"Simply by existing." Hijiri broke away from his hands and hugged her stomach. Stoffel's charm evolved. It stole her personal feelings. Made them bigger and poisonous. Like her tears, she couldn't stop the words from falling. "Everything is fake. You're not mine. You weren't made for me. You can't love me."

Ken shook his head, his jaw tight. "That's the charm speaking, right? I thought we . . . we were getting closer. That you were starting to see me as a real boy."

Her heart withered so fast, she doubted even a microscope could find it. So she said the most hurtful thing she could think of to make him go away. "I wasted *so much time* on you, Ken. Instead of trying to solve you, I could have been doing something more productive. Like crafting my love charms."

Ken's breath hitched. "Is that how you really feel?"

Hijiri scooted farther away from him. Her heart raced, though it didn't seem to know where it was running to.

Ken dug his fists into his knees. His chin sank to his chest. "Sorry for being such a burden. I was just weighing you down," he said brokenly.

The school nurse came, Nico on her heels.

Ken stood up on unsteady legs, his eyes to the floor. He had to push past the onlookers to leave the hallway. Fallon, who had watched the exchange, bit her lip.

Hijiri doubled over, her palms pressed to the floor. She expected tears, but nothing came. She was dry. Empty. Her eyes fell closed when she hit the tile.

Chapter 17

HOME AGAIN

When Hijiri woke, she was in a cot in the nurse's office, sheets tangled at her waist.

"You were kicking up a storm," Nurse Geerts said, handing her a cup of water. "After you're feeling better, Principal Bemelmans wants to see you in his office."

She nodded and drank. Her throat was scratchy from crying.

Stoffel's charm had wrung out her heart like a wet towel until nothing was left of her but damp wrinkles and soreness in her bones.

A few minutes later, Nurse Geerts escorted her to the office. The woman's gnarled but gentle hand gripped Hijiri's shoulder, holding her steady.

Hijiri avoided making eye contact with the students she passed on the way. Her heart retreated to a quiet corner behind her rib cage, angry and jagged. *My own heart is mad at me*, she thought. *That's not fair. It was Stoffel's fault that I broke down in the hallway.*

But the words she had slung at Ken were true. She wasn't strong enough to believe in something that didn't exist, no matter how wonderful he was. *I can't give my heart to a walking, talking love charm. That's going too far. That's a line no love charm-maker should ever cross.*

Her heart shrank and grew pointier. It jabbed her between the ribs.

"Come inside, Miss Kitamura," Principal Bemelmans called from his office.

The sunlight pouring into the office nearly blinded her. Nurse Geerts helped Hijiri into a sun-warmed chair and left.

Principal Bemelmans opened the drawer at his elbow and plucked an envelope from inside. "This just arrived from your parents."

Hijiri took the envelope from him and hooked her finger to neatly tear it open. Inside was one round-trip train ticket to Lejeune and back.

"Your parents called this morning to check on the delivery of the ticket," he said. "They want you to come home to see them. To know that you're okay."

They wouldn't come to Grimbaud. She knew her parents. With winter on the way, they were busier than usual. Snow caused accidents. The insurance company was, therefore, a flurry of activity. Lejeune was already snowy, even though Grimbaud had yet to shed all its leaves.

Principal Bemelmans sighed. "In light of the circumstances, I think it's important for you to see your parents. They must be worried about you, no matter how . . . uniquely they show it."

Hijiri stared at the ticket. She could use it whenever she wanted since it was already paid for. Tuck it away in her room for when *she* decided to go home. Normally, she'd have ignored her parents' invitation. Being alone, never really needing them, was part of her life.

But her life had not been normal for months.

Stoffel ran free through Grimbaud, infecting more townspeople with each passing day. Gage's arrest hadn't made a difference. Her missed-connections charm would leap off the pages of her notes any day now if she kept working on the last few details. Then there was Ken.

Hijiri held her head in her hands and whimpered.

"Miss Kitamura," the principal said. His chair slid back from his desk. "You don't look well. The incident in the hallway must have . . ."

Hijiri looked up, her eyes blurry. "I'll go see them. Today."

He looked relieved. "I'll let your teachers know."

❧⟶

Hijiri had never left school early before. Tourists ruled the streets. They unfolded maps and consulted them on street corners and in the shade of cafés. Her head throbbed as she fought off overzealous shop owners trying to lure her into their shops with coupons and special offers. By the time she got to her apartment, she stumbled into bed and napped, her eyes so heavy that she thought the twins had snuck into her room to glue them shut. The ticket crunched under her chin.

Eventually she got up, yawning so hard her jaw popped, and stuffed her backpack with some clothes and other necessities. Taking the golden cupid she had painted felt right so she threw that in too. After having consulted the pocket train schedule she kept in the kitchen (so she could plan her winter breaks at home accordingly), she saw that three trains were leaving for Lejeune, ranging from two to eleven at night. If she left now, she'd be able to take the two o'clock train.

Hijiri almost stopped in her tracks when she saw Fallon at the complex gate. "What are you doing here? School's not over."

"When you didn't come to lunch, I got worried. Principal Bemelmans said you were going home. You're not running away, are you?"

"From what?" Hijiri said, playing dumb. This wasn't a conversation she wanted to have right now.

Fallon fell into step with her, her expression tight. "I heard everything you said to Ken in the hallway."

Hijiri looked at her feet. She couldn't remember where

Fallon had been after Nico ran off to get the nurse. "You were there?"

"Didn't want to leave you alone. When Ken came, I thought maybe you'd be okay, but then . . . what you said to him . . . that wasn't just Stoffel's charm talking, was it?"

Hijiri hailed a cab, ignoring the sluggish thudding of her heart. She and Fallon rode in the back of the cab in silence. *Punishing silence*, Hijiri thought, staring at her hands. She could tell Fallon was angry.

Grimbaud's train station shone in the sunlight. The perfect escape from this uncomfortable conversation. Hijiri left the cab, only to have Fallon slide out after her.

"You didn't follow my advice," Fallon stated. "About listening to your heart."

"I told you I tried," Hijiri said.

"*That* back there in the hallway never would have happened if you'd tried harder," Fallon said.

"How do you know?" Hijiri shouted. Her eyes started to itch with new tears. Just when she thought she was empty. "You don't understand."

"I understand enough to see that you're being senseless. You've plugged up your ears so that you can't hear what your heart is telling you about Ken. All you're doing is hurting yourself and him."

"He doesn't have real feelings to hurt."

Fallon groaned. "I'm not getting through to you, am I?"

"I appreciate your concern," Hijiri said carefully, "but

you shouldn't be encouraging me to fall in love with a charm-boy. You're too practical for that, Fallon. I'm surprised."

"Well, for someone who's fake, he's awfully thoughtful," Fallon said. She pulled something out of her schoolbag and placed it in Hijiri's hands. "When he heard that you were going home, he told me to give you this."

Hijiri uncurled her hands to find a little golden bell.

"It's a hearth charm he's been meaning to give you," Fallon said.

"What does it do?"

"It's like a magnet, drawing the people you love home. Just ring it."

"Thank you," Hijiri said, pocketing the bell.

"After what you said to him in the hallway, Ken skipped his classes and sulked in the boys' bathroom. Sebastian had to drag him out of there." Fallon frowned. "Ken's our friend too. We're going to take care of him while you're away."

Hijiri's cheeks burned with shame. "I'm not running away."

"No, but you're falling apart," Fallon said with concern. "Go see your parents. Recover. Trust us to keep everything under control here. The twins are already brainstorming a plan to capture Stoffel. When you get back, we'll have it ironed out."

Hijiri didn't need to say thank you. She let out a relieved sigh and hugged Fallon tight.

The Kitamuras lived in the better part of the city, but still surrounded by Lejeune's noisy traffic and crowded lakes. Their house had a view of Juu Roku Lake—or "sixteen," as each lake was named after numbers because there were so many. Darkness had fallen by the time her train pulled into the station, but night was never *night* in Lejeune. Too many neon lights and beam-bright streetlamps.

"I'm home," Hijiri called, dropping her backpack in the hallway. She kicked her snow-soaked shoes off and hung her damp coat on the rack. Her whole body trembled with cold. Her heartsickness thawed as she did. She had the sudden urge to curl up on her bed and cry while listening to love ballads. *Lucky my tape player broke over the summer,* she thought, rubbing her moist eyes, *and I was too busy crafting to replace it.*

The Kitamura household did not provide any warmth beyond the heating system. Her parents preferred slippery stained wood floors and sleek leather couches with silver buttons swirling on the armrests. The kitchen chairs made Hijiri's back ache the longer she sat in them. The interior designer her parents hired came once a year to survey the house for any potential upgrades to the modern style. Hijiri wished for coziness though. A hearth charm to brighten up the place.

The lovesickness tugged her toward the kitchen where she spent ten minutes writing terrible poetry all over the report her mother left out on the counter. After writing five haikus, Hijiri dropped the pen as if it burned and let it clatter on the tile. She stumbled to the cabinet above the microwave and opened it so hard it smacked against its neighbor.

"I know my stash of tea is still here," she muttered, standing on her toes to reach the back of the cabinet. She felt around behind the stacks of fragile rice bowls until she found the small tin squeezed behind it.

Hijiri made quick work of brewing the Heart's Ease tea. Her lovesickness melted off her bones after the first few sips.

With a much clearer head, she looked around. "Hello?" she called, hoping to hear her parents answer her from somewhere in the house. She found a note on the fridge written by her mother: both her parents would be getting home late but they would all go to dinner as a family. Her shoulders sagged.

Ken's hearth charm was still in her pocket. Hijiri picked up the golden bell, keeping it silent by pinching the clapper with her fingers. *Why did he still want to give me this after I lashed out at him? I made him angry. No, not that. Worse. I punched a hole in that fake heart of his. Yet, here he is, still being kind,* she thought.

Her parents were supposed to take care of her, yet they

left her at home. Again. She knew better than to believe them when they said they'd take her to dinner. She wasn't sure if the hearth charm would make a difference, but she wanted to try. After a few moments, she let go of the clapper and rang it.

For such a tiny bell, it had a deep, sweetly weeping tone. The charm spread with each toll, wider and wider until the sound left the room entirely to reach whoever needed to come home. Her parents.

The bell reminded her of Grimbaud's belfry. Of Ken aiming his slingshot at the empty nest.

Hijiri stopped the clapper and put the bell in her pocket. Her heart ached to return to Grimbaud already.

Her bedroom was on the third floor of the house, alone but for a small bathroom and balcony. Hijiri went directly upstairs with her backpack and turned on every lamp to chase the night away. When she opened the balcony windows to see her neighbors across the lake, many rooms still flickered with light. Snowflakes drifted on the wind.

For once, her mind didn't spin with love charm ideas. Her mind was, in fact, quite empty.

Snowflakes melted on her upturned face. Her eyelashes. Like rain. Before her heart responded to that memory, Hijiri pushed the image of Ken's wet eyelashes into the old box she always used.

"We're going to sort this out," she hissed into the night. "But not now. Please, give me some peace."

Hearts didn't take requests often, but that night, her heart crawled willingly into the box and shut the lid.

➻━▷

"Hijiri, where are you?" Mrs. Kitamura called.

I'm just dreaming, Hijiri thought, rolling over in her bed. The blankets were toasty warm. Her nose had thawed with the help of the nap she had taken after coming home. The golden cupid stared at her from its perch on the desk.

"We have *reservations*," Mrs. Kitamura said, echoing from the staircase.

Hijiri pushed the sheets back. She ran to the top of the stairs and squinted. Yes, that was her mother standing there. "Where?" she croaked.

"Dinner, of course," Mrs. Kitamura huffed. "Your father and I got home as soon as we could. Luckily we chose a restaurant that's open late. Put some nice clothes on and we'll leave in ten."

Nodding, Hijiri scampered back to her room and threw on a long-sleeved dress and tights she had in the back of her closet. She slipped on her coat and brought the bell with her, unwilling to part with it. When she reached downstairs, her parents were waiting at the front door. "You're here." Hijiri breathed.

Mrs. Kitamura frowned. "We *said* we were taking you to dinner."

"You say those things a lot," Hijiri said, "and they don't happen."

"Honestly, you act as if we don't take you anywhere."

Hijiri rubbed her eyes. Not even Stoffel's charm could distract her from this anomaly.

She sat between her parents in the cab. Her mother shifted uncomfortably, complaining about the shoulder pads in her blazer. When her father's stomach growled in response, the three of them laughed. Hijiri felt the mood lighten in the cramped cab.

They dined on raw tuna served on toasted chips covered with avocados, tomatoes, and olive oil. The butter was shaped like a puffer fish. The sharp blue lighting made her feel as if she were eating underwater; imposing octopus statues lurked in each corner of the restaurant.

They didn't talk much with the food as delectable as it was. Still, Hijiri felt a little less anxious sitting with her parents, and a little less lonely. Her father didn't complain about his boss. Her mother even asked her what kind of love charm she was working on—and listened.

"I've entered a love charm-making competition," she said, taking advantage of their attention. "The town's going to pick the best love charm-maker on November thirtieth. I'd like you to come, if you can make it."

Her parents exchanged a look. Mrs. Kitamura wrote the date down on her napkin and folded it into her purse. "We'll check our schedules, dear."

Hijiri wondered if Ken's bell was in any way responsible for this wonderfully bizarre dinner. She curled her fingers around the bell while they waited for dessert. Her parents smiled at her. She smiled back.

The trouble with visiting working parents on a weekday was that she only had a rushed breakfast to share with them. Hijiri rose at dawn on Friday, knowing that her father was already shaving and her mother spritzing orchid perfume on her collarbone and wrists.

Hijiri raked her long hair out of her face and padded down the two flights of stairs to the kitchen. She helped herself to bread and salted butter for her toast, everything tinted pink by Stoffel's charm. Halfway through her glass of orange juice, Mr. and Mrs. Kitamura made their entrance into the kitchen.

"There you are," Mrs. Kitamura said, as if Hijiri had been hiding in her briefcase all along.

Mr. Kitamura laid his stuffed file folder next to the unused mixer and knelt down to study his daughter. "You're still not feeling well, huh? That was quite the illness you caught."

Hijiri frowned. "Yes, and yet you made *me* get on a train to see *you*."

Mrs. Kitamura popped the lid on her usual breakfast shake. "Missing school is very bad, Hijiri, but we had to know that you were okay. And it looks to us that you do need the rest. I can't imagine you recovering in that rowdy apartment complex."

"How long are you staying?" Mr. Kitamura asked, standing up and rubbing his knees.

"I don't know," Hijiri said. "Not long."

Mrs. Kitamura checked her watch. "Hitomu, we're going to be late."

Mr. Kitamura nodded and kissed his wife on the cheek. Then she smiled at Hijiri and told her that they'd both try to get home early again.

Hijiri watched them dance around each other in the kitchen until they gathered their briefcases and materials. The front door shut with a lonely creak. Would the magic of Ken's bell last another night? Hijiri promised herself she'd ring it again later.

Being home distracted her from the worst of Stoffel's charm, but it was still there, slowing her movements, making her want to cry. Hijiri filled her parents' soaking tub and added her mother's orchid bubble bath. She slipped underneath the steamy water and stayed there until her skin pruned. *I've got to fight this charm*, she thought weakly. *I can make more tea here. I'm sure I have the ingredients.*

Hijiri dried her hair and got dressed. Lejeune called her. A symphony of barking dogs and screeching tires when the traffic lights turned yellow, then red. Joining the early morning joggers and dog-walkers, Hijiri stayed on the path circling Juu Roku Lake. The water was pale blue, mirroring the cloudy sky. Fishing boats bobbed on the water. Minnows and catfish were plentiful. Most restaurants served them. Hijiri never got sick of eating fish, but she appreciated the variety of food in Grimbaud. *And the sweets*, she thought, missing the chocolate-drizzled waffles fiercely enough to make her stomach grumble. She didn't deviate from her walk. There was one particular place she had to go, because putting off speaking to her heart had gone on long enough.

Halfway around the lake, Hijiri found a woodsy gap between houses, partially obscured with unpruned bushes. She covered her hands with the sleeves of her coat and pushed the branches back, careful not to release them too soon and get her face scratched. The path took her deep through the overgrowth separating one house from the other. If she craned her neck, she would be able to see the skyscrapers through the tree branches. But, as most people did in Lejeune, she kept her eyes in front of her.

The path turned sharply to the right. A wooden sign, faded with age, read:

SWAN LAKE

In middle school, she had heard rumors about the dried-up lake the city drained and the secret path to get there. Hijiri had ached for a secret at that time, even if she had to borrow one. Trees still masked the lake's graveyard from sight. Snow covered the ground and fallen branches in white. She broke through more bushes and reached the lake.

Swan Lake was a pit in the ground, holding leaves, scavenging birds, and dry soil. Hijiri didn't know the lost lake's story. When had it dried out and why? Where were the swans? Why had no one thought to revive the poor lake? Grimbaudians would have found this place enchanting. She could picture amorous couples sneaking away to come here.

She walked to the center of the dead lake and sat cross-legged. Hijiri took out her golden cupid and set it down in the wet leaves in front of her. The paper heart curled at the edges. The pipe cleaners around its neck had twisted oddly while traveling in her backpack.

"Okay," Hijiri said, breathing in the wet air. "Listen up, little heart. You and I are going to have a talk."

"Hearts don't like words," the golden cupid said. "Bartering with feelings would get you better answers."

Hijiri yelped and fell back on her elbows.

The golden cupid laughed and notched an arrow. When it let go, the golden arrow whizzed past her ear and landed in a tree trunk.

When Hijiri looked behind her, she saw a figure emerge from behind the wounded tree. A woman in her late forties with golden-blond hair and foxlike eyes. A key hung from her neck, swinging back and forth like a pendulum.

Chapter 18

HEART-TO-HEART TALK

"Love," Hijiri gasped, struggling to her feet. She ran for the woman, arms out, only to pass through her like fog.

"Sorry about that. I'm not exactly corporeal right now," Love said, twisting a golden lock of hair around her finger. "I'm still on my inventory trip but I borrowed that cheeky cupid over there to reach you. Like making a phone call."

Hijiri pulled the golden arrow out of the tree trunk. It fit in the palm of her hand. Her vision swam deep pink. Her chest burned with pent-up tears. "Stop this game now," she said, bitterness straining her words. "Stop making me fall in love with Ken. You're *ruining* my heart."

Love snorted.

Hijiri growled and wiped tears from her eyes. "Don't laugh at me!"

"Your heart needs bending and stretching to grow. Not that it wasn't already a proper size before I brought

Ken to your door." Love shrugged. "Your heart is not *ru-ined*. It's stronger than ever."

"How can that be?"

"Because you're learning to pay attention to yourself."

Hijiri inhaled sharply.

"The world's great love charm-maker cannot neglect her own heart, can she?"

"I've been doing fine so far." Hijiri sank to the ground, her back rubbing against the tree trunk.

Love sighed so loudly that her fog-body disappeared. She rematerialized next to Hijiri and crossed her legs too. "You remind me of someone. This is not a conversation I ever hoped to have with you . . . but it seems you need it."

Hijiri drew her knees to her chest and waited.

"When I offered you Zita's position last year, I meant it. I do think you're brave and honorable and worthy of being an influence not only on Grimbaud but far beyond the town. I know you are capable of great things. However, you're also a lot like Zita."

Hijiri felt as if she'd been slapped. Never in her wildest dreams would she seek revenge like Zita had, distorting people's love fortunes in the process. "I'm *nothing* like her."

"You could be," Love said softly. "It's very easy to ignore your heart when you've had plenty of practice."

Hijiri hugged her knees tighter.

"Zita chose to ignore her heart to escape the pain of Dorian jilting her. She did such a good job that when she tried listening again she didn't understand what her heart was saying."

At some point, Zita must have decided that her heart was only a nuisance. Why listen to it when building her power and making the Barringer family miserable brought her such satisfaction?

"She interpreted it her own way," Hijiri said.

Love nodded. "It gave her no peace."

Hijiri moved her feet, causing the leaves to crackle around her. "Am I in danger?"

Love twisted a thicker coil of hair. "You need to keep working at it," she said finally, "but you will be fine. You've already started listening."

"What about Ken?" Hijiri said. "How could you give me a fake-boy?"

"Real or fake, should it matter?" Love said. "Either way, he found a way to make you care about him."

"Of course he did. Ken's perfect."

"Perfect?"

"For me. Just as you designed him." Hijiri squeezed her eyes shut. "He's kind and endlessly patient with me. Best of all, he's *interesting*. I've been trying to solve him for weeks."

"What have you discovered about Kentaro?" Love said more gently.

"You charmed his throat to make him keep your secrets," Hijiri said, opening her eyes.

Love looked smug.

"He's got a scar over his heart that blushes when he does. He's good at archery. He also has a strange passion for hearth charms." Hijiri frowned. "I don't know why you gave him that attribute."

"What do you want from him?" Love asked.

To keep holding his hand. To feel his arms around her. To laugh at his bulky sweaters and dorky backpack. To know what kissing Ken would feel like. Loving Ken was like dreaming. One day, she would wake up and he'd be nothing but a series of broken charms.

"Most of all," she whispered, "I want him to stay."

Love's ghostly hands framed Hijiri's face. "You've earned my help. If I let you go back to Grimbaud in your current state, Stoffel would have an unfair advantage."

Lovesickness blinded Hijiri again; she dug her hands into the snowy-wet leaves and tried not to panic. The charm crawled through her veins, burning her fingertips, dredging up her insecurities to morph into bad poetry and cutting words.

"Miss Kitamura," Love said, adopting a clinical tone. With the snap of its fingers, Love morphed into a surgeon. Dark blue scrubs, face mask, plastic gloves. "Your heart-strings are clogged with pink muck like a bad cold. Even that wonderful tea of yours couldn't clear it up for good."

Wind screeched through the trees, stealing leaves from the dead lake. Hijiri felt as if her heart was leaving her body. Love pulled her heartstrings taut and plucked away the sticky, cotton-candy manifestation of Stoffel's charm clinging to them until the strings were clean. Her eyesight returned with normal colors: the white of the snow, crackly brown leaves, the fierce gold of the cupid.

"You'll have to destroy Stoffel to destroy the charm," Love said after yanking its face mask down.

"Thank you," Hijiri said, sighing. She felt fine. More than fine. Like she was fully human again.

Love nodded. "My town is waiting for you."

"Ken's waiting for me," Hijiri said.

"The big question still remains. Does it still matter to you whether Ken's real or fake?" Love asked again.

Hijiri inhaled deeply and paid attention to her heart. With the lovesickness gone, her heart snuggled back into her chest, beating strong and sure again. *Does it matter? Tell me*, she thought, closing her eyes. Hand over her heart.

The answer came immediately.

Hijiri took a shaky breath and opened her eyes. "It matters to my brain because I want to solve him," she said, a small smile dawning. "You know how much I love puzzles. But my heart . . . my heart says something different."

"If you're fishing for clues, you won't get them from me," Love said, crossing its arms. "Solving my charm-boy is still your responsibility."

"Of course," Hijiri said. She didn't expect that part of Love's game to end so easily.

Love winked and faded out, the termination of a radio signal.

⌖⟶

When Mr. and Mrs. Kitamura dropped Hijiri off at Lejeune's train station late Friday evening, they looked sorry to see her go.

"But I'm all better," Hijiri said, giving her parents' hands a squeeze before climbing out of the backseat.

"Maybe we should eat at fancier restaurants more often," Mr. Kitamura said, bemused.

She put on her backpack and checked to make sure she had her ticket in her coat pocket. "It wasn't the food. I liked your company."

She turned on her heel and dashed into the station before she could see her parents' faces. Her smile didn't fade until the train carried her away from the city.

The trip back to Grimbaud was a blur. Hijiri clasped Ken's bell to her chest, listening to it chirp like a baby bird whenever the train car bumped along uneven tracks. Back to a warmer autumn. The beginning of November.

One month left to craft her missed-connections charm.

Her other deadlines were much shorter. Stop Stoffel.

Catch the culprit. Find Ken. Tell him what her heart was feeling about him.

She took a cab back to the Student Housing Complex; walking such a distance alone wasn't an option with Stoffel lurking. Posters with the charmed robot's face on it had tripled since she was away. Grimbaud held its breath, waiting. She felt fear in the air.

When Hijiri reached her apartment, she unpacked and put the bell on top of her card catalog. Her fingers itched to get to work on her charm, but her heart demanded something different. Hijiri swore she'd listen, so she did: it wanted to sniff out Ken, even if it had to search every building in Grimbaud. And when it found him, her heart wanted to curl up inside his hands and stay there.

"Not shy anymore, are you?" Hijiri huffed. She took a steady breath, slipped her coat back on, and climbed the stairs to Ken's apartment. She knocked hard enough to make her knuckles sting. He didn't answer. She called his name and checked the windows, but all the lights were off. "Where could he be?" she asked.

Then she remembered what Fallon had said. That her friends would take care of him. Maybe he was with Sebastian and Fallon now?

Hijiri flew down the stairs and knocked on Sebastian's door.

Sebastian opened the door. He was still wearing his leather hip holster from his grooming job, dog hair covering his shirt and skin. "You're back," he said, smirking. "Thought you'd be gone longer. A vacation before winter vacation."

"I was ready," she said.

The apartment smelled like onions and fresh bread. Fallon closed a cabinet door and brightened when she saw Hijiri. Relief lit every feature. "Your teachers missed you too," she said, heading over. "I have the homework you missed."

Hijiri smiled at her friends, but her eyes flickered over the rest of the apartment. A blanket had been draped over the back of the couch, a stack of pillows shoved in the corner. Her heart squeezed when she saw Ken's duffel bag next to the couch. "Where is he?" she said too softly, her voice cracking.

Sebastian and Fallon exchanged a look.

"There's something else you need to know," Fallon said carefully.

"I've only been gone a day and a half," Hijiri said, unable to mask her irritation.

"That's like a thousand years for the brokenhearted," Sebastian said. "Ken's been staying here since you left."

The bathroom door opened, releasing steam and a shirtless Ken, towel-drying his soft, dark hair. The scar over his heart was purplish. No blush to be found.

She said his name.

Ken turned still as stone at the sound of her voice.

Slowly, he draped the towel over his shoulders and crossed his arms.

Hijiri fidgeted. "I was looking for you."

Ken's answer was little more than a sigh. "Oh."

This wasn't how she had imagined seeing him again after her trip home. Sure, she had expected his sadness, even anger, but not this quiet, moping version of the charm-boy she knew. "I used the charm you made me," she ventured. "The hearth charm bell."

Ken shifted his weight. He studied the radio sitting on Sebastian's coffee table.

"It worked," Hijiri blurted. "My parents took me out to dinner Thursday night, just like they promised. I can't remember the last time they kept their promise. I know it was thanks to you. The charm called them back to me."

Ken's mouth twitched. After seeing so many of his smiles, she couldn't pretend that this one came anywhere close.

Fallon grabbed Sebastian's arm and led him into the kitchen, giving Ken and Hijiri more space. Sebastian looked like he wanted to get in the middle of it, but Fallon's grip was unyielding.

"Please go back to your apartment," Ken said.

"We need to talk. I saw Love while I was in Lejeune and this amazing—"

"*Please*," he said, holding up his hand. "Just go."

Hijiri swallowed thickly. "You're mad. I get it."

Ken let out a dry laugh.

His laugh wasn't right. It was broken, wrong-sounding. Hijiri's pulse quickened. "Is your heart okay?" she asked softly. "Did I break it?"

Ken pressed his fingers against the scar and shook his head.

"Let me see," she said, stepping toward him. Several love charms came to mind. "I bet I can fix it."

"You've done enough, thank you," he said harshly.

Hijiri flinched. "But you love me."

Ken turned away.

"You *do*," she said, her voice rising. His feelings for her had always been a constant. He bluntly told everyone he could about his love for her. He said it without words: through his unwavering belief in her, his touch, his tender smiles. He wouldn't deny it now, would he? "I dare you to say otherwise. Tell me when you first fell in love with me. Was it on your first day of school? When you popped out of the giant present?"

Ken looked over his shoulder, about to say something, when his hands flew to his throat and he hunched over, coughing.

Hijiri lunged forward and grabbed his shoulders, holding him upright as he coughed into his hands. Her mind raced. *Love's charm is stopping him from saying . . . what?*

Ken sucked in a few deep breaths and leaned on his knees.

Hijiri bent down in front of him. Her eyes searched his face. "Did you love me . . . before you hid in that box?" *Before you ever met me?*

He pushed away from her.

Hijiri waited another minute, but Ken stubbornly refused to open his mouth. She wished she had thought of complaining to Love about his charmed throat. Get that obstacle out of the way. But perhaps that was something she had to get rid of herself.

She clenched her jaw and said, with the absolute certainly of a love charm-maker, "If you won't tell me now, then maybe you will later. When I give you a better way of sharing the story."

The florist had called that night to tell her that the hibiscus petals came in. Hijiri ended up making enough Heart's Ease tea to last for about a week—now that an entire hospital wing was occupied with Stoffel's victims. She warned Dr. Vermeulen that she couldn't keep up with the demand. He told her that Detective Archambault was still trying to squeeze a confession out of Gage, but the old man claimed innocence.

No chance of a real cure anytime soon.

That weekend, Hijiri holed up in her hermitage of an apartment, determined to finish her missed-connections love charm. When she worked hard, and her focus was at its best, she forgot everything else. No breakfast. No lunch. Her stomach growled and her laundry piled up, but Hijiri barely noticed. Her card catalog's open drawers looked like loose teeth, sticking out for hours before she remembered to close them.

Hijiri realized what was missing from the basic construction of her missed connections charm: heartstrings. Zita had used the townspeople's heart's threads to control them, but thanks to Love, Hijiri now knew that the heart had many strings—connected to destiny, perhaps, but also to other people.

Her run-in with Love made her even more sure that heartstrings were the key to her love charm. *It makes me believe that our hearts can be tangled and tied to each other, no matter how far away we are or how much time passes between,* Hijiri thought, bent over her table. *Our hearts remember more than our brains do. Even missed connections from many years ago can be found again,* she thought, *because that moment imprinted itself on the heart where it stays, long after the brain forgets.*

She drew up new blueprints. Changed her materials. Then put her plans into action and crafted. Hijiri wiped the sweat from her face and finally took a break to eat hours later. When Fallon knocked on her door, she didn't even bother fixing the weak bun barely holding her hair back.

"I see you're putting your own heartbreak to good use," Fallon said mildly. "When was the last time you took a shower?"

"Not heartbroken," Hijiri insisted. "Just bruised. But if this charm works, I might finally solve Ken. Everything will be okay."

Fallon tucked her hair behind her ears and lifted her chin. "I'm here to make sure you get to our charm theory club meeting today."

"It's not Wednesday."

"This is a special meeting. We really need you to be there."

"Can we stop somewhere first? I need to see Ms. Ward. Urgently."

"As long as you wash up," Fallon said. "And change out of those pajamas."

Hijiri made herself presentable with a quick shower and a change of clothes. *I hope this works*, she thought, wrapping her finished missed-connections charm in newspaper so that the glass bottle wouldn't break on her way to Ms. Ward's apartment. She put the bottle in her messenger bag and nearly ran out the door.

"Slow down," Fallon called.

"I thought you said we have a meeting to go to," Hijiri said, looking over her shoulder. "I'm hurrying."

She and Fallon arrived at Ms. Ward's apartment, out of breath and sweaty.

"What a pleasure to see you two," Ms. Ward said. Her brows furrowed. "Is there some kind of emergency?"

"I need your help," Hijiri said, her heart still pounding from the brisk walk.

Ms. Ward flushed and welcomed them inside.

Hijiri moved a stack of hardcovers off the couch so she could sit while Ms. Ward brewed tea. Her stomach whined when the bitter scent reached her nose.

"If I understand you correctly," she said, carrying the tea tray into the living room, "you've crafted a missed-connections charm."

"That's right." Hijiri snatched her teacup and drank, burning her tongue.

Fallon blew on her cup of tea. "She's going to use it for the competition."

"I need to know if it's going to work. Would you like to try it?" Hijiri asked.

Ms. Ward's face flushed with pleasure. "I'd love to."

Hijiri wasted no time in grabbing the charm from her bag: a green glass bottle with a red string tied around the neck. "This is it."

"What does it do?"

Hijiri drew in a breath. She'd been practicing how to explain it clearly. "No matter how short an encounter is with someone, our hearts can remember forever. The memory is like a thread, connecting one heart to the other, and most of the time, we never realize the hearts we touch and those that touch ours.

"This charm taps into that connection. It's the same principle as using paper cups and string to communicate with a friend. You leave a message, the bottle carries it by following the string, and your missed connection receives the message. He or she can respond back the same way."

Ms. Ward gasped. Her hands shook as she held tight to the bottle. "Am I dreaming?"

"I hope not. I don't know if it really works yet or not. Would you do me the honor of trying to contact one of your missed connections?"

The librarian didn't hesitate. "How?"

"You're going to send your memory of him," Hijiri said. "Hold the bottle to your heart and remember. The charm will absorb the memory. You can also 'think' a message to go along with the memory if you want. Either way, I've included instructions for the receiver. I'll get that while you remember."

Ms. Ward grabbed Hijiri's elbow. "But I don't even know his name."

She grinned. "You don't need to know where this person is, or his name, or if he's balding or has three kids by now. All that matters is that you remember him as he was then."

"Okay," Ms. Ward breathed more than said. She looked nervous. After a moment, she pressed the bottle to her heart and closed her eyes. The bottle began to glow.

Hijiri plunged her hands into her bag and felt around for the rolled-up instructions. If the charm worked, she'd need to print the instructions rather than handwrite them. Her handwriting was pretty neat, but not if she had to write hundreds of instructions at a time. She looked up in time to see golden sparkles fill the bottle and melt away.

"I think I did it," Ms. Ward said, looking down. "The bottle feels heavier."

Hijiri popped the instructions into the bottle and corked it. "Last step. You have to throw it."

"Miss Kitamura," she said, astonished, "this isn't a plastic bottle. It'll smash against the floor."

"It won't *touch* the floor."

Ms. Ward frowned.

"Go on. You have to be the one to do it. It's like throwing a bottle into the sea."

Ms. Ward stood up, squeezed her eyes shut, and threw the bottle as hard as she could. The bottle sparked and disappeared in a puff of smoke before it could collide with the wall.

"There. It's sent," Hijiri said, sighing.

"What happens now?"

"We wait for a response. I don't know how long it'll be before he sends the bottle back with his message. It could take minutes or days."

Ms. Ward wrung her hands, a blush to her cheeks.

"Do you mind if I ask who you sent my charm to?" Hijiri said when the silence grew between them. It wasn't a question she'd normally think of asking, but it felt right. This wasn't just about the charm working. This was Ms. Ward's past love. No matter how fleeting.

"He was a street performer," Ms. Ward said, "playing the violin so fiercely I wanted to dance right there on the sidewalk. I remember the pitch of his whistle when he saw me coming, the zipper on his leather jacket gleaming in the light of the shop he stood in front of. Even though our eyes met, and it looked like he wanted to play for me, I had no change. I ran into the shop and got stuck waiting in line for the cashier. By the time I had my change, the violinist was gone."

Hijiri could picture the missed connection perfectly in her head. The heart's memory must be even better. "Maybe you'll find out what happened now."

Ms. Ward burst into a grin. "Maybe I will. Thank you."

Chapter 19

SPOKEN AND UNSPOKEN

Fallon told Hijiri that they would be meeting at an outdoor café notorious for its noise level—the perfect place to hatch a plan without being heard. Also, with so many tables clustered together along the sidewalk, the twins would have to behave themselves.

The café spanned half a block, the open kitchen providing hungry patrons a view of their dishes being cooked. Femke, Mirthe, Ken, Nico, and Sebastian had already pushed together two tables.

Ken sat next to Sebastian, picking at the remains of a grilled ham and caramelized endive sandwich. His dark eyes were twin lakes at midnight, unfathomably deep and sad. If she looked too long, she'd drown in those eyes. Lucky for her, Ken had been avoiding her gaze.

Hijiri unbuttoned the top of her coat's collar to let in some air. She suddenly felt too warm in her layers. "My competition charm is just about finished," she announced when she got there.

"That's great," Sebastian said. "Can we see it?"

"Ms. Ward's testing it for me," Hijiri said. "We'll all have to wait and see if it works first."

"Have a seat," Mirthe said.

Ken lifted his backpack off the ground and put it on the empty chair next to him. He went right back to his sandwich, his shoulders hunched.

Hijiri felt his rejection like a slap. She inhaled sharply and tried not to let the hurt show on her face. The only empty seat left was between the twins. She sat down. Having grown used to him sitting beside her, she felt disoriented without him. Like she wasn't where she was supposed to be. Femke passed her a laminated menu.

Nico looked at his watch and checked the street. No sign of Martin yet.

Fallon cleared her throat. "I think we should catch Hijiri up on the plan."

"Last Wednesday's meeting was a success," Mirthe said, "because I came up with a way to stop Stoffel."

"Why are you taking the credit?" Femke muttered.

"Because the plan was mine first."

Femke plunged her hands into her pockets. Bits of fog curled out.

"That's enough," Fallon snapped. "No charms. Put. Them. Away."

Femke slumped back in her chair, but the fog stopped.

"I think *we'd* better continue," Sebastian muttered to Fallon.

Fallon nodded gravely and stood up, commanding the attention of the group. Even though the police had spread news and warnings about Stoffel all over town, including on Bram's radio show, that hadn't stopped couples from going out on Friday nights.

"Date nights," Sebastian clarified. "Apparently, Stoffel attacks the most people on weekends."

"The police can't figure out Stoffel's behavior patterns beyond that. They're running out of time. If Stoffel isn't caught, Detective Archambault is going to have the competition canceled."

"She *can't*," Hijiri said, gritting her teeth.

"I know. That's the last thing any of us want to happen," Fallon said, "but pretending that everything's fine while a dangerous charm roams the town is not right either."

They couldn't let this happen. If the competition got canceled, the rivalry it had bred between the new love charm-makers would only continue. The entire town could become a battleground instead of just Verbeke Square's stage. *Someone wants to be crowned the best in town*, Hijiri thought grimly. *Better it happens with the police watching and rules in place.*

"Detective Archambault arranged for a stakeout next Friday."

Nico checked his watch again. His brow creased.

"Grimbaud has a curfew now. We're all supposed to be inside with our doors locked starting at six in the evening. Only the police are allowed to be out." Sebastian smirked. "We're ignoring those rules, of course."

Hijiri rested her elbows on the table and told them about meeting Love in Lejeune and how her lovesickness had been cured. "Love said that Stoffel needed to be destroyed for the lovesickness charm to stop."

"That's exactly what we're going to do," Mirthe said.

In groups of two, the ex-rebels would pick spots around town to wait for Stoffel. Mirthe was already working on weather charms to use against the robot and asked the other club members to carry helpful charms with them for the night.

"If we're separated, how will we know if someone sees Stoffel?" Hijiri asked.

"My father has communication charms as a backup in case the radios on our boats ever broke," Nico said. "He won't miss them for one night."

"Bram and Ms. Ward have agreed to help us," Femke said. "I don't think either of them could pass up another adventure. Fallon said she'd find a way to ask Anais and Bear to join us too. We could use Bear's strength for catching Stoffel."

Fallon laughed. "Believe me, they'll say yes. Anais is always up for some mischief."

As intimidating as the robot was, Hijiri had no doubt that Bear could throw him to the ground with his judo training. Of course, Bear needed to be where Stoffel was. And avoid getting locked in a hug. Hijiri hoped that they could stop Stoffel with charms, but she had to be open to different solutions if they were going to pull this off.

"What about the police?" Hijiri asked.

"Oh, I'm sure they'll see us, no matter how careful we are," Femke said, unconcerned. "We'll have to dodge them as best we can."

"Until one of us finds Stoffel."

"That's right." Femke frowned. "It's hard to trust the police after everything that happened with Zita. We can't leave this problem up to them."

Hijiri nodded. "Sounds like as good a plan as any."

"Then let's pick the groups and locations," Fallon said.

Sebastian's hand shot up. "I choose the princess."

Fallon huffed and wrote their names, her lips curling into a smile. "Okay. Next?"

"Martin's still not here yet," Nico said, his worry showing, "but I'm sure he'd want us in a group together."

Fallon scribbled their names down. She also put down Anais and Bear as a group, as well as Ms. Ward and Bram. "Who else?"

Mirthe stared at Femke.

Femke stared at Mirthe.

Neither budged.

Hijiri was about to raise her hand when Ken beat her to it.

"Pair me and Femke together," he said.

Hijiri gripped her menu painfully. Her heart flinched like a shot bird and fell somewhere by her feet.

"Fine," Mirthe said sharply. "Hijiri goes with me. The *best* group. We have the moped."

Fallon hesitated a moment before writing their names down. She chose the locations and then passed the notebook around for everyone to see:

Sebastian and Fallon: Grimbaud High
Nico and Martin: The Main Barnes Canal
Cruises Booth
Anais and Bear: The Belfry
Bram and Ms. Ward: Love's Park
Femke and Ken: The Tunnel of Love
Mirthe and Hijiri: Verbeke Square

"Keep my sister out of trouble, if you can," Femke said to Hijiri.

Ken kept his head down. He didn't seem the least bit upset that they weren't in the same group.

Verbeke Square and the Tunnel of Love weren't terribly far away if something happened. If *Stoffel* happened. Hijiri tried not to show her disappointment. She hid her face behind the menu.

After discussing further details, the meeting ended. The twins ducked out, going their separate ways. Ken lingered, finishing his sandwich, while Sebastian commended Fallon on leading the meeting.

"They're like children," Fallon said, rubbing her temples. "Someone needed to step in."

Hijiri was about to sit down next to Ken and pry answers from him, if need be, when Nico shot out of his chair with a huge smile.

"Martin," he called, "you missed the meeting!"

The student government president hugged a folder to his chest, his glasses sitting crooked on his nose. He was out of breath. When he bumped against a woman pushing a carriage, the folder spilled from his hands and papers flew out.

Nico rushed over to help him grab the papers.

"Don't touch them," Martin snapped, scrambling to pick them up.

Nico ignored him and chased after a stray page that danced down the sidewalk. He read the page and gasped. "This is . . . a college acceptance letter."

Martin grabbed it from him so quickly that he tore the page. "It's nothing. Just forget it."

Nico looked weary. He dragged a hand through his hair. His eyes were wet. "It's your life, Martin. I care."

"Maybe you shouldn't care as much," Martin said. He crushed the folder and tossed it in the nearest garbage bin.

Hijiri turned her frustration and cracked heart on the boys. She grabbed both Martin and Nico by the wrists. "That's enough," she hissed. "You're going to talk this out. Now."

While Hijiri sat them down, Fallon retrieved the crushed folder from the bin.

"Thanks," Hijiri said, taking the folder from her. "You can go back to the complex. I'll handle this."

"Yes, you will." Fallon smiled. "I believe in you."

The compliment warmed her. It sounded like something the charm-boy would say, if he wasn't busy brooding over a sandwich. Hijiri looked over at him. Ken was still sitting at the table. *Perhaps he wants to see if I can fix this*, Hijiri thought, biting her lip. *I hope I can. He should be here to see me do it.* Knowing Ken was there, sulking or not, gave her a burst of confidence.

Nico and Martin sat down, their chairs facing slightly away from each other. Nico slumped forward, his elbows on his knees, head bowed. Martin crossed his arms tightly and tapped his foot.

Hijiri opened the folder with the torn acceptance letter on top. She had a quick look at the pages underneath and discovered that it was a welcome package for Martin—a potential student. A political science major. The university was in Wuyts, a city close to Lejeune. The commute by train would be almost as long as hers. "Do you want to tell us about this?"

Martin's fingers turned white.

Nico noticed and looked worried.

Hijiri waited a few moments, hoping her stare would be pressure enough to get Martin talking. It wasn't. "Let me tell you what Nico's been feeling, since you're not talking," she said.

"I can guess," Martin said solemnly.

"I should hope so," Hijiri said harshly, "since he's been telling you this whole time. But you haven't been listening enough to do something about it, so maybe you need to hear it from me."

Martin dug his nails into his arms. He kept his eyes on the ground.

Hijiri knew how Nico was feeling, now more than ever. She felt something like it herself after Ken pushed her away. "When you're not talking to him, it makes him feel deserted. It makes Nico question your trust in him. It makes him wonder if this one thing you're not telling him will lead to other things. More secrets. Martin, is this a secret you want to hide from him?"

Martin drew in a shaky breath. He dragged his eyes up to Nico. "I had wanted to keep it secret," he confessed, "because I didn't want to confront it."

"What do you mean?" Nico shifted in his chair to face Martin.

Martin nodded at the folder. "I'm not going to Wuyts."

Hijiri handed Nico the folder.

Nico flipped through the pages. "Why not? Looks like a good university, at least from the pictures."

"My parents made me apply there," Martin said. "Both my mom and dad went to universities far-flung from Grimbaud and they think that I need to do the same."

"Distance isn't a problem. It's not going to be easy, but we'll work on it," Nico said, tentatively touching the back of Martin's hand. His voice trembled. "Just please don't tell me we're not worth trying, Martin."

Martin looked incredulous. He stared at his boyfriend, wide-eyed, and shook his head. "Is this what I've been making you think?"

"Seemed like you had an expiration date on us," Nico offered. "Doesn't graduation do that to people? Start a new life, forget the old one."

Martin yanked Nico by his collar and kissed him fiercely. "Erase that from your head immediately," he said hoarsely.

Nico caught his breath, his face flushed.

Hijiri hadn't thought to look away when they had kissed. She was still confused. "If distance isn't the problem, what is?"

Martin ran his hands over his thighs. "My parents want me to study politics at Wuyts, become some big-city senator. They love that I'm the student government president and expect me to pursue a career in that vein."

"It's the paperwork you like," Nico said with a soft

smile. "You happen to be the only teenager on this planet who relishes filling out forms and using accordion files."

Martin tried to smile back. "I didn't tell my parents that I applied to Lambrechts College as well. I want to study business management. Those times I disappeared on you," he told Nico, "I had actually scheduled a campus tour and a few appointments with Lambrechts College's business department. It was easy to get there from Grimbaud High."

The neighboring town of Lambrechts was only fifteen minutes away from the western edge of Grimbaud: beyond the greenbelt, following the main road. Hijiri remembered that the twins had driven their moped there last year to buy formerly banned magazines with love charms inside for the rebellion.

"Sly," Nico said. "I had no idea where you were."

"Have you heard back from Lambrechts College?" Hijiri asked.

Martin shook his head. "It's still early."

"Are you going to show your parents the Wuyts acceptance letter?" Nico asked.

"That's what's been eating away at me," Martin said. He rubbed his temples and squeezed his eyes shut. "They've always been strict with me, but this is too much. I've tried to tell them that I don't want to study politics. I don't want to go to Wuyts. I've been arguing with my parents since July about this. I can't go home without the pressure weighing me down. Even my sisters joined the great family debate; they like siding with my parents for kicks. They're too young to understand."

Nico inched his chair closer and took his boyfriend's hands in his. "Why couldn't you tell me about this?"

Martin bumped his forehead against Nico's. "I'm selfish. I gave up, in a way. I thought if I could forget about it during the day and focus on you, then I could feel relief. And I did, for a while."

"But you didn't focus on me. You were too worried and you wouldn't let me help you," Nico said. "Will you let me help now? Together we can come up with a way to tell your parents about Wuyts. And *when* you get accepted to Lambrechts, they won't stop you."

"How will we do that?" Martin said, bemused.

"Maybe they just need to know their son a little better," Nico said. "You could open up to them a bit more. Show them what you really love. Kind of like what you're learning to do with me."

Martin grimaced. "I still need to work on that. I'm sorry."

"Your glasses are crooked," Nico said, leaning forward to adjust them.

Martin held his breath.

"There," Nico murmured.

Hijiri watched their exchange with satisfaction. Nico could be quite clever when he needed to be, especially when it came to getting out of his ticket-selling duties at the booth, so she felt sure he'd be able to help Martin.

"Say, Hijiri, you wouldn't happen to have charms for talking to oppressive parents?" Martin asked.

Hijiri thought of three charms right away, but she shook her head. "You don't need charms. You can talk to them just fine yourself."

Nico stood up. "Then the same goes for you."

She raised her eyebrows. *What does he mean?*

"Thank you for making us talk," Martin said, standing too. "It must have been hard for you not to use a love charm on us, but I'm glad you respected our wishes."

"It wasn't hard," Hijiri said, flustered. "I just had to use my own . . . heart." The realization startled her. *My own heart. That's right.* The empathy she felt for Nico came from within her. She knew that pain, thanks to Ken, and she was able to untangle Nico and Martin's problem by tapping into her emotions.

When she felt particularly philosophical about charm-making, she used to think that the love charms she made had lives of their own. That the ideas came out of nowhere and she captured them in her net, making them real at her worktable. *I can't think like that any-more. I was always in control. My heart and mind desired the charms, and so I made them. I never gave myself enough credit.*

Nico and Martin held out their hands.

Hijiri shook both of their hands and smiled. She looked back at Ken.

He leapt from his chair, almost knocking it over. Ken's gaze clashed with hers for a second, jolting her heart, before he left, abandoning his empty plate for the busboy to collect.

Hijiri would be walking back to the complex alone. Again.

❦→

Hijiri hadn't seen much of Ken over the weekend, though she tried to catch him around the housing complex. She knocked on his door and even waited outside of it for a while before realizing he wasn't there. He had become Sebastian's unofficial roommate, sleeping on his couch.

"He just needs the company," Sebastian said, standing in the doorway. He wouldn't let Hijiri pass. "I'm the closest friend he has besides you, and *you're* the one that broke his heart. Who else can he turn to?"

Hijiri's own heart stung. "Are you sure he doesn't want to see me?"

"Quite sure." Sebastian sighed. "Sorry. Give him time."

Hijiri couldn't break into Sebastian's apartment to reach Ken, though she thought about it, so she turned to other pressing concerns. Bringing charms to the stakeout was critical, so Hijiri planned and made charms whenever she had the chance. She also slowly made headway on the homework she had missed while in Lejeune. Fallon came over for support. They both sat at the kitchen table, textbooks and worksheets scattered between them. Hijiri tried not to think about Ken. Or the fact that Ms. Ward hadn't contacted her; the librarian must not have received a response from the missed connections charm yet.

"Concentrate on your essay," Fallon said, tapping her pencil on Hijiri's notebook.

Hijiri grumbled.

"You'll have four days to craft charms for the stakeout," she said. "Your teachers expect their assignments turned in much earlier."

Having her friend there to keep her focused, Hijiri managed to work through the pile of essays, worksheets, and readings for all her classes. She'd never been a bad student, but as the semester progressed, her priorities often got shuffled around—in the wrong direction. Midterms had passed with a whisper, which meant that the finals would probably be twice as hard.

"I can't do anything about Ken or the competition until I find out if my charm works. I hate feeling helpless," Hijiri said.

Fallon made a sympathetic noise. Then she handed Hijiri a new eraser.

After making up a quiz she had missed in her history class, Hijiri dropped her textbook off in her locker. The halls were empty since the first bell hadn't rung yet. She yawned and considered going back outside to stand with her friends in the shady tunnel.

Footsteps echoed through the hallway. Ms. Ward ran, albeit wobbly, in her heels, a look of excitement and fear in her eyes. "I got my reply!"

"Did you open the bottle?" Hijiri said, her own smile growing.

She shook her head.

"Do you need me there?"

Ms. Ward looked relieved. "If you don't mind."

They jogged their way up the stairs and to the library. Ms. Ward ushered Hijiri into her office and shut the door tight behind them. The librarian's office was an extension of her home, books spilling from their shelves and a map of the world hanging behind her desk.

Ms. Ward unlocked her desk drawer and pulled out the green bottle. Her hand hovered over the cork.

Hijiri leaned forward.

When Ms. Ward pulled the cork, the *pop* preceded glowing that bathed the room in soothing green. The image of a man formed above the neck of the bottle, flickering like film reflected on water.

Hello, Emma, came a soft, raspy voice as his image came into focus. *I'm glad to know your name at last.*

Chapter 20

IT'S ALL IN THE CHASE

The violinist was a thin man in all black with red side-burns and a goatee. He leaned against the shop window, playing tune after tune while his open violin case filled with coins. His name was Sid, he said, narrating just as Hijiri had hoped, as the image changed and showed him in a bright white apartment.

I can't return your feelings, but I'm glad you told me. I always thought we had a connection that night. I wouldn't whistle at just any girl.

Ms. Ward nosily searched her desk for a tissue. She dabbed at her eyes, a small smile on her lips.

Sid showed Ms. Ward his family—his lovely brown-eyed wife and their daughter, who had taken up the drums. By the time the image faded into ghostly, glittery trails, Ms. Ward wiped her eyes with her tissue and sighed.

"One missed connection down," Hijiri said. "How many more did you say you had?"

Ms. Ward laughed. "Be careful. If you tease me too

much, I just may buy you out of all your charms. You won't have any in time for the competition."

Hijiri thanked her. She felt like crying herself. "I have to go," she said, almost tumbling out of her chair.

Ms. Ward raised an eyebrow. "Trying the charm yourself?"

"Something like that," Hijiri said. "There's someone I want a green bottle from."

Her love charm *had worked*! Victory was a heady feeling. It carried her through the day and gave her the energy she needed to prepare another missed-connections love charm.

↦

The next morning, Hijiri knocked on Sebastian's door. Her hands were full. The sun hadn't even risen. No matter how thick her knee-high socks were, the high school's uniform offered little reprieve from the cold.

Sebastian answered the door, specks of dog hair pressed to his cheek. "My alarm didn't even go off," he complained.

"Where's Ken?"

"Still sleeping," he said with a tired smirk.

"Will you let me through today?" Hijiri *needed* to see him. She hoped she looked as desperate as she felt.

Sebastian scrutinized her. Then he shrugged. "By all

means, wake him up. I'm feeling jealous already that he slept through your knocking." He leaned out of the way so she could see behind him.

Ken was curled up on the couch, the gentle rise and fall of his chest showing that he had, in fact, slept through the noise. One hand behind his head, the other in a loose fist by his cheek.

"Did you come to woo him?" Sebastian said, making her jump.

"Only you would use a word like that," she said, blushing.

Sebastian shrugged. "You brought him a present. I'm just assuming."

Hijiri put the present down on the floor and perched on the armrest. If she raised her hand, she could feel his warm breath on her palm. "Some privacy, please."

"Not like this is *my* apartment or anything," Sebastian grumbled. He said something about taking a shower and wandered back to his room.

One way or another, she had to wake him up, even if she was worried about his reaction. Hijiri shook his shoulder.

"I'm your alarm clock today," she said, daring herself to say it in his ear.

Ken groaned, his forehead scrunching.

Hijiri leaned back quickly, almost falling off the armrest.

He opened his eyes and yawned. His toes peeked out of the other end of the blanket when he stretched. "What are you doing here?" he asked, not quite awake yet.

The present she'd so artfully wrapped with red ribbon and shiny paper slipped from her mind. Instead, her skin tingled at the sound of his sleep-rough voice. Ken's hair looked as if it had been attacked by a whisk overnight; some pieces stuck up and his bangs fell messily over his eyebrows. There were pillow creases on his neck and collarbone. Hijiri sank down to sit on the couch cushion. Her heart reached for him as she leaned over the blanket and brought her lips close to his.

Ken pushed her back, covering his mouth with the back of his hand. "What are you doing?" he rasped, his eyes wide.

Her body was fire, blue flames of severe embarrassment and frustration. "You wouldn't listen to me when I came back from Lejeune," she said. "I still haven't told you . . ."

"You don't need to say anything. We're friends. We'll always be friends, no matter how you feel about me," Ken said carefully. He still kept his hand where it was.

"I miss our walks to school," she said.

"You have more time for charm-making brainstorming now," he said. "I thought you said I wasted enough of your time."

Hijiri winced. "Okay. I deserved that," she said. "Stoffel's charm dragged some terrible thoughts to light. You never should have heard them. Besides, they're not really the truth. Not anymore."

Ken slowly lowered his hand. "I can't walk with you this morning."

"Tomorrow?"

"No."

"Can I visit you at the library?"

"I'd rather you not."

Hijiri inhaled sharply. What if Ken was broken? *When a charm breaks, it can't be repaired. You have to throw it away and start over.* If she broke the charm-boy's heart, he wouldn't recover on his own. The thought of Love throwing Ken away gave her goose bumps. She looked down at her hands. Pressed her lips together. *Then this is my responsibility. I have to heal him somehow, starting with what I know.*

"I brought you something," Hijiri said, grabbing the present off the floor.

"What's this?" Ken asked.

"Open it, please," she said.

Ken gave her a small smile and took the present apart with care, unknotting the bow and winding the ribbon neatly around his finger. Peeling the wrapping paper rather than tearing it down the middle. When he found the green glass bottle and set of instructions, he gave her a questioning look.

"My charm for the competition is finished," Hijiri said. "The missed-connections charm."

"Why," he said, hesitating, "why are you giving it to me?"

"Love's stopping you from telling me secrets, but this charm is all about *showing*. This may be a way around your charmed throat."

Ken rested the bottle against his chest. He closed his eyes and sighed deeply. "You don't know if it will work. If we don't have a missed connection . . ." His voice broke off with a cough.

"Don't you want to try?" Hijiri asked. "If it works, you'll be able to share whatever Love's made you hide."

Ken deliberately plunked the glass bottle on the table next to the couch. Out of reach.

Hijiri flinched.

"Please leave," he whispered. His hand drifted to his heart.

Hijiri stumbled over Sebastian's shoes as she ran out of the apartment. Her toes hurt from the impact, but that wasn't why she was crying.

The first time she had been on a dangerous adventure, Hijiri felt the delicious *wrongness* of it in her bones. Slipping away from the Welcome Love Festival to battle Zita.

Breaking the rules in order to free everyone from Zita's clutches.

This time, she just felt cold.

Snow flurries dusted the town all day and got worse by the time school ended on Friday. To avoid suspicion, Hijiri had gone straight for her meeting spot at Verbeke Square rather than going back to the Student Housing Complex first. Mrs. Smedt had warned the boarders that she would be patrolling the complex for any students out after curfew. All doors had to be locked. Lights turned off. Hearts safe and snug inside their apartment walls.

A waffle and creamy hot chocolate served as her dinner. Then she went to her meeting spot while the square was still full of people.

She and Mirthe agreed to meet behind the shops in Verbeke Square. Tourists never wandered back there. Nothing to see but garbage bins, back staircases, and a small, cobblestoned walkway. Hijiri blinked back snowflakes as she pressed herself against the back of a lace shop. She was only a few feet away from the door to the sewers that the twins had discovered last year—the door that had led them down into the darkness of Zita's hideaway.

Hijiri stamped her feet and rubbed her shoulders. Waited. She shivered in her thin, royal-purple coat, even though she had tied the belt at her waist and buttoned the collar up to her chin. Her sweater, black jeans, gloves, and boots did little to keep her warm, but sitting still was not on her agenda anyway. She had pulled her hair into a loose bun with a knitted headband over it to keep her ears warm. Her crossbody bag held a plethora of charms she had crafted for the stakeout.

With five minutes until curfew, the square emptied. She heard the last few footsteps and locks clicking as the shop and café owners closed early.

"Sorry I'm late," Mirthe whispered, creeping around the back of the shops. "I parked the moped over there, 'cause we're going to need it."

The belfry bells rang. Hijiri counted the six strokes.

Mirthe unzipped her backpack. "Take this," she said, handing Hijiri a pin. "Nico's communication charm. The others should already be wearing theirs. We're late to the conversation."

The golden pin had been shaped to look like one of the Barneses' canal boats. She pinned it on the collar of her coat and the charm activated, allowing her to hear the other rebels from around town.

"Hijiri and I are at the square now," Mirthe said, leaning into her pin. "No sign of Stoffel."

Nothing is happening at the high school, Fallon said.

Good, Bram said. *It would take too long for the rest of us to get there if the charm makes an appearance.*

He's right. We can't take a cab, Ms. Ward said.

Unless we want to ride in the back of a police car, Sebastian added dryly.

Hijiri listened as the others chimed in. The sunset bled the world orange and bruising purple.

Mirthe peeked around the corner of the building, checking the square for any sign of police officers. She wore all black, from her boots to the cap hiding her hair, except for the shiny velvet-red mask over her eyes. Hijiri wondered if Femke was wearing the same clothes.

An hour dragged by. The weather made waiting worse. At least the police force sat cozy in their heated cars.

Mirthe didn't handle the boredom any better. She stared at the dark rooms above the shops and paced. "Stoffel *has* to find us," Mirthe muttered, too low for the charm to pick up. "We have stormy enough hearts to attract it."

Hijiri couldn't feel her nose. She blew on her gloved hands and rubbed them together for warmth. *Mirthe has a point. She's extremely upset with her sister and I'm hurting because of Ken. If Stoffel seeks out heartbroken people, there's no way that robot will miss us. Unless . . .* Hijiri gasped. She unpinned the communication charm so the others wouldn't hear her. "Femke isn't as vocal as you, but she must be just as distressed that you're both fighting, right?"

Mirthe grudgingly agreed.

"Then there's Ken," she said. He was much worse than she was. Kentaro had been nothing but gentle and easygoing from the moment he popped out of the gift box. But his broken heart had changed him dramatically. The purple scar. The moping. How desperate he'd been to push her away. "I tried to apologize. He just brushed me off."

Mirthe sighed. "Apologies don't fix everything."

"You don't understand," Hijiri said, her panic growing. "That's not Ken. He never shuts me out."

Her brain and heart reached the same horrifying theory: *What if he was letting his heartbreak fester on purpose to attract Stoffel?*

"Stupid," Hijiri whispered, curling her hands into fists. Tears stung her eyes. How selfless and stupid of him to draw the robot away from her. "We have to go to Femke and Ken," she said fiercely. "They're in danger!"

Mirthe threw up her hands, startled by Hijiri's outburst. "Okay, just hold on . . ."

Hijiri pinned the communication charm back on and listened. Then the bells rang for seven at night.

Femke's short gasp broke the silence. *A flyer just tumbled past us.*

Four more flyers underneath the bridge, Ken said.

"Where are they coming from?" Mirthe asked.

"That's not important right now." Hijiri spoke over Mirthe. "What do the flyers say?"

They waited a few breathless moments. Then Femke said, *I can read them quite clearly. They have Stoffel's message written on them, just like you said, Hijiri.*

STOFFEL'S HUGS HEAL HEARTS

Hijiri grabbed Mirthe by her coat collar. "We have to go *now*."

Mirthe nodded, too excited to speak.

They both ran for the moped. The other rebels scrambled to get moving also. Their words melted in the background of her racing heart.

Mirthe peeked around the corner of the shop while Hijiri put on the spare helmet. Mirthe muttered something under her breath and kicked the side of the building. "What luck. I think I see two policemen at the entrance."

Be careful, Anais said. *They could still check the back of the square.*

Mirthe shrugged off her warning, but Hijiri tensed when she heard the police officers talking. They were drawing closer, lazily making their way through the middle of Verbeke Square.

Hijiri panicked. How would they escape without being seen?

Mirthe rolled her eyes. "I didn't come into this empty-handed. Get on the moped."

She did as the twin said, lifting one leg over the side of the moped and finding the dip in the seat for a second passenger. She noticed a familiar charm tied to the handlebars. Bram's silencing charm. It was shaped like a pair of lips stitched together with thread. When the threads were tied, a thick and overpowering silence would blanket everything nearby.

Mirthe reached into her bag and pulled out a trembling, midnight-blue vial. She pitched the vial like a bowling ball toward the police officers, then ran over to put her helmet on and tied the strings on the silencing charm.

In seconds, Hijiri couldn't even hear her own heartbeat. The pure silence made her grip Mirthe's waist tighter.

Mirthe started the engine and they shot out from behind the shops. Hijiri turned in time to see the vial collide with one of the café tables. Upon impact, the vial shattered and released a tremor that shook hard enough to knock the policemen to the ground. Neither officer saw them escape as Mirthe drove them through the empty square, impervious to the earthquake illusion.

Wind whipped Hijiri's body as they sped down barren streets and over lonely bridges. She had never seen Grimbaud looking so dead. Without the energy and lights, it looked more like a model of a town rather than a real one. *People* made Grimbaud as magical as it was. Not just the shells of buildings and parks.

They were riding in the dark thanks to the silencing charm. No one could hear the moped's engine or the tires rolling against the earth, but it went both ways. The communication charm wasn't working. Hijiri tried not to panic as the minutes passed. *Ken has to be all right*, she thought, gritting her teeth. *We're almost there.*

When Mirthe turned a sharp right, bumping against

the sidewalk in her hurry, Hijiri caught sight of Detective Archambault. The detective leaned against the front of the police car, parked on the opposite end of the street. Her eyes narrowed when she saw Hijiri and Mirthe fly by. Mirthe flashed the detective a thumbs-up as they passed.

The detective shouted a curse smothered by the silencing charm and climbed into her police car. No doubt she'd be following them. Hijiri held on tighter. Mirthe wasn't going to make it easy.

Chapter 21

CROSSFIRE

The moped flew across town. Mirthe took the shortest route possible to the Tunnel of Love, careful to use her mirrors to keep an eye out for flashing lights. Mirthe drove her moped down alleyways too tight for the police cars to fit through. Leaves cracked like bones under the wheels. Hijiri pressed her face against the twin's back, wishing as hard as she could that the detective wouldn't stop them. Stoffel was moving. She needed to reach Ken and Femke.

Mirthe chose footbridges that a car wouldn't have access to. Hijiri almost bit her tongue as the moped trembled over the cobblestones. To her left, she saw the canal stretching into the night and Stoffel's flyers littering the water's surface. *Where are they?* Hijiri thought, squinting across the water to the bank where the Tunnel of Love's boats had been tethered.

When they reached the other end of the footbridge, Hijiri could make out three figures crossing under the streetlamps. The largest one, Stoffel, in hot pursuit of two teenagers running for the water.

"Ken!" Hijiri bellowed. "Femke!" Her words were lost in the silencing charm.

The moped sliced through tendrils of fog as Mirthe headed for the closest streetlamp to park underneath. "A fog charm, really?" Mirthe growled as soon as she killed the engine and untied the silencing charm. "What was she thinking? That's not going to help!"

Hijiri's heart caught in her throat when she saw Ken and Femke leap into the water. The canal water only came up to their waists, but their clothes got wet and heavy as they weaved between the boats.

Water should have stopped the robot. But this was a charmed hunk of metal. It didn't fear breaking. Stoffel dipped one skeletal leg into the water. Then the other. The robot shoved the boats aside and waded farther out into the canal. *Thanks to charms, no doubt*, she thought.

Hijiri stumbled off the moped and ripped off her helmet. "Come on!"

She and Mirthe sprinted for the bank. Hijiri shoved her hand in her bag as she ran, searching for the charm she needed. Her fingers wrapped around a knot of bracelets. She untangled one and tossed it at Mirthe. "Put this on," she yelled, "but it'll only work once."

"What's this one?" Mirthe puffed back, pumping her legs.

"This one," Hijiri said, breathing fast, "encourages personal space."

When they reached the edge of the bank, Hijiri called Ken's name and threw a bracelet at him; she had a terrible arm, so the bracelet plunked into the water a few feet away from him.

Ken ran to where it fell and plunged his hands in the water.

Femke whispered a few words and a cloud drifted down from the night sky to wrap itself around them. This fog was thick enough to completely mask her and Ken.

Stoffel's heart-shaped head spun on its axis, red eyes scanning for its lost victims. Flyers spilled from its mouth.

Bram and Ms. Ward came running toward the bank. Bram must have felt nostalgic about the adventure because he wore the same fedora and trench coat from last year. Ms. Ward carried a book in her arms, her cheeks flushed from running.

"Who's in the water?" Bram shouted, pulling a handgun out of his trench's pocket.

"Ken and Femke. They're hidden in the cloud. Don't you dare shoot," Mirthe said.

"Every time," Bram muttered.

"Get out of the water," Ms. Ward shouted. "If Stoffel breaks . . ."

Electrocution. Hijiri couldn't find her lungs.

"Will you put down that book?" Bram yelled, stuffing

the gun back in his pocket. "I don't know why you brought the thing."

Ms. Ward hugged the book closer. "It's an electrician's guide—more useful than you right now."

Bram's mouth twitched. He looked hurt. A sharp, old kind of hurt. The kind that Stoffel would pick up.

The robot locked on Bram, its body twisting to face the bank. It spewed more flyers and trudged through the water.

Bram cursed and reached for his gun again.

The robot was charmed to move quickly and gracefully; the water didn't slow it down as it landed on the bank and ran up toward the ticket booth and Bram.

"Why is he after you?" Ms. Ward asked.

Bram grunted. "You wouldn't know, would you?"

When Stoffel drew close, Ms. Ward slammed her book against the robot's left hand. The electrical guide was a rugged hardcover with peeling edges and over five hundred pages, by the looks of the thing. While the heavy impact could have taken down a bank robber, the robot barely acknowledged the attack.

Ms. Ward tried again, lifting the book over her head this time.

Stoffel knocked her over with one gloved hand. The book flew from her fingers and tumbled down the bank, into the water.

Ms. Ward gasped and struggled to sit up.

"Stay down," Bram warned, rushing to shield her. He

aimed his gun between Stoffel's glowing red eyes and fired. The bullet went through, but the robot kept moving. It grabbed Bram by the arm and dragged him forward.

"Mirthe, now!" Hijiri yelled.

The twin removed her gloves, whispered something that rhymed, and snapped her fingers: the sound echoed. The air around Stoffel and Bram rippled and grew sharply cold within seconds. Ice formed on Stoffel's arm, gluing its fingers together. Bram wrestled his way out of the robot's grip and backed off.

The cold was gone as soon as it had come. Stoffel flexed its fingers and the ice cracked.

"Cold snap," Mirthe explained, catching Hijiri's eye. She motioned in the direction of the water. "Get down there."

Hijiri nodded and ran down the bank toward the cloud-covered canal.

Mirthe must have unleashed another weather charm because she felt the rush of hot wind at her back. Hijiri's hair whipped around her face and she felt the pull of what was probably a tornado tug at her bones. But she wasn't going to stop. *I have to find them. They're in the fog somewhere, I know it.*

She plunged feetfirst into the water and squinted as the cloud obscured her vision. She adjusted the strap on her bag to keep her charms dry. The canal water numbed her legs as she waded, searching for any sign through the thick cloud that her friends were okay. After a few breathless moments, she saw shadows in the water ahead of her.

Femke had her eyes closed, whispering a charm that thickened the cloud around her even further. Sweat beaded at her temples.

Ken stood close by her, fingers wrapped tight around Hijiri's charmed bracelet. When he saw Hijiri, his eyes flashed with worry. "What are you doing here? Stoffel could come back any minute."

"It's busy with Mirthe," Hijiri said. Her teeth chattered.

"It won't be with you here," Ken said, his eyes wide with fear. "You need to get somewhere safe."

"What are you trying to do?" Hijiri said, not budging.

"My heart is calling Stoffel," Ken said. "Any minute now, my heartbreak will tempt it back here."

Hijiri grabbed him by the elbow, digging her nails into his sweater. "I *knew* it," she whispered. "You're the bait."

"Femke needs time to craft a stronger charm. She asked me to think of you, to feel every sharp edge of my broken heart."

"Like pouring salt on a cut," Hijiri said.

Ken raised his fingers to her lips, silencing her. He closed his eyes and listened. The faint sound of heavy splashing and gears met their ears. "See? It's coming back. You have to go."

No way, she thought, gripping his elbow harder. *I'm not*

leaving him and Femke alone with Stoffel. I need to stick a bandage on his heart, however temporary.

Hijiri wanted to kiss him. Kisses were miracles. They solved problems. But the last time she had tried, Ken pushed her away; the memory was like a scorch mark on her heart. So she hugged him instead. Her arms snug around his waist. Her nose buried in the crook of his neck.

This wasn't like the last time she had hugged him, sobbing with relief when they met Sofie and Lars after the first challenge. Hijiri focused on him, finding him as real in that moment as she ever thought with her body pressed against his. He smelled of boy and evergreen. His skin was soft at his neck.

Ken rested his chin on her head with a shaky breath. They soaked in each other's warmth for a few precious seconds. Hijiri felt their heats beating together through their coats. His sounding as healthy as it could be with the break she had given it. Just enough.

Stoffel's wet footsteps stopped. Its head creaked as it turned. After a few seconds, it started walking back to the bank again.

"I think . . . that worked," Ken said, letting her go.

Hijiri shivered when the chill came rushing back, but she knew they needed to keep going. Through the thick cloud, she heard Bram and Mirthe goading Stoffel from the bank.

Femke's green eyes flashed. She stopped whispering

and the cloud started losing its sticky thickness. "I can't do this alone."

"What can we do?" Hijiri asked.

Femke bit her lip. "The fog is only obscuring the robot's vision. Without another weather charm, it won't do much more than that."

"What will you use?" Ken asked, looking through the twin's backpack.

Femke let out a humorless laugh. "I didn't pack anything but cloud and fog charms. I thought I'd show off and finally impress my sister, but Stoffel's charms guard him from water. I'm stuck."

Hijiri stepped toward her. "Do you need Mirthe?"

Femke's face crumbled. "We're still fighting. She's not going to help."

"Mirthe would have *flown* here to save you if your moped had wings," Hijiri said.

"Really?"

Hijiri nodded.

Femke dragged her fingers through the foggy air, collecting it in thick bunches. She threw it over her shoulders like a cloak. "I need my sister," she said with new determination. "Let's go."

They ran for the shore. Femke's charmed cloud thinned, revealing the struggle onshore. Mirthe's tornado had torn the grass and clods of dirt from the bank. The material covering Stoffel's chest had a few more tears than before.

Fallon and Sebastian had arrived, both of them helping Bram and Ms. Ward to their feet. Meanwhile Mirthe tried to distract the robot by taunting it with wind charms that pushed at its metal frame.

Stoffel's head creaked as it turned this way and that. Hijiri noticed that it had lost one of its red eyes. She wondered if Bram's gun or Mirthe's tornado had been responsible.

Mirthe saw Femke coming. "It's about time," she yelled. "You're okay?"

Femke tugged the fog around her tighter. "Fine. Pay attention to what *you're* doing," she snapped.

Mirthe frowned and was about to spit back a reply when Stoffel grabbed her around the waist. The charmed bracelet activated, pushing girl and robot apart with unseen force.

Femke raced to her sister and helped her up off the cobblestones. "Listen," she said, "I was trying to craft something big to stop this robot, but I can't do it without you."

Mirthe dusted off her knees. "So you're going to change your specialty?"

"Absolutely not," Femke said. Then she smiled. "But fighting about it is ridiculous. We should be supporting each other's decisions."

Stoffel got to its feet as well and scanned the rebels for its next victim.

Mirthe grabbed her sister's hand and shook it. Then she drew Femke into a hug. "Let's blow this robot to pieces," she said, her voice muffled in Femke's shoulder. "Together."

The twins ran back into the water while Hijiri turned to the robot. *We have to protect the twins long enough for them to craft whatever powerful weather charm Femke has up her sleeve*, she thought.

Stoffel scanned the rebels a few times over, its head gliding back and forth. One red eye piercing their hearts with its inhuman gaze.

Ken inched forward, intent on shielding Hijiri.

Bram's hand hovered over his gun.

Stoffel's head and body started spinning. The charms and wiring within hummed.

"What's it doing?" Sebastian asked.

Stoffel's red eye dimmed slightly. It started walking back into the water with a different course in mind.

"Is it . . . retreating?" Ken asked.

Maybe it sensed the shift in their hearts; none of them ached strong enough for it to stick around. "We can't let it get away," Hijiri said.

"When our charm's ready, we'll find you," Mirthe yelled from the water. The fog had thickened again, this time with tendrils of lightning tangled inside.

"Stoffel's entering the Tunnel of Love," Fallon said, squinting.

"Then why bother chasing it?" Sebastian asked. "The tunnel loops. Stoffel will just come out on the other end."

"Not necessarily," Nico said, arriving just in time with Martin at his side. They were both panting from having run across town. Nico fished a ring of keys out of his pocket and dashed to the control box. He jammed the key in and twisted, awakening the Tunnel of Love. The lights flickered on and the music began mid-note.

The bank showed signs of their earlier struggle with the torn-up grass and cracked cobblestone on the street. Bram jogged down to the water and bent down on his knees. He dragged something heavy out of the water. The thoroughly ruined electrician's guide.

Ms. Ward clasped her hands together, looking as if she might cry. "My book."

Bram wiped droplets off the ruined cover and handed it to her. "Figured you'd still want it."

"I do," she insisted, opening to the first page and surveying the smudged type. Ms. Ward sniffed and choked out a laugh.

Hijiri nearly jumped when she heard the sirens. Three police cars pulled up across the canal, clogging the road with flashing lights and disgruntled police officers.

"Oh no," Ken said.

"We can't let them stop us," Hijiri said, "not when we're so close to stopping Stoffel."

"Some of us need to stay behind, then," Sebastian said.

"And if Stoffel *does* come out the other end, we'll be here," Fallon added.

"This is my family's attraction. I have to go in," Nico insisted.

"I'm going too," Martin said.

They quickly decided that Fallon, Sebastian, Ms. Ward, and Bram would stay behind to deal with the detective.

Detective Archambault ran to the edge of the bank, looking angrier than Hijiri had ever seen the cool, stern woman.

Good thing Fallon's staying behind, Hijiri thought as they took off running. *She'll be able to keep her cool with the detective much better than I would.*

Nico led the way into the water. They stuck to the right side of the tunnel where a narrow path had been built in, hidden by the mood lighting, googly-eyed stuffed animals, and walls covered with enlarged love letters.

Stoffel had chosen the left side of the tunnel. Its legs kept getting caught by the soft fur of the bow-tied bears and cats. Nico let out a low whine when he saw the destruction the robot had already caused. Without a path on that end, it smashed whatever it walked through.

"Dad's going to kill me," Nico said. He looked ready to plunge across the water.

Martin grabbed Nico's shoulders. "Stay focused. It's going to be okay."

Hijiri felt for him. There was nothing they could do

to stop the robot from breaking the items in its path; it was still a robot, charmed or not, without any care for stepping around the delicate heart-eyed plushies and toys.

When the tunnel curved, she lost sight of Stoffel.

"There," Ken said, pointing over her shoulder.

Stoffel had ripped open the tunnel's ceiling—no, it was a door—and was pushing itself up.

"We're going to lose him," Hijiri said.

"There's an emergency door on our side too," Nico said. "And a ladder. We can follow it." Nico pushed back the dark pink curtain on the tunnel wall to get the ladder hidden behind it for the emergency door.

Hijiri's boots slipped on the ladder's rungs as she climbed. The cold air bit her skin when she reached the top. The door led them behind the tunnel where a bicycle path separated the backs of houses from the Tunnel of Love's unmemorable stone outside.

"Hurry, he's going north," Nico shouted.

Hijiri took a deep breath and hoped her lungs could hold out for another chase.

With nothing blocking Stoffel's way, the robot practically glided up sidewalks and across empty streets. Nico and Martin slowed down after a few blocks, having run farther than Hijiri and Ken had throughout the night. Nico unzipped his windbreaker and tugged off his scarf. Martin wheezed. Hijiri passed them, her eyes never leaving the robot. *I know this street,* she thought. *We're so close to Heartwrench.*

"Why are we here?" Hijiri whispered. "Gage is already behind bars. He can't be controlling Stoffel from his jail cell."

"Someone is," Martin whispered back.

"Someone who's still trying to get Heartwrench pulled from competition, perhaps," Ken said.

"Sabotage," Hijiri murmured. *It's possible. Clea and Sanders certainly seemed capable of it.*

The robot slowed its steps as the love charm shop came into view. The lights were on inside Heartwrench, oil stains from the car repair shop next door illuminated on the concrete. The electric sign flickered.

The door opened, revealing a tired-looking Ryker. His slicked-back hair and glasses absorbed the colors from the neon sign.

"Watch out," Hijiri warned. "Don't let it hug you."

Ryker startled at her voice. Far away, sirens started up again.

Stoffel came to a stop in front of Ryker, arms slack and head bent forward.

"Stand back, Ryker, while it's not moving," Hijiri said. "We have to destroy it to end the charm Gage put in it."

Ryker's eyes slid from the robot to the charm in Hijiri's hand. His expression hardened. "Don't you dare touch my creation."

Hijiri gasped. Did she hear right?

"Stoffel," Ryker said coolly. "That girl's heart is in terrible pain. You didn't do your job."

The robot trembled and spun around, red eye trained on Hijiri. It wiggled its big, gloved hands and reached for her.

Ken pushed her out of the way. They both fell onto the cobblestones.

Hijiri's fingers searched the cobblestones for anything to throw at the approaching robot. Ken groaned beside her and shook his head.

Then she heard a battle cry come from behind the robot.

Chapter 22

AIM AND FIRE

Anais and Bear, late but still right on time, came charging. Anais sat on Bear's shoulders, cheering and whooping like a victorious army general. Bear held tight to her ankles and tried not to laugh.

"Pick on someone smaller," Anais said. When they came to a stop, she climbed off his shoulders. "I'll pull that other eye out of your face!"

"You can't do that yet," Bear muttered.

Anais didn't hear him. She ran at the robot as if it were made of straw. She dug her fingernails into Stoffel's torn middle and attempted a foot sweep. Her boot collided uselessly with the endoskeleton, pinging loudly.

Bear wrenched her away by grabbing the back of her coat. He ducked under Stoffel's hands and used his weight and momentum to perform a sweeping hip throw. With years of practice under his belt, Bear succeeded in knocking the robot to the ground.

Stoffel landed facedown, its arms and legs creaking and groaning as it struggled to pull itself up.

Bear rolled away, only to have Anais kiss him soundly and declare she had it covered.

"The charm's still working," Hijiri said, scrambling to her feet. Stoffel could find a way to get back on its metal feet again, even with Bear's throw.

Ken had his slingshot, aiming at the other eye. The marble he had notched glinted under the streetlamps. "Love is blind," he whispered.

"That's it," Hijiri said. She lowered his arm so that she could pluck the marble from him. "Stoffel's attracted to heartache. Its scanners must be in those eyes." She rubbed the marble between her palms, drawing strength from the hug she had shared with Ken. The marble grew hot, glowing a soft, rosy pink, when she handed it back to Ken.

As Ken notched the charmed marble, she saw Ryker lunge.

Ryker slammed into Ken, knocking them both to the ground. Ryker landed a punch on Ken before Bear and Nico were there, pulling Heartwrench's assistant off of Ken. Ken's cheek was already starting to bruise from the punch. Ken winced and crawled to his knees, reaching for his slingshot and the rolling marble.

Hijiri pulled her Blinded by Love charm from her bag. Opening her compact mirror and tossing the glitter on its surface, she blew—Bear and Nico were smart enough to close their eyes when the blinding flash of light lit up the area like a lightning bolt.

Ryker screamed and struggled against the boys' holds.

Still kneeling, Ken turned, notched the marble, and shot Stoffel's remaining eye.

The hairs on her arms stood on end when the robot's eye shattered; a wave of charmed magic rising, then melting, covered the area. Stoffel's neck sparked like a dying breath but its limbs kept moving, grabbing and reaching with aborted movements.

Hijiri covered her mouth with her hands, feeling ill. Ryker hadn't been lying when he said that Heartwrench married technology and charms—the fact that the mechanics still worked after the charms were gone was baffling and more than a little creepy.

"Incoming," Femke and Mirthe called in unison, raising their hands to the swirling night sky above. A rumbling cloud formed and hovered over the Tunnel of Love. The twins pressed their foreheads together and it began to rain.

The rain was soft and translucent, ice crystals and liquid merging in a soft fall to earth. Hijiri felt the snow and warm rain hit her skin. The rain and snow seeped into every nook and cranny in the robot. Without the charm to protect it, Stoffel became a collection of broken parts. Its movements slowed, the cogs underneath grinding to a halt. It stopped moving completely. The twins ensured that no one would be able to salvage the remains. Mirthe uncorked a bottle, releasing a hot, tropical wind that felt delicious and dried their cold, wet bodies.

"Freeze," Detective Archambault called out, arriving on the scene with two police officers in tow. Her eyes flickered from Stoffel to Ryker and the rebels.

Officers replaced Bear and Nico in holding Ryker down. Ryker started crying, tears mingling with the rain as he rocked back and forth. "What have you done?" he demanded. "My Stoffel, my *creation*. You've ruined it."

Detective Archambault slowly approached Ryker, stepping over one of Stoffel's hands. "Am I to understand," she asked, "that your uncle didn't make this?"

"My *uncle* doesn't have the skills," Ryker spat. "He tried making a hugging machine, but it was nowhere near operational. I had to step in and make Stoffel my own. Heartwrench would fail without our success in the competition."

Detective Archambault frowned. "Why did you do it?"

Ryker seemed almost eager to tell her. "I was supposed to go to college, but my uncle persuaded me to use my funds to start this business with him. It's my business more than his." His jaw tightened. "We were losing the challenges. Heartwrench was empty most days without profits to even cover the rent. He was holding us back. Holding *me* back."

Hijiri curled her hands into fists. "How dare you call yourself a love charm-maker," she said to Ryker. "Stoffel had nothing to do with love."

"Love doesn't solve everything," Ryker said, his handsome face marred by a sneer.

She'd seen so many broken and bruised hearts these past few months. It would take more than just love to fix some of them. But love was a spark in the darkness. It was a beginning.

She hoped that there was still a beginning for her and Ken.

>—▷

As Detective Archambault had the police shoving Ryker in the back of the police car, Hijiri saw that her fellow rebels had gotten a ride with the other police cars from the Tunnel of Love.

"You're okay," Fallon said, jogging over to them with Sebastian in tow. Bram and Ms. Ward followed.

Hijiri tried not to flinch when Fallon hugged her hard, oblivious to her sore muscles.

"I missed all the fun *again*," Sebastian said, crossing his arms. He didn't seem too upset about it when he saw the darkening bruise on Ken's face. "What happened to you?"

"I came between a love charm-maker and his creation," Ken said, grimacing.

"Yeah, you should have known better," Sebastian said, snorting.

Anais chatted animatedly with the twins about the charms and judo moves she had used. Bear shook his head and insisted she needed to practice more before she put herself in danger like that.

"Danger?" Anais laughed. "I knew you were with me. I didn't have a reason to be scared."

Bear blushed furiously.

The twins walked side by side. At some point, Femke had tucked her hair into her cap, exactly the way that Mirthe wore hers. Their clothes were still different. But the smiles were the same. Perfectly alike. Looking at them, Hijiri felt another imbalance start to melt away.

"What are Mom and Dad going to find missing this time?" Femke asked.

Mirthe shrugged. "The southerly. I was going to use it to celebrate our victory, but we actually needed it a lot sooner."

"That was an expensive amount. Very potent."

"Doesn't matter. You and Dad can always catch another one."

"And you're okay with that?" Femke asked.

"Becoming a master of crafting *every* kind of weather is my dream. Choosing just one specialty is absurd. Especially boring old clouds and fog."

Femke rolled her eyes.

"Apprenticeships aren't forever," Mirthe said, sounding like she was trying to convince herself of this truth.

"So pick something already," Femke said, holding out

her hand. "When we both return to Grimbaud, our little town won't know how to handle us."

Mirthe shook her sister's hand, the old spark of mischief returning to her brown eyes.

Hijiri bit her lip, stopping the laughter threatening to shake her body. It wasn't hard to imagine the twins starting their own empire of bold weather charms.

Martin sighed heavily.

"What's wrong?" Nico asked. "We caught Ryker. You should be happy."

"I am," he said, frowning. "But honestly, I was hoping that Sanders was behind the robot. I *still* have to keep my sisters away from his shop."

Martin has a point, Hijiri thought. *We took care of this crisis, but I'll be facing Sanders, Clea, and Mandy onstage soon enough. They're still dangerous. I can't forget that.*

Even though Grimbaud remained unusually quiet, the weight that had fallen heavy and cold upon its shoulders lifted. The shops and houses didn't feel as empty. Windows glowed like fireflies as they turned on one by one. The townspeople must have sensed the change in the air. Those already sleeping had been pulled from their dreams.

"What I don't understand," Detective Archambault said, her tone cutting like a knife through their joy, "is why a group of teenagers decided it was a good idea to take on a hazardous charm. *And* defy a direct order from Grimbaud's police force. Your parents will hear about this and, of course, you are all disqualified from the competition."

The rebels paled. *Disqualification? That can't be!* Hijiri swallowed a lump in her throat. As grateful as they were for Detective Archambault's timely intervention, none of them had thought about the repercussions of getting caught. The police hadn't been an issue with Zita. But this was a different situation. They had all deliberately ignored the curfew.

"I'm an adult," Bram said. "If you're looking for someone to blame, choose me."

Ms. Ward gasped. "Me too! I was with these students, encouraging their plan to stop Stoffel. Please don't be too hard on them. They should finish the competition."

Fallon shook her head. She drew herself up, posture perfect, and said in a loud, clear voice, "Please don't take credit for my idea."

Detective Archambault crossed her arms. "Care to explain yourself, Miss Dupree?"

Fallon gestured at Stoffel's remains. "Look at how proactive I've been. My friends and I have helped you close the case on the charmed robot. I put together this team knowing that if we worked together, we'd stop Stoffel quickly. Finding Stoffel's real creator in the same night was a bonus." She smiled politely. "Do interns get extra credit?"

The twins hid their laughter well, but Anais tried to cover up her bark of laughter by coughing.

The stunned detective blinked. "You're serious."

Fallon raised her chin. "We're not the saboteurs. Find another punishment for us if you must, but please keep us in the competition. We did save the town, after all. You can't deny that."

Detective Archambault narrowed her eyes and appraised the group. "We'll talk about punishments after the competition, then." Her eyes pinned Hijiri. "If I see any hint of foul play, I'll pull you out of the contest."

Hijiri nodded, relieved and thankful for Fallon's quick thinking. She went over to see how Ken was doing. One of the officers gave him a cold compress for his bruise.

"Here, let me," she said, taking the compress and holding it against his cheek.

Ken hissed. "My brain's still trying to catch up. Did I really shoot a robot in the eye?"

Hijiri grinned. "Yes, you really did."

Now that the danger was over, fatigue caught up with them. She tried pushing her hair back over her shoulders and caught her fingers in the fresh knots. Ken slumped against the police car's hood, his eyelashes stiff and casting shadows on his cheeks from the streetlamp above.

"I knew it was Stoffel's charm that made you say what you did," Ken said quietly, "but hearing the words aloud reminded me of my own insecurities."

"You?" Hijiri couldn't fathom it. "With Love in your corner?"

Ken flinched when she moved the compress higher. "You believed so fiercely that your heart was tiny. That nothing and no one could *make* room in there."

"The boys I dated never interested me for long. I was *scared*. I thought there was something wrong with me. That I couldn't love someone else properly," she admitted.

He tried to say something, determination furrowing his brow. When the first word hit his lips, it went out like a flame. He kept trying, choking and coughing. She had to tell him to stop.

When he finally caught his breath, Ken looked more miserable than before. "This . . . this isn't okay, Hijiri. We can't have a relationship if only one of us shares her heart."

"We can work around the charm if we can't break it," Hijiri said.

"You don't deserve that," Ken said. "The boy you date shouldn't be made of shards and secrets. You need a whole boy."

She still had hope that the missed-connections charm would work. But he'd have to be willing to try. Hijiri swallowed back her tears and said, "You always told me to trust my instincts and believe in myself. So show me that you believe in me too. That you believe in us."

Ken winced when she touched his bruise. His eyes dropped to the ground.

Hijiri left him to his thoughts.

❧⟶

The news of Stoffel's destruction and Ryker's arrest spread quickly through Grimbaud. The townspeople celebrated their regained freedom by staying out late; cafés served hot chocolate and melty-sweet desserts until midnight and couples strolled through gardens under the stars. Dr. Vermeulen reported that the lovesickness plaguing Stoffel's victims went away for good. All the victims had been sent home with dry eyes and tired but happy hearts. The town hummed with anticipation of the competition's end.

November thirtieth was not cold enough for the competition to be relocated indoors. Fallon and the twins had helped Hijiri pick an outfit from her closet: a soft, creamy-pink empire-waist dress, silver gloves and boots, and thick black stockings. A red scarf hung loosely at her neck. Hijiri pulled her long hair into a braided bun and thought about her parents. They knew about the event, but she hadn't heard from them. *Maybe they couldn't clear their schedules for today*, she thought, smoothing down her bangs. *I shouldn't be surprised. Though I wish Mom and Dad would be here for this. I want them to see me compete. The Hijiri they know would never have stood onstage before hundreds of people.*

Before she left, Hijiri picked up the charmed bell Ken had given her. She took a deep breath and rang it, letting the sound wash over her. She hoped it would reach her parents somehow.

Verbeke Square had never been so intricately decorated for an occasion. White and gold streamers miles wide stretched across the square from one roof to another, forming a flimsy canopy overhead. Paper lanterns burned in the gray daylight. Confetti congregated in the cracks between the cobblestones. Vendors pushed their carts through the crowds: sausage and onion baguettes, waffles dripping with slices of plums and walnuts, and tea hot enough to melt bones.

Hijiri waited for the competition to begin, standing with the other love charm-makers on the side of the stage. Everything she needed was already onstage: a rolling cart carrying her missed-connection love charms. The green glass bottles twinkled.

Mandy and Clea wore their smocks and crystal butterfly pins over their coats. Makeup couldn't hide the bags under Mandy's eyes; she leaned on Clea, hiding a yawn with her hand. Battling the lovesickness in the hospital must have sapped her energy. Clea glowered at Hijiri.

She must still blame me for Mandy being attacked. Not that it's my fault her fiancée is unhappy with her. Hijiri glared back.

"A fine day for a spectacle," Sanders muttered beside Hijiri. The stoop in his shoulders was more pronounced, his forehead creasing as he watched the crowd grow.

Hijiri noticed that he was wearing a chef's coat under his jacket. Whatever he had brought with him was going to be edible. "Your charmed sweets have created enough of a spectacle," she said, "and yet you're going to keep making more."

"Mind your own charm," he said, frowning.

Bram took the stage in his usual noir garb, this time decorated with some romantic touches—a red-ribboned fedora, a masculine yet lacy brooch pinned to his trench coat. He looked uncomfortable with the frilly additions to his outfit, a far cry from his anti-love reputation, but he gamely took the microphone with a smile for the audience. "Finally, it's time to see what our love charm-makers have been working on these past months," he said.

The rest of his opening speech was a blur as Hijiri searched for her friends in the audience. Gage was there; he had been released after being proven innocent, though disqualified from participating in the competition. Ms. Ward's eyes followed Bram's strides as he crossed one side of the stage to the other. The rebellion stood in front of her: Femke and Mirthe side by side, Martin holding his little sisters in a tight grip, Nico, Sebastian, Anais, and Bear. But where were Fallon and Ken? Hijiri squinted and tried looking again. Neither of them were short enough to disappear in the crowd. Panic crawled its way up her spine. *Where are they?*

Her parents not showing up was one thing: it hurt, but she was used to the disappointment. Her best friend and the boy she loved not being there? Was this a nightmare? Her palms felt clammy.

"The rules are simple," Bram said, drawing Hijiri back to the task at hand. "The love charm-makers will each present their best love charms. After the last charm-maker is done, it'll be time for the audience to vote for the last time." Some volunteers wheeled three tables in front of the stage: red, yellow, and purple. A box and bowl of marbles sat on each of the tables. "We're going to vote via marbles again, Grimbaudians. One vote per person. Put the marble in the box belonging to the love charm-maker whose charm impressed you the most. Detective Archambault will be watching to make sure there's no cheating with the voting."

The detective looked sharply at Bram and nodded.

"Repeat after me: yellow for Love For All, red for Metamorphosis, purple for the charm theory club. Got it? Great. Let's begin with Sanders of Love For All!"

Sanders met a rise of boos from disgruntled parents and cheers from the younger children in the crowd. He ignored both, talking to the space just above everyone's heads. "I won't bore you with the details," he said. "The chocolates I've made for you today are my finest creations. You'll see what makes them charming. Let's start with the taste-testing."

He gestured at the sides of the stage, where employees from his shop sprang forward, each carrying trays of square chocolates. Martin struggled to hold his sisters back, when the younger one started crying and hit him in the leg. The crowd lurched forward, hands reaching for the trays.

"Nobody touch that chocolate!" shouted a voice from the back of the crowd.

A man and woman wearing health inspector uniforms loudly made their way through the crowd, led by none other than Fallon Dupree.

Mrs. Dupree hadn't needed a microphone. Her voice carried all the authority and assurance Hijiri had come to see in Fallon, only amplified. "Sanders Lemmens, you are in violation of"—she paused, consulting her clipboard—"*numerous* health code violations."

Sanders balked. "This is ridiculous! You have no right to stop me."

Hijiri chewed on her lip, waiting. Sanders had managed to worm his way out of trouble until now, but the Duprees were different.

"Look at them," he said, sweeping his hands across the crowd. "They love my charmed sweets. This town is practically begging for them. Grimbaud shouldn't be deprived of my superior confections. Not even the local chocolatiers can compare."

"Your 'superior confectionary talents' won't erase the *months* of flagrant disregard for the health and wellness of minors in this town," Mr. Dupree said firmly.

"If Detective Archambault would kindly escort Mr. Lemmens off stage, we will let you get back to your competition," Mrs. Dupree said.

From the matching dirty looks the Duprees gave the

detective, Hijiri knew that Archambault would get an ear-ful about her neglect in private.

The twins, nearly identical in matching red dresses stitched with lace shaped like snowflakes, high-fived Fallon and snickered at Sanders's retreating form. In the commotion, Hijiri stood on her toes and searched again for Ken and her parents. Still not yet. She wished she could ring the hearth charm again, just to feel better.

Chapter 23
UNMEASURABLE

"Looks like we're down to two competitors," Bram said, drawing the crowd's attention. The yellow table was wheeled away. "That just means we'll be drinking hot chocolate and congratulating the winner much sooner. How about we continue with Metamorphosis?"

"We're ready," Clea said.

They dressed the stage like a makeup station. Mandy wheeled a bouquet of eye shadows onstage, every color under the sun, while Clea carefully chose a brush to start with.

"They say that eyes are the windows to the soul," Clea said. "So what if we could unlock those windows?"

While Clea pulled a volunteer from the crowd, Mandy explained their newest product. Eye sockets held power in forming the face. They acted as window frames. With proper attention, frames could provide a different view of the world—or in this case, heart—within.

The woman Clea had chosen sat stiffly in her chair; she had small, pebblelike eyes and flushed cheeks.

"Tilt your head up," Clea said, bending over the woman like a surgeon. "There we go."

Mandy followed Clea with the eye shadows, murmuring suggestions as Clea dipped different brushes in various colors. The end result was not one of beauty.

Clea had covered both of the woman's eye sockets with grays, charcoals, and purples that produced a vortexlike effect. Hijiri couldn't look away.

As a fellow charm-maker, Hijiri was allowed a closer look at the charm first. When she was only inches away, she was able to see a series of faint images flashing in the woman's eyes—her inner heart. It felt so personal and strange to witness. Her dreams of love, the man at the grocery store she hoped to attract, and her disappointments when it came to romance.

Even Bram was unsettled by the charm. "Clea and Mandy will escort our brave volunteer off stage so you will be able to see the charm at work. Informed voters are fair voters," he said. The crowd pressed in on the woman and the Metamorphosis owners.

Hijiri felt uneasy about Metamorphosis's charm. She couldn't imagine anyone willing to wear makeup that made them look zombified, even if it exposed the heart like no other love charm. *That type of exposure is dangerous*, Hijiri thought. *What if the wrong person happened to catch your eye and see something precious and private? It would just make things like blackmailing and heartbreaking so much easier.* She couldn't let their love charm win.

"Hijiri Kitamura, are you ready?" Bram asked.

She felt the weight of this moment heavy on her shoulders. *Don't fail now,* she told herself. *Love is on your side. Your friends believe in you.*

Friends. But what about her charm-boy?

Hijiri mechanically walked over to the rolling cart. Her fingers tightened on the cart as she pushed it to the center of the stage. When she heard the pregnant silence of the audience, everyone waiting for her to speak, the words were ice frozen in her throat.

Hijiri searched the crowd once more. Her friends held their breaths, looking worried as the silence stretched. Fallon pressed her hands together and mouthed for her to *go on.*

All the way in the back of the crowd three figures were running. The two in front looked remarkably like her parents. Mrs. Kitamura held on to her husband's collar as they maneuvered through the crowd. They were wearing their office clothing, of course, and looked severely overdressed among the Grimbaudians.

Ken cupped his hands around his mouth, telling them to keep going, to push through the crowd to see their daughter better. His cheeks were red from running. His eyes met hers, burning with something stronger than affection. His look melted the ice in her throat.

Hijiri's heart fluttered in her chest and she smiled. Any last tendrils of tension left her body, replaced with excitement. She was ready.

"Everyone has missed connections," she started. "They come and go, perhaps lost forever. Until now. The heart is capable of remembering what the head has forgotten. Even if years pass, the threads that connect you to the lives you've crossed and connected with never break. You might know them as heartstrings.

"Imagine your heartstrings as telephone wires, stretching as far as the horizon, lines unused but connected to loved ones and strangers. My love charm taps into that power. With it, you'll be able to send a message to your missed connection and receive an answer in return."

Hijiri took one of the glass bottles. "When you open the bottle, think about your almost-love, your missed connection. My charm will help your head remember as the heart pours the memory into the bottle. Once you're done, send the charm off into the world—it will find your lost love and deliver the message." Hijiri put the bottle down and turned to the audience. "Ms. Emma Ward has agreed to demonstrate how my charm works. If you would please come to the stage."

Ms. Ward blushed at the applause and slowly made her way to the stage.

Hijiri took one of the bottles, about to uncork it, when she noticed something green flash and disappear above the crowd.

Seconds later, a green glass bottle shimmering with memory materialized in front of her. Hijiri gasped and nearly dropped the one she was holding.

"What's this?" Bram asked, teasing. "Is that bottle for you, Miss Kitamura?" He took the bottle she had been holding for Ms. Ward from her hands. "What do you say, folks? Should she open this mystery bottle?"

The crowd cheered. Bram was doing her a favor, giving her time to recover from her shock. This hadn't been part of the plan, but . . . there was only one boy in the world the bottle could be from, and after waiting for so long, it felt almost unfair that she had to uncork it in public. But she wasn't about to wait any longer.

Hijiri pulled the cork out and a memory began to form in the air for all of Grimbaud to see.

She saw a boy in a hospital bed. He was Ken, but not the healthy, lively Ken she'd been spending the semester with. His skin was unnaturally pale, as white as the sheets tucked around him, and his lips were cracked and dry. His eyes opened from time to time, hazy from pain and medication. Doctors and nurses came and went like his memory was on fast-forward. A man and woman, his parents, held their son's hands when the doctor showed them diagrams of hearts, when he shook his head and pointed at a list, Ken's name toward the bottom.

The memory shifted to a common room in the children's ward. Soothing green curtains framed the windows and toys for the younger children littered the floor. Ken slumped in his wheelchair, facing the window and breathing shallowly.

A nurse stepped into the room pushing a snack cart, with empty cups and a teapot losing curls of steam out its snout. A girl trailed behind the nurse. She had her hands in her pockets, timid and sticking too close to the nurse. Her clumpy, oily hair hid her face. Hijiri Kitamura.

Hijiri knew then when this memory was: middle school, when she had been obsessed with wearing the same lavender T-shirt because it had a sparkly heart on it—she had considered it a proper charm-maker's uniform at the time.

Ken shifted his wheelchair to better view the cart and the girl.

"Is this everything you need, Hijiri?" the nurse said to the girl. "I'll let you handle it from here."

Hijiri glanced at the door, plainly wishing she could leave. But as soon as her eyes landed on the teapot, she seemed to relax a little. She poured the first cup. The scent of hibiscus filled the room. Children stopped playing and sniffed the air. Ken breathed in the tea's scent and faintly smiled. He felt warmer, less achy already.

The children who were well enough to walk approached the cart. Hijiri didn't look at them as she poured and handed out the tea. Her face flushed and her hands shook.

Ken wheeled himself over, letting the others cut in front of him. When it was finally his turn, he took his cup of tea and asked, "What is it called?"

Hijiri started. A few drops spilled on the cart. "H-Heart's Ease," she said. Her voice was croaky, like she didn't use it much.

"Charmed?"

She nodded. "A love charm. Takes away anxiety for a short time."

Ken took a sip. The tea soothed him down to the tips of his fingers. "Maybe you need a cup for yourself."

Hijiri looked at him for the first time. Their eyes met and his heart stopped. For once, it wasn't a medical emergency.

He never got a response. The nurse came back just then and told Hijiri that her parents had arrived to pick her up. The girl breathed a sigh of relief and didn't look back when she left.

She remembered the trip as just one more failed attempt at overcoming her shyness that summer. People indiscriminately made her nervous. A full pot of Heart's Ease had sloshed in her stomach and she still hadn't been able to say hello to anyone. She tried to forget those summers and succeeded—wiping out the boy with it. Tears burned the back of her throat.

The charm kept going, showing her another memory.

A different hospital room this time. Ken's cheeks had hollowed out. He barely stirred in the bed. His father snuck a slingshot into the room and lined up empty plastic cups for Ken to shoot. His mother read to him from long, rambling novels. They tried keeping him in good spirits, but his name hadn't risen to the top of the list yet.

A doctor entered the room.

His mother looked up from her book, face collapsed in grief. "Did Doctor Petit send you?" she asked. "He said he was sending a specialist. In what? All my boy needs is a heart."

The doctor calmly entered the room, stethoscope hanging from his neck. "Special circumstances require special attention," he said. The doctor had a plain, gentle face with a graying beard. His coat was open, revealing a long gold chain with a key swinging from the end. "I'm here to make a deal with you and your son."

Mr. Oshiro shifted closer to Ken. "We don't make deals with crooked doctors."

"That's a healthy attitude. Good thing I'm not a doctor." Love wiggled his fingers, palm out, and a beautifully new beating heart appeared. "Kentaro gets this heart if he helps me with a little project."

Ken winced as he sat up in bed. He was mesmerized by the magical heart.

"There's a young charm-maker in Grimbaud who believes she has a tiny heart. You've met. In fact, if I know the dying thing in your chest as well as I do, you want to meet her again." Love grinned. "Come with me to Grimbaud. You'll go to school, make friends, study charm-making. You'll have to do some pretending while you're there, but I'll make it easy for you to keep your identity a secret."

"What will Ken be doing?" her mother said warily.

"Showing my charm-maker that her heart is bigger than she thinks. If we're lucky, she may fall in love."

Ken's attention shifted from the heart to Love. "Who is she?"

"You've never forgotten the tea she served you," Love said. "Hijiri Kitamura."

Ken reached for his parents' hands. A smile pushed its way to his lips.

The charm had held all the memory it could; Ken's memory abruptly dissolved.

Hijiri pressed her hands over her heart. She thought she knew where the edges of her heart were, so tiny she could pinch it between her thumb and index finger. What she felt beating under her curled hands had slipped beyond the confines of her rib cage.

Her heart was on her tongue, twisting her speech into impossible knots. In her knees, keeping her standing upright. In her toes, turning her to face Ken, who had made his way to the side of the stage while his memories played.

Ken stepped up onto the stage, breathing clouds. He stopped a few inches from her. Snowflakes melted on his red cheeks. If he was blushing there, his scar must have been glowing furious-red under his wool coat. "You're my missed connection," he said. Out loud. Without choking or coughing or covering his tracks with thin lies. Delighted, he shouted it again.

Hijiri's hands moved from her heart to her mouth. She cried. Tears and snow burned her skin. "I can't feel my heart," she confessed. "I think it's everywhere."

Ken let out a soft laugh. "An extraordinary heart."

The townspeople woke from their spell of awed silence. Men and women alike dug handkerchiefs and tissues from their pockets to dab their eyes. Femke and Mirthe whistled.

This was the part in the presentation where Hijiri was supposed to explain how the responses from almost-loves worked and what to do when you received one. *I never thought in a million years I'd be demonstrating it*, she thought fuzzily.

And that was where her thoughts ended. She threw herself at Ken and kissed his face, wherever her lips landed. His blushing cheeks. The line of his jaw. His eyelashes, spiky and wet from the snow. She almost made it to his mouth before the volume of claps and whistles grew too deafening to ignore.

Oh, right. The competition. Hijiri reluctantly drew away from Ken and gave the audience an awkward bow. "Meeting your missed connection might not go as smoothly as this one," she said, cobbling together the last of her speech, "but it gives you the chance to find out."

The crowd cheered. Stamped its feet. Ken, still befuddled from the flurry of kisses, flashed her an adorably shy smile.

Her insides melted.

"Please, if you can possibly *bear* it," Bram said with some impatience, "we have a winner to vote for. How about it, Grimbaud? Do we know which love charm-maker is the best?"

As each townsperson approached the tables to drop their vote into the appropriate table's box, Hijiri waited. She didn't want to make herself more anxious by watching the length of both lines, trying to guess which one was longer. So she tried keeping her mind blank. Hard to do when Clea shot her daggers.

Counting the votes had to have taken a significant amount of time, but Hijiri couldn't remember it passing slowly. One minute, she was standing with Ken, wishing and waiting, and the next, Hijiri stumbled back to center stage in front of a roaring crowd. Confetti rained down on her head.

"Congratulations, Hijiri," Bram said with not even a speck of cynicism in his tone.

Hijiri wiped the golden confetti from her face and joined Bram. She tugged Ken along with her. As far as she was concerned, their hands had melded together. There was no way she was letting him go.

Her friends rushed the stage for a group hug. Chins bumping, shoulders pressed together, the twins' hearty laughter, and Bear's too-strong handshake. Bram plucking a missed connections charm from the table, slipping it into the pocket of his trench coat with a wink at Hijiri.

She saw Clea and Mandy walking away—Clea clenching her fists, almost in tears, while Mandy looked happier than ever. "We lost, so you have to keep your promise," Mandy said. "No makeup for a whole week . . ."

When Hijiri turned back to her friends, she saw her mother crying happy tears, then her father's arms were around her. "Thank you for coming," she said into her father's suit jacket. "It means everything to me."

Her mother wiped her eyes. "You've grown so much. I can't believe . . ." She looked at Mr. Kitamura. "Hitomu, we shouldn't miss these kinds of things anymore."

Mr. Kitamura pretended to consult his planner, then laughed. "Perhaps you're right."

"If it wasn't for Ken, we would never had made it here in time," Mrs. Kitamura said, smiling at Ken. "He found us at the train station."

Hijiri looked at him, eyes wide. "So that's where you were."

Ken squeezed her hand.

"Mr. and Mrs. Kitamura? I'm Fallon," Fallon said, flashing a knowing look at Hijiri. "I'm Hijiri's best friend. My parents would love to meet you. . . ."

Then there was Ken, his breath in her ear. "Hurry," he said, "before we lose another chance."

Hijiri jumped off the back of the stage with him and ran across the cobblestones. For the second time, they sprinted through a ghost town. Their feet moved faster than their heartbeats.

"Let's go somewhere warm," Ken said.

Hijiri tugged on his arm. "We're warm enough. Let's go there," she said, pointing to Love's park. Snow camouflaged the white marble of Love's statue with the boy and girl. Hijiri sat on the lip of the fountain. The water had been turned off, but the coins hadn't been picked up yet. She stared at the twinkling metal peeking starlike through the snow when she felt something hot being pressed into her hands. *Tea.*

"This is my favorite tea," Ken said, pouring himself a cup of tea. Through all their running, his portable tea-for-two set had survived—a hearth charm in disguise, perhaps, crafted to withstand household accidents. The ceramic cat's head painted on the top made her smile.

Hijiri smelled the hibiscus of her Heart's Ease tea. The first sip soothed her tired muscles.

Ken shifted so that their knees touched. "So you solved me," he said.

He was real. He had always been real. Kentaro Oshiro hadn't been born in a gift-wrapped box, but he was a little weird anyway. He had a heart transplant scar that glowed and blushed for him. A heart that was probably not real, but still worked better than his old one.

For some reason, the truth didn't hold as much power as she thought. Instead, it felt like the beginning. "I haven't solved you yet."

"You haven't?"

"I don't think I'll ever solve you. There's so much I

want to know about you, and even if we sat like this for years asking and telling, I still wouldn't know it all. And that's thrilling. I can keep unfolding parts of you, the good and bad sides of Kentaro Oshiro, and you would . . . you would do the same for me."

"I want the same thing." Ken swallowed thickly. His eyes went glassy. "I want you to know everything."

Hijiri finished her tea and carefully put it down behind her. She moved closer. "I've unlocked one door, but I have so many more to open. This time, when I ask you questions, you *have* to answer."

"With pleasure," he breathed.

"Did your dad really sneak a slingshot into the hospital?"

"Yes."

"You've never been to school?"

"Homeschooling was my only option. I'd been sick so often."

"Why do you like hearth charms?"

Ken shyly drank the last of his tea. "My parents are hearth charm-makers. They run a shop in Lejeune. Actually, I convinced Ms. Ward to order from our shop for the library."

Hijiri placed her hand on his knee. *For balance*, she assured herself, even as her cheeks burned.

Ken's eyes flickered to her hand. He gently removed it, only to stand up and adjust himself on the lip of the fountain so that they were close, so so so close. He brushed his nose against hers and her fingers dug into his rough wool coat.

"You fell in love with me *twice*," she murmured, closing her eyes. "How?"

Ken kissed the corner of her mouth first, then pressed smaller, soft kisses that made her heart twist and her hands creep up to his neck. He tasted like hibiscus and spicy cinnamon, a new, more delicious way of drinking her tea. They kissed with time to spare; Grimbaud was celebrating for them back at the square.

"I don't think," he said, pulling back, catching his breath, "I can put that answer into words."

Her charm-boy. Her puzzle-boy. Hijiri tucked away her box of questions and enjoyed letting her heart roam free.

Acknowledgments

Until I finished revising the last few lines of *Love Fortunes and Other Disasters*, I hadn't known that Hijiri Kitamura still had a story to tell. Thank you, Swoon Reads, for helping me find out and giving me the chance to share her story. To my editor, Holly West, for solving the puzzle of my first draft and helping me reshape it into something magical. Special thanks to Lauren Scobell and Emily Settle for teaming up with Holly and bringing the awesome. To Eileen Savage for the adorable robot ARE cover and her work on the final cover's layout. To Zara Picken for returning to the sequel with another gorgeous cover. Thanks again to the Swoon Reads community and the growing list of wonderful authors I'm happy to call my extended writing family.

I need to thank my zany coworkers for their support and making the cubicle life a fun one. To Andres Unda, for believing that robots in love would be more interesting than just robots. To Steven Georgeson, for answering my even stranger questions about hearts this time. To the Bemelmans family in Florida and their relatives in Belgium for the authentic Flemish names for pets. To the dueling pianists and staff of Jellyrolls, for providing a musical reprieve from reality. Lauren Christian, for your unfailing belief in me and your friendship. To the real Hijiri, who I was lucky enough to meet by chance at Epcot years ago—thank you for letting me fall in love with your name.

Many thanks again to the Figgies Underground crew: Lydia Albano, Kristin Yuki, Cara Clayton Olsen, Emily Rose Warren, Hannah Horinek, LiAnn Yim, Samantha Chaffin, Patrick and Janelle Labelle, Savannah Finger, Reagan Dyer, and Enaam Alnaggar. Phillippe Diederich, for sharing our author experiences and inspiring me to keep writing as prolifically (or close to it) as I used to in graduate school. JB Lynn, thank you for falling out of the sky and into my life just when I needed your friendship; may we continue being quirky and write like the wind.

To my family, for all the love and well-wishes and sending me surprise photos of my books out in the wild. Thank you, Mom and Dad, for understanding when I passed up on going to Disney to keep to my writing deadlines—it was only a temporary sacrifice. Biggest thanks of all to Misty, who did not change her ways just because I'm published now: she still sits on my lap and rests her head on my keyboard.

Turn the page for some

Sw♥♥nworthy
Extras...

Hijiri's (BAD)
Love Sickness Poetry

My tears are waterfalls
Dripping with longing for you.
Where are my tissues?

~~If you~~

If I stole your sock
would you mind if I kept it
for posterity?

No cure for a heart
that loves because it is ~~for~~ charmed.
What did my heart want?

If I have feelings
they are buried underneath
fictional heartache.

A Coffee Date

"Getting to Know You (a Little More!)"

HW: What is your favorite word?

KK: My favorite word *at this very moment* is "toothsome." I love what it means and how it sounds. I like to use it when describing the perfect scoop of gelato or spotting a cute boy with rolled shirt-sleeves.

HW: Nice! If you could travel in time, where would you go and what would you do?

KK: There are so many time periods I'm fascinated by, but I think the 1920s would be my first choice. Frankly, I'd try to track down silent-film comedian Buster Keaton and see him in action—maybe during the production of one of his films. I'd have lunch at a Horn & Hardart Automat. The fashion of the period was gorgeous; I'd probably be popping in and out of shops in the hopes that my time machine had room for the clothes!

HW: Ooooh! Good answer! I want some fun flapper dresses too! Do you have any strange or funny habits? Did you when you were a kid?

KK: I eat cereal without milk. I have trouble opening and closing umbrellas. One of my big goals is to rewatch all my favorite child-hood shows and cartoons (I'm at least thirty episodes into *Legends of the Hidden Temple* and loving it—go, Blue Barracudas!).

Swoon Reads

When I was a kid, I was obsessed with watching Disney's *The Little Mermaid*. I always had to dance at the end! My parents said I had terrific concentration, especially when sitting with a book. I never ripped the pages and they had to shout to get my attention if I was reading.

HW: Who is your current book boyfriend?
KK: Nawat from Tamora Pierce's *Trickster's Choice* and *Trickster's Queen*. He was a crow who took the form of a man to help the main character, Aly, and fell in love with her. He won my heart with his crow-isms as he adjusted to living as a human and how deeply he cared for Aly as the story progressed.

HW: I *love* Nawat, although Numair Salmalin will always hold a special place in my heart. And speaking of love, if you could have any love charm, what would it do?
KK: I still suffer from shyness, so a love charm that would arrange a meet-cute would be awesome. But then, I think the confidence charm that Fallon found would take care of that since having confidence is half the battle when meeting new people.

"The Swoon Reads Experience (Continues!)"

HW: Did publishing *Love Fortunes and Other Disasters* change your life?
KK: My life is full of bookish surprises now. I'm excited to open my email in-box each morning knowing that I may find fan emails,

interview requests, or even news from Swoon Reads itself! I can attend conferences and literary events as a guest author. It's surreal. I used to dream about this. Now that it's happening, I'm enjoying every moment.

HW: What has been your favorite thing about being a Swoon Reads author?

KK: I love that readers have such a big voice in my Swoon Reads publishing journey. One of the most exciting moments for me was when readers voted on their favorite cover concept for *Love Fortunes*. That choice led to *Love Charms* having another fantastic Zara Picken–illustrated cover.

HW: What is the oddest thing a fan has ever said or done?

KK: While I was on the Summer of Swoon Tour, I had two different fans from two different cities tell me that I reminded them of Cather from Rainbow Rowell's *Fangirl*. At the time, I hadn't read *Fangirl* yet, but I knew enough about the book to feel flattered and kind of in awe by that comparison. I snagged a copy and devoured the book within two plane rides toward the end of the tour. They were totally right. Cather and I have a lot in common!

HW: I can see that. And what a nice comparison! What was the most unexpected thing for you about being a published author?

KK: Taxes! I didn't know much about the financial side of being an author before Swoon Reads, but I've learned a lot over the past few months. Makes me feel like I'm adulting correctly.

Swoon Reads

HW: Do you have any advice for aspiring authors on the site?

KK: Read other manuscripts on the site and get comfortable with giving feedback through the comments and rating system. As exciting as it is to upload your manuscript on Swoon Reads, it means so much more when you engage in the process. You may find your next favorite book—and new writer-friends—along the way!

"The Next Phase of the Writing Life"

HW: If you could change one thing about your writing habits, what would it be?

KK: I wish I used outlines more often. Outlines and I don't always mesh (if I get too detailed, I get bored), but when we do, it works beautifully. Trying out different outline techniques is definitely something I'll be doing in the future so that I can have a better balance between planning and experimenting.

HW: That could be fun. You know that I'm a big fan of outlines. ;-) Where did you get the inspiration for *Love Charms and Other Catastrophes*?

KK: By the time *Love Fortunes* had been revised and off to print, I knew I couldn't leave Grimbaud just yet. Out of all the voices begging to tell their stories, Hijiri's was the loudest (ironically). I wanted to know what kind of future a love charm-maker would have in this newly liberated town and what kind of boy would capture her stubborn, "tiny" heart. Once I knew those answers, Kentaro was born. I've always loved those funny and heartwarming scenes where a person surprises loved ones by bursting out of a cake or a

box. I knew Ken was going to surprise Hijiri by popping out of a box. It was one of the first images I started with when dreaming up *Love Charms* and the scene was so fun to write.

HW: Second books are notoriously difficult. What was the hardest part about writing *Love Charms and Other Catastrophes*?
KK: The tricky part about writing the second book was learning how to do so as an author, rather than an unpublished writer. People are finding *Love Fortunes* in stores. They're leaving reviews. I can't *not* see these things, yet at the same time, I had to learn how to balance that new dimension of my writing life with trusting my instincts and skills as a storyteller (and my fabulous editor!).

HW: One last question. What do you want readers to remember about your books?
KK: I hope readers will think of my books as quirky adventures with characters who never give up on their dreams.

LOVE CHARMS
and other
CATASTROPHES
Discussion Questions

1. Hijiri is a love charm-maker, while Ken makes hearth charms and the twins control the weather. If you lived in Grimbaud, what charms would you make?

2. For much of the novel, Hijiri feels that her heart is too small to ever find love. Have you ever worried that you didn't have room for more people in your life?

3. During the first part of the contest, the love charm-makers had to come up with a single question to help someone choose the perfect date. What question would you have asked?

4. If you had access to Hijiri's missed communications charm, who would you contact?

5. Throughout the novel, Femke and Mirthe are fighting over their future plans. If the choice was yours, would you have specialized in a specific type of weather as Femke did or tried to be good at everything as Mirthe wanted?

6. Hijiri's first instinct was to solve Nico and Martin's problem with a love charm, but Nico refused. What would you have done in that situation?

7. Of all the charms mentioned, which is your favorite?

8. Hijiri refers to Ken as her "puzzle boy" and tries to solve him.

When you are attracted to someone, do you enjoy a sense of mystery, or do you prefer to know everything you can about them?

9. While checking out the competition, Hijiri thinks about how love charms are usually monitored as potentially dangerous since they impact a person's emotions and thoughts. What do you think about love charms?

10. While under the influence of Stoffel's lovesickness, Hijiri says some things to Ken that really hurt his feelings and damaged their relationship. Have you ever accidentally hurt someone like that? What did you do to repair your relationship?

In which plans for a season without romance are unapologetically foiled.

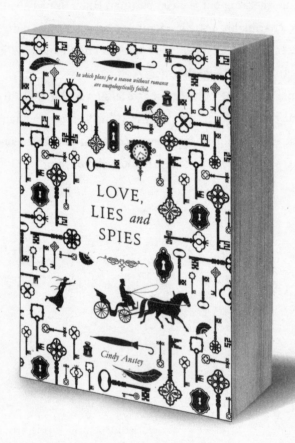

In this hilarious homage to Jane Austen, a lady
with a penchant for trouble finds a handsome
spy much more than merely tolerable.

CHAPTER

1

In which a young lady clinging to a cliff
will eventually accept anyone's help

"OH MY, this is embarrassing," Miss Juliana Telford said aloud. There was no reason to keep her thoughts to herself, as she was alone, completely alone. In fact, that was half of the problem. The other half was, of course, that she was hanging off the side of a cliff with the inability to climb either up or down and in dire need of rescue.

"Another scrape. This will definitely give Aunt apoplexy."

Juliana hugged the cliff ever closer and tipped her head slightly so that she could glance over her shoulder. Her high-waisted ivory dress was deeply soiled across her right hip, where she had slid across the earth as she dropped over the edge.

Juliana shifted slowly and glanced over her other shoulder. Fortunately, the left side showed no signs of distress, and her lilac sarcenet spencer could be brushed off easily. She would do it now were it not for the fact that her hands were engaged, holding tightly to the tangle of roots that kept her from falling off the tiny ledge.

Juliana continued to scrutinize the damage to her wardrobe with regret, not for herself so much as for her aunt, who seemed to deem such matters of great importance. Unfortunately, her eyes wandered down to her shoes. Just beyond them yawned an abyss. It was all too apparent how far above the crashing waves of the English Channel she was—and how very small the ledge.

Despite squishing her toes into the rock face as tightly as possible, Juliana's heels were only just barely accommodated by the jutting amalgamate. The occasional skitter and plop of eroding rocks diving into the depths of the brackish water did nothing to calm her racing heart.

Juliana swallowed convulsively. "Most embarrassing." She shivered despite a warm April breeze. "I shall be considered completely beyond the pale if I am dashed upon the rocks. Aunt will be so uncomfortable. Most inconsiderate of me."

A small shower of sandy pebbles rained down on Juliana's flowery bonnet. She shook the dust from her eyes and listened. She thought she had heard a voice.

Please, she prayed, let it be a farmer or a tradesman, someone not of the gentry. No one who would feel obligated to report back to Grays Hill Park. No gentlemen, please.

"Hello?" she called out. Juliana craned her neck upward,

trying to see beyond the roots and accumulated thatch at the cliff's edge.

A head appeared. A rather handsome head. He had dark, almost black, hair and clear blue eyes and, if one were to notice such things at a time like this, a friendly, lopsided smile.

"Need some assistance?" the head asked with a hint of sarcasm and the tone of a . . .

"Are you a gentleman?" Juliana inquired politely.

The head looked startled, frowned slightly, and then raised an eyebrow before answering. "Yes, indeed, I am—"

"Please, I do not wish to be rescued by a gentleman. Could you find a farmer or a shopkeep—anyone not of the gentry—and then do me the great favor of forgetting you saw me?"

"I beg your pardon?"

"I do not want to be rude, but this is a most embarrassing predicament—"

"I would probably use the word *dangerous* instead."

"Yes, well, you would, being a man. But I, on the other hand, being a young woman doing her best not to call attention to herself and bring shame upon her family, would call it otherwise."

"Embarrassing?"

"Oh, most definitely. First, I should not have gone out in the carriage alone. Carrie was supposed to come with me, but we quarreled, you see, and I got into a snit, and—" Juliana stopped herself. She was beginning to prattle; it must be the effects of the sun. "Second, if I had not been watching the swallows instead of the road, I would have seen the hole before my wheel decided to explore its depths—very scatterbrained of me. And third, if I return home, soiled and in the company of a gentleman with no acquaintance to the family, I will be returned to Hartwell forthwith in shame. All possibility of a Season and trip to London will be gone completely."

"Well, that is quite an embarrassing list. I do see the problem."

"Is there someone down there?" another voice asked.

The head with the blue eyes disappeared, but Juliana could hear a muffled conversation.

"Yes, but she does not want to be rescued by us. She says she needs a farmer."

"What?"

Juliana leaned back slightly to see if she could catch a glimpse of the other gentleman, but that dislodged a cloud of dirt.

"Achoo."

"Bless you," one of the voices called from above before continuing the conversation. "Yes, it seems that we are not the sort—"

Juliana's nose began to itch again. She scrunched it up and then wiggled it, trying to stop another burst. To no avail. *"Achoo."* This time her left hand jerked with the force of the exhaled air and broke several of the roots to which she was clinging. Slowly, they began to unravel, lengthening and shifting Juliana away from the cliff's side, out into the air.

Looking for more charming Grimbaud adventures?

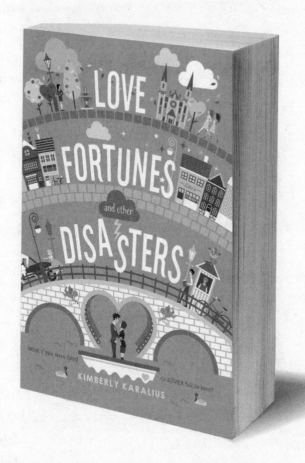

Learn the full story of Zita's defeat and how Fallon and Sebastian defied fate in Kimberly Karalius's first novel *Love Fortunes and Other Disasters*.

In love with Nico and Martin?

Check out their e-novella,
First Kisses and Other Misfortunes

READ YOUR HEART OUT

Join the hottest community of Young Adult readers and writers online now at swoonreads.com

KIMBERLY KARALIUS is the author of *Love Fortunes and Other Disasters* and its sequel, *Love Charms and Other Catastrophes*. She holds an MFA in fiction from the University of South Florida and has been sharing stories on Figment.com with a strong following of enthusiastic readers since the site's inception. Although Kimberly lives in sunny Florida, she prefers to stay indoors and sometimes buys a scarf in the hopes of snow. She loves watching really old cartoons and silent films. Being in Florida certainly has one big perk: going to Disney World. Which she does. Frequently.

kimkaralius.com